"*Going Down in La-La Land* is Perezcious! This sexified tale of drugs, sex, power, sex, money, sex, and sex would make a Hilton blush. And that's saying something! This is one of the most brazilliant books— gay or straight or bi or curious—of the year. A must-read!"

—Perez Hilton
Gossip Gangsta,
PerezHilton.com,
Celebrity Fluff and Stuff

"Andy Zeffer has written perhaps the first 'I was there' book about the backstage sex life of Hollywood that rings bitingly true. His lightly veiled sexual encounters for money with some of the heavy-hitters in the movie community are anything but fictional. And they're pretty easy to guess who they are, too. At last, a hard-edged report with no glitter, no glamour. I loved it."

—David Leddick
Author, *The Millionaire of Love*
and *The Handsomest Man in the World*

"*Going Down in La-La Land* takes a concise, unflinching look at the seamier side of Hollywood. Andy Zeffer manages to make the absurdity of Tinseltown funny without insulting. As sunny and juicy as endless groves of oranges and avocados, *Going down in La-La Land* is a great read!"

—Ben Patrick Johnson
Actor, activist, and best-selling author
of *In and Out in Hollywood* and *Third and Heaven*

"The pages were so hot they burnt my fingers. I closed my eyes and visualized one of my movies!"

—Chi Chi LaRue
Legendary porn director and drag delight

"A racy romp through the dark and funny sides of Hollywood, porn, drugs, and the closet."

—Michael Musto
Columnist, *Village Voice*

Going Down in La-La Land

HARRINGTON PARK PRESS®
Southern Tier Editions™
Gay Men's Fiction

Elf Child by David M. Pierce

Huddle by Dan Boyle

The Man Pilot by James W. Ridout IV

Shadows of the Night: Queer Tales of the Uncanny and Unusual edited by Greg Herren

Van Allen's Ecstasy by Jim Tushinski

Beyond the Wind by Rob N. Hood

The Handsomest Man in the World by David Leddick

The Song of a Manchild by Durrell Owens

The Ice Sculptures: A Novel of Hollywood by Michael D. Craig

Between the Palms: A Collection of Gay Travel Erotica edited by Michael T. Luongo

Aura by Gary Glickman

Love Under Foot: An Erotic Celebration of Feet edited by Greg Wharton
and M. Christian

The Tenth Man by E. William Podojil

Upon a Midnight Clear: Queer Christmas Tales edited by Greg Herren

Dryland's End by Felice Picano

Whose Eye Is on Which Sparrow? by Robert Taylor

Deep Water: A Sailor's Passage by E. M. Kahn

The Boys in the Brownstone by Kevin Scott

The Best of Both Worlds: Bisexual Erotica edited by Sage Vivant and M. Christian

Tales from the Levee by Martha Miller

Some Dance to Remember: A Memoir-Novel of San Francisco, 1970-1982 by Jack Fritscher

Confessions of a Male Nurse by Richard S. Ferri

The Millionaire of Love by David Leddick

Transgender Erotica: Trans Figures edited by M. Christian

Skip Macalester by J. E. Robinson

Chemistry by Lewis DeSimone

Friends, Lovers, and Roses by Vernon Clay

Beyond Machu by William Maltese

Virginia Bedfellows by Gavin Morris

Seventy Times Seven by Salvatore Sapienza

Going Down in La-La Land by Andy Zeffer

Independent Queer Cinema: Reviews and Interviews by Gary M. Kramer

Planting Eli by Jeff Black

Going Down in La-La Land

Andy Zeffer

Southern Tier Editions™
Harrington Park Press®
An Imprint of The Haworth Press, Inc.
New York • London • Oxford

Published by

Southern Tier Editions™, Harrington Park Press®, an imprint of The Haworth Press, Inc., 10 Alice Street, Binghamton, NY 13904-1580.

PUBLISHER'S NOTES
The development, preparation, and publication of this work has been undertaken with great care. However, the Publisher, employees, editors, and agents of The Haworth Press are not responsible for any errors contained herein or for consequences that may ensue from use of materials or information contained in this work. The Haworth Press is committed to the dissemination of ideas and information according to the highest standards of intellectual freedom and the free exchange of ideas. Statements made and opinions expressed in this publication do not necessarily reflect the views of the Publisher, Directors, management, or staff of The Haworth Press, Inc., or an endorsement by them.

This is a work of fiction. Names, characters, places, and incidents either are the products of the author's imagination or are used fictitiously, and any resemblance to actual persons, living or dead, business establishments, events, or locales is entirely coincidental.

Cover design by Jennifer M. Gaska.

Cover photograph by Dennis Dean (www.dennisdean.com)

ISBN: 978-0-7394-6864-7

CONTENTS

Acknowledgments

Special thanks and gratitude go to my friends and family who shared the journey of this book, especially the following individuals. Dennis Dean for his spectacular images. Chip Starkey and Ray Zglobicki at the Flamingo Guesthouse in Fort Lauderdale for their generosity. The entire team at The Haworth Press for their support; you have been a joy to work with. Karen Dale Wolman of Lavender Writes for providing an invaluable haven for writers. David Leddick, a true Renaissance man and visionary artist. Jay Quinn, who became a mentor and a guiding force. My parents for their constant love. Clare Donahue who told me to look within. Jeff Allen, a pal who is always there. Lisa Calli for her endless encourgagement. And Wendi Russo, a delightful muse and dynamite individual.

The land of sunshine and oranges? Once there, they discover that sunshine isn't enough. They get tired of oranges, even of avocado pears and passion fruit. Nothing happens. They don't know what to do with their time. They haven't the mental equipment for leisure, the money nor the physical equipment for pleasure. . . . Their boredom becomes more and more terrible. They realize that they've been tricked and burn with resentment. . . . The sun is a joke. Oranges can't titillate their jaded palates. Nothing can ever be violent enough to make taut their slack minds and bodies. They have been cheated and betrayed. They have slaved and saved for nothing.

Nathanael West, The Day of the Locust

Candy Girl

"Maybe we'll run into one of the gay guys from my alcohol and drug education program," Candy commented out of the blue as she raced her Benz north along Robertson. She was in a fifteen-week court-ordered class after being pulled over intoxicated one night racing her diabetic cat to the twenty-four-hour emergency pet clinic.

"Isn't the whole point of dragging your ass there that you people are supposed to stay away from bars and clubs?" I asked wryly.

"Yeah." Candy sighed apathetically. "I always see this one guy in particular. Our conversation is always the same—I won't tell if you won't. Oh, I don't care. Me neither. So, how's it going?"

I pushed the seat back and stretched a little as she pressed the pedal to the metal. As with everything else in her life, when driving she was a wild woman.

"Anyways, I've never been arrested so many times in my life until I got here!" she laughed.

I looked over at her glossed lips puckered together at the side of her mouth the way she did when in thought. My zany friend. I always gravitated toward characters that aren't altogether there. A little left of center, you could say, maybe missing a link or two. I tried not to think about this tendency too often, because God only knows what it reflected in me.

Candy zoomed her way in and out of the dense traffic heading east on Santa Monica Boulevard. I was amazed at how well she maneuvered the road, considering there was construction and gridlock on every other block. It seemed the streets yearned for more pedestrians and less cars, and I'd wondered if I'd done the right thing by coming out here.

Would I, Adam Zeller, find the fame and fortune that eluded me in New York? Would I become a star instead of a half-starved waif endlessly pounding the pavement for chances and golden opportunities?

For now it was just a relief not to be behind the wheel after making the five-hour drive from Vegas to LA. I always hated that drive, because it was just plain ugly. It seemed an endless voyage, hot and dusty with a stretch through San Bernardino that never seemed to end.

Candy insisted we hit West Hollywood so she could give me a quick tour of the neighborhood and then have dinner at a gay bar and restaurant called The Abbey.

"Over there are Mickey's and Rage," she pointed with a perfectly lacquered nail, the soft pink polish glistening under the street lights. "I'll drive up a ways toward Fairfax just so you get an idea of the neighborhood. Oh! Look! Isn't that place with the neon dog cute? I get my cat food there!"

Candy rambled on as I struggled to keep up with her. My blood sugar was low. I was zonked from the drive and still stunned by being here. I really needed to eat.

"Let's just eat. I feel like I'm gonna pass out," I finally broke in.

"Okay!" Candy chirped in her girlish way.

Then she proceeded to bring the car to a screeching U-turn and just missed slamming into oncoming traffic by a matter of a few seconds.

I hated when she did that.

I had met Candy three years earlier in Manhattan while making a no-budget independent horror film called *Sect of Lucifer*. Both of us answered an ad in *Backstage* looking for actors. She landed the plum role of Morgana Sateen, the vampire woman, while I bagged the choice part of Tor the zombie. Sharon Stone and Johnny Depp, look out! I was so proud to have been chosen for my role. Surely Bela Lugosi was just green with envy in his grave. After all, there are tons of hungry actors in the city competing for parts. These were our first starring roles, the beginning of what we hoped would lead us to successful acting careers.

Yes, I was that naive back then. For a month and a half in the sweltering summer humidity the job consisted of parading around in gauze bandages, a cheap latex mask a half an inch thick, oily stage makeup, and a heavy black robe. I lost about ten pounds through the whole ordeal, which was not a good thing, as keeping weight on my lean frame has always been a challenge for me. The first night of shooting took place at the filmmaker's home on Long Island, which was catered with every conceivable junk food imaginable from chips to doughnuts to greasy pizza. Candy showed up forty-five minutes late in a brown suede minidress, complete with a long blonde hairpiece right out of *Barbarella,* and carrying White Castle hamburgers for everyone there.

Boy, is this one a piece of work, I thought after first laying eyes on her. Blonde, blue-eyed, with a great body, not to mention breasts almost falling out of her dress, she was a sight to behold. A pretty face with nice bone structure, she looked like a St. Pauli Girl advertisement.

Immediately the rest of the crew smirked and joked when this brassy hurricane left the room. But I just looked at her quizzically, thinking I had met a modern-day Jayne Mansfield. While the other cast members discussed one cast member's lactose intolerance, Candy and I stood side by side and giggled.

"If I have one piece of that pizza I'll be knocking down the bathroom door to get to that toilet!"

As filming progressed, both of us laughed uncontrollably as we, along with the other characters, were expected to fall down around a pentagram made with lime powder on the filmmaker's backyard lawn. While this was happening, it was like the Halloween amateur hour. The neighborhood children taunted us over the back fence.

"Ohhh, monsters! I'm so scared!" they yelled in teasing voices as we just stood there stupidly.

Before the night was over, it was obvious we were right up each other's alley. We fell down on the ground a total of fifteen times with the rest of the haphazard cast before landing at the same time like we were supposed to. A cheap contraption coughed up puny puffs of smoke while fake tombstones fit for a house decked out for trick-or-treaters dotted the yard.

The filmmaker, Vinnie, was a full-time transit worker with a beer gut who wore his hair in a mullet. His other pursuit besides film was organizing Renaissance fairs. Vinnie's fat, cross-eyed best friend spit whenever he spoke and played the mad professor. The best friend already resembled a monster, therefore requiring no makeup whatsoever.

Early that first evening, Candy flashed the whole cast by revealing she wore no panties under her skirt, giving the oddball men there a bigger thrill than they could remember in years.

The female lead was a catering waitress named Darlene who was already busy psychoanalyzing everyone else present, and it was only the first night of filming. The guy who played the sea monster was riding the high of his life because he had landed a spot in a Snapple commercial after writing a letter to the company informing them how much he loved their iced tea.

Overall, the whole cast appeared to have escaped from a mental institution. This was hardly the filming of *Gone with the Wind*. More like *One Flew Over the Cuckoo's Nest* with a good dose of *Ed Wood* thrown in.

Throughout the next few months that the two of us dedicated ourselves to this cinematic masterpiece, I hitched rides with Candy back and forth from locations. Her company made me look forward to the tedious treks to various shoots on Long Island and a shitty neighborhood in Queens, where the filmmakers had rented a suffocating room to film interiors. It was in a dark and filthy industrial building that made you feel as though you were going to be mugged, beaten, and raped the moment you stepped inside.

"Are you all making a porno?" a bunch of big black guys who had a makeshift recording studio down the hall kept asking us.

If it weren't for the amusement Candy provided, and the fact that the guys behind the project were pretty nice people, the whole thing would have been unbearable.

After *Sect of Lucifer* was in the can, I continued to hang out with my former costar. Candy's life read like something from a wacky television show, and I was like an appreciative viewer who tuned in each week to witness her latest adventures and travails. She had two boyfriends: the wealthy and older Frank and the young, good-looking, but basically useless moron, Dean. Most of her time was spent shopping, and every salesperson at the city's finer boutiques knew her well.

When we first met she lived in an Upper East Side high-rise (care of her then boyfriend Frank), and later moved into Beekman Place before eventually leaving Manhattan. The latter address was a spot any gay man would appreciate. It gave Candy a spectacular view of an old brick building across the East River that when illuminated at night looked like a castle.

Being a fan of the movie *Auntie Mame,* I was thrilled when hearing the news Candy was moving into Beekman Place. And just like Mame, she herself was a larger-than-life character, so you couldn't find a more appropriate address for her to live. You couldn't get much more glamorous in my eyes.

Candy was no dummy, just quirky and eccentric. She grew up in Connecticut and held a business degree from what was widely considered a public Ivy League university. It also happened to be rated the number four party school by *Playboy Magazine* her senior year, a fact she was more proud of. After being bored to tears with her pharmaceutical sales job, Candy decided to pursue a career as an actress. Eventually the pharmaceuticals job came to an end when a two-faced co-worker informed her superiors Candy was leaving work at 4 p.m. on Fridays to take classes at the Actors Studio and writing off the parking as a company expense.

She was promptly fired.

By that time Frank had come into her life along with the Mercedes, the apartment, and a showcase closet of Versace, Chanel, Dolce & Gabbana, Pamela Dennis, Vera Wang, Richard Tyler, with a few Fendi furs thrown in for good measure.

"I'm such a fruitcake. Can you believe I bought this thing?" she'd laugh while tossing a periwinkle fur scarf around her neck.

Faithful dedication to acting classes and auditions filled the rest of her time. With Frank's help she even created her own calendar, involving countless photo sessions with a photographer named Rocco. She later introduced me to him, and he took nude pictures of me for a sex mag called *Hotguy,* which was quite a few notches below *Playgirl.*

"Turn your torso a little more to the right," he would say.

"That's good. Hold it there," he went on as he held the camera with only a T-shirt on and his cock flopping around. Despite having bad teeth and being completely lit on pot, Rocco was a lot of fun and had a dick like a log. This made our photo sessions a very interactive and enjoyable experience. It also made it much easier for me to get aroused and hold a boner for the pictures.

After *Sect of Lucifer* Candy decided to take a few agents' advice and move to Los Angeles where they felt she could make it in movies and television. She had since married Frank, and he was willing to finance her career aspirations. I stayed in touch with her while finishing my degree in theater from Eugene Lang College/The New School in Greenwich Village.

Eugene Lang College could only be described as a bizarre amalgam of characters that weren't exactly cut out for your typical state university. The student body consisted of militant lesbians with shaved heads, aspiring live poets, drugged-out club kids, and students who wanted to go to school in downtown Manhattan but couldn't get into NYU. These were the people who were freaks and outcasts in high school. To say the curriculum was a little out there was putting it mildly. Classes included "The Drama of Opera" and "Sex and the City," long before the book or television series existed. Participation in the latter class included a field trip to go witness a fisting take place. Hardly the course work taken by sane people with direction in their lives paying tens of thousands of dollars in tuition.

Parsons School of Art and Design was the sister school to Lang, so everyone in the dorms saw themselves as the next Calvin Klein, Andy Warhol, or Madonna. Living in such an out-there environment fueled my visions of becoming a great star on stage and screen despite having no prior experience in either acting, singing, or dancing, and only contributed to my delusions of grandeur in general.

While waiting for stardom to touch down on me, I acted in plays at school and took dance classes around the city. Part-time jobs came and went, and included such stints as a gym receptionist at half of the better gyms in the city. The pay sucked, but the job provided a place to work out for free, which I learned was a must as a gay man upon moving to Manhattan. That is, if I ever hoped to have a date or be looked at twice, an unfortunate but harsh reality of gay social life. Then there was the shoe sales job at the Capezio store in Times Square. It was right above the Winter Garden Theater where *Cats* played, which attracted busloads of tourists. That meant fitting tap shoes on gaggles of dancing girls and drill teams on field trips with Miss Katy's Dance School, or whatever the fuck small-town dance studio they took the bus from.

That was always fun, having some fat slob of a mother stand over you repeatedly asking, "Does she have enough room at the toes?"

Needless to say, shoving tap shoes on sweaty feet was the closest I got to being on Broadway.

Don't let me forget the waiter gig at a bistro in Chelsea working for a grumpy family of Persians. I can't remember any one of them smiling a single time when I was there.

I was also registered with more than one temp agency that sent me on assignments all over the city, which included everything from stuffing envelopes to fetching Diet Coke for a rabbi who ran a charitable organization.

Finally there was my occasional night job, turning tricks as a male escort. I always swore it would never happen again after each call. But a few months later I'd find myself so far in the hole that I had no other choice.

So no, I wasn't completely innocent before moving to LA. But at least I was still hopeful.

I think the event that really convinced me to take a break from New York was when I was rushing through wind and torrential rain to get to my apartment on East 11th Street and Avenue A. It was one of those days when you see dozens of battered black umbrellas sticking out of every garbage can on the corner. Walking up my doorstep I looked through the glass door into the foyer in disgust. Sitting in the corner was a big brown pile of shit. What made it even worse was that I knew it didn't come from a badly trained dog. No dog in creation takes a dump that big.

I'm paying hundreds of dollars a month on rent to live in an apartment the size of a coat closet and be greeted by someone's feces when I get home? I thought to myself.

I loved Manhattan and my friends but felt it was time to get out for a while and get my thoughts together. Not having a clear path just made life depressing, even debilitating. I thought I could move someplace where it was possible to save some money and start thinking about graduate school. It was time for me to get a dose of reality and come back to planet Earth. At least, that's what I had in mind.

Hollywood or Bust

When I mentioned the idea of moving back into my parents' home in Las Vegas for a short time my mother almost had a cardiac arrest. The thought of having either one of her two children back in her house frightened her beyond imagination. I suppose I would have taken it harder if she hadn't felt the same way about my older sister, who is the opposite personality type of myself, mainly heterosexual and, for the most part, conservative.

Mom had always been irritable and nervous when we were around, even as children. As a child I could play at the neighbor's house till 9 p.m. and she wouldn't have noticed. Actually I could have been out till dawn and she would have preferred it. She was loving and generous in her own way, always sending help when I needed it most, but at the same time, her kids just drove her plain nuts.

It didn't help that she was a tad bit on the obsessive-compulsive side when it came to keeping her house clean. She ran around the place with a DustBuster in hand 24-7. She could give Joan Crawford a run for her money when it came to having an obsession with cleanliness.

"Ish! Ish!" and "Kaka!" were her favorite expressions as she raced around the house with a dust cloth and a can of Pledge.

"I can't believe how much cat hair there is around this place from just yesterday. Adam, did you brush the goddamned cat today?" she'd bellow across the house.

The DustBuster was her most favorite object in the whole world. If you left one crumb on the counter you risked having her shout expletives at you for an hour, despite the fact it gave her the opportunity to use her favorite toy. All the while she'd go on at length and berate, "Do you know how long and hard your father stands on his feet to pay for a nice home while you do your best to shit the place up?"

While my dad is the most easygoing and loving guy on the planet, the idea of having his wife going nuts every day and fighting back and forth with his kid didn't appeal to him. My mother always wore the pants in the house anyway. So my idea of returning back home a little while to save money, look into grad school, and get grounded never stood a chance to begin with.

I continued to weigh my possibilities. By luck, I had joined the Screen Actors Guild a few months before deciding to move. I was working a nowhere job in an ugly payroll office in Midtown near Grand Central and was bored out of my skull. One day someone tipped me off that there was a call for extras in Woody Allen's new film that very afternoon. The casting happened to be two subway stops from where I was working, so I decided to check it out, figuring if it was mobbed by people I would just get a slice of pizza and hop back on the number 6 train.

Surprisingly there turned out to be only a small line at the church where the call was. Even more surprising was the presence of Woody Allen himself, sitting at a table surrounded by casting women and assistants. They all wore Prada outfits and had their hair pulled back the same way, reminding me of the type who recently graduated from Vassar and worked a job in a PR firm. Woody Allen looked like the result of a Dr. Moreau experiment with an owl. I stood there in front of him for less than a minute while he looked me over and then scribbled something on my head shot that had been handed to him.

"Okay, thanks," the production assistant standing next me said after he finished scribbling and placed my picture aside.

A few weeks later the phone rang and someone asked if I would like to be an extra in the film. For three days I stood next to Leonardo DiCaprio outside the Stanhope Hotel with a prop camera hanging around my neck. The gig consisted of yelling and grabbing at him along with a gaggle of annoying preteen girls and actors impersonating the paparazzi and police officers.

In the extra list my name was described as "oddball fan." One of the crew informed me that at first Woody Allen had me in mind to play a stalker, but that idea was scrapped. Something about the way I looked must have really disturbed Woody Allen, because a few times

I caught him gazing at me with fear in his eyes. Despite the fact he thought I made a convincing fanatic, during filming when I asked him to sign my wardrobe snapshot, he graciously obliged. Soon-Yi made a visit to the set carrying a really ugly straw purse that she probably shelled out more money for than what most people make in a month.

I said nothing to Leonardo DiCaprio the whole time, figuring he did not want to be bothered by some tall, gay extra looming beside him. Besides, he had his hands full with the obnoxious prepubescent girls.

"Girls, relax!" an exasperated Leo snapped on the third day of filming, up to his wits' end with their constant screaming.

"Oh, whatever," one of the more overconfident and smart-ass prepubescent teens rolled her eyes and shot back. "Listen to you trying to be all cool. *Girls, Relaaax!*" she proceeded to impersonate and mock the world-famous heartthrob, leaving him speechless and feeling a bit stupid.

By the third day the little bitches became so bratty that I wanted to bitch slap them across the street into Central Park. I'm sure Leo would have liked to join in.

A few months later *Titanic* opened and I found myself standing next to him in various fanzines. I looked like an out-of-place dolt in those pictures, with a camera hanging around my neck and wearing ugly corduroy pants given to me by wardrobe. It didn't help that I was standing next to the hottest young star in the world wearing a great pair of black leather pants.

On the brighter side, the gig made me eligible to join the actors union, an opportunity many people would kill for. So I borrowed money from an ex-boyfriend and joined, thinking it would help lead to the dreams of stardom that had brought me to New York in the first place.

If I moved to LA, at least I could work as an extra with my SAG card if a job didn't turn up right away. Since my degree didn't even qualify me to get a job as a waiter, my SAG status made me feel a little more secure. A more important influence in my decision was when my parents told me there was no way I could stay with them for an extended period of time.

Candy came to my rescue and offered to let me stay at her place until I got settled. We had spoken to each other regularly since she moved to LA. I was always waiting to hear when her big break would come

"Adam, I'm telling you, you'll love it out here. The weather is great. Today we had sun all day long," she would tease over the phone after I had trudged home in the frigid cold.

I reasoned my parents were only five hours away from LA, so if worse came to worst I would have family nearby. Okay . . . well, at the very least I hoped if things got really bad my mother wouldn't let me live in the streets.

So with that all in mind I began packing my bags. I hung around New York long enough to get my security deposit back on the apartment, then jumped on a flight to Vegas, to start what I envisioned would be a less stressful life filled with promise.

The two weeks in Vegas were excruciating. The heat was brutal, and my cousin was staying for the summer so my mother was already on the brink of a nervous breakdown. My arrival nearly drove her over the edge. To earn a little extra money and stay out of my mother's way I paraded around Caesar's Palace in Roman soldier gear, even though I didn't quite meet gladiator standards. Having Japanese tourists giggle and pose for pictures with me was better than arguing at home.

My mother was still pissed I didn't follow her advice and get a job with an advertising agency back in New York. I used the two weeks to find a car, stay out of my mother's way, and head for LA.

Candy had given me directions to her place a few days earlier. Halfway through the drive there I was already sick of being in a car, stuck on overcrowded freeways. Not a good sign for someone about to settle in southern California. It was a typical LA moment when I arrived at her apartment to find Candy was at the gym. Her ex-boyfriend Dean, who was just as stupid as ever, answered the door. Apparently he had followed her to LA with aspirations of becoming an actor himself.

I gathered he hung around her apartment when Frank was out of town, which was most of the time. He was probably crashing from place to place, a total mess. Long ago I had given up trying to understand Candy's relationships with men. As far as I was concerned it was her business.

"Yeah, man, I love Vegas," Dean grunted while I prayed for Candy to get home soon. "Lots of good pussy there, man."

Luckily I only had fifteen uncomfortable minutes of trying to make conversation with the moron before Candy came back.

"Hi, Adam!" she called as she bounced in through the front door, dressed in designer workout gear from head to toe.

"Hey you!" I jumped up in relief at the sight of her and ran to give her a hug.

"Are you hungry?" she asked.

"Starving."

"Damn it, Dean! I thought I asked you to put the dishes away!" she yelled toward the bedroom before telling me "We'll go to the Abbey. It's really nice. We can sit outside, and there's plenty of hot gay guys there."

For some reason Candy always felt compelled to integrate a gay destination when we went out together. After my tiring day I wasn't really thinking about meeting somebody. We could have gone to a taco stand and I would have been just as happy.

Waiting for her to shower and get dressed, I looked forward to my first night out on the town and going somewhere where the two of us could catch up, minus the on-again, off-again, temporary lunkhead boyfriend of hers.

As we walked out of the apartment toward the elevator the door to the adjoining apartment opened and a petite dark-haired woman appeared. Her face had obviously been lifted and was heavily made-up. Her dark hair shined with vibrant copper streaks. Gold and diamonds glittered from her neck, wrists, and hands. She was wearing expensive low-slung jeans and a tank top that had BEBE written across in little rhinestones.

"Cahn-dee!" she pronounced in a shrill accent. "Did you know zee ex-ter-mee-na-teer did not come deese month for zee bugs to spray zem with?"

"Really Orly? That's terrible," Candy answered, trying to appear concerned.

"Yes!" The woman's eyes grew big. "But I call zee manager already, so he tell me zee man come tomorrow!" She finished with satisfaction, apparently very proud at having taken control of the missing exterminator. I could now place her accent as Middle Eastern. It had that heavy wail to it.

"Orly, this is my friend Adam. He will be staying with me for a while, so I wanted you to meet him. He just moved from New York," Candy said.

"Ooohhh! Heellooo!" Orly practically screeched. "I love New York See-teee. So bee-eww-tee-ful!" she gushed and went on with an enormous smile.

We stood and listened to her babble for what seemed like forever until Candy was finally able to break us away.

"Just so you know," Candy warned on the way to her car, "she is the eyes and ears of the building and complains about everything, so just be real nice and butter up to her. At first she hated me, especially when Frank and I would fight. The woman can't stand noise. But I've managed to warm up to her, and have even had her over for coffee a few times, so now she's cool with me. Otherwise she is kind of a trip. She'll keep talking to you for hours about when she was Miss Israel 1967, or some shit like that."

The Abbey was a classy place, with a coffee bar where one could order a nice meal and an outside bar where one could get drinks. A courtyard surrounded the outside bar and was filled with tables and statues behind a wrought iron fence. When you stepped inside you really did feel as though you had entered a real abbey, that is, an abbey filled with cruising gay men instead of nuns. Surrounding the preening and posing queers were tall outdoor heat lamps placed around the outside bar, meant to keep people warm during the winter months. A lot of outdoor places in LA had them, and I would soon find I had to be careful whenever I was around them to keep my head from getting singed, a hazard tall people in LA deal with on a seasonal basis.

In the middle of her dinner Candy spotted an actor she was friendly with named Kyle, who was one of the stars of a network sitcom called *She's On Her Own.* He was walking around with another guy, looking about the crowd as if expecting something to happen.

Candy grabbed his arm and shouted up, "Hey! Kyle!"

Hey looked down, surprised for a moment like he had no clue who she was.

"It's me. Candy. Gary's friend," she said sweetly.

His eyes got really big behind designer horn-rimmed glasses, and he said in an overly enthusiastic and affected voice "Hey! How are *you?*"

It turned out they knew each other from New York, where they had a mutual friend named Gary, a gorgeous gay guy and sex addict who after realizing that jerking off in front of his apartment window for various neighbors every night wasn't acceptable behavior began attending Sex Addicts Anonymous meetings.

As Kyle sat down I wondered if he had ever fucked Gary. From what I knew of Gary's track record I decided the answer was probably yes.

Kyle's friend Collin worked for one of the studios in town. Both guys seemed friendly when introduced to me. Tinges of excitement and delight came upon me when they pulled up their chairs. My first night in LA, and here I was dining outside under the stars in a trendy hangout and already mingling with the stars down here on Earth. It was a very cool start to my new life in sensational southern California. If meeting people was going to be this easy, I shouldn't have any trouble building a career and finding my niche in the world of entertainment.

"It's Adam's first night in town; he just got here!" Candy announced.

"Really?" Collin said. "What brings you here?"

"Well, I just felt it was time that—" but before I could finish Kyle suddenly cut me off and said, "What is with that guy's shirt? Is he working a landing strip? That color would stand out on the stage of the *Moulin Rouge*!"

The two were full of more stinging comments. Their body language, such as the way they splayed their legs out and the disinterested expressions on their faces, gave a clear message of cocky arrogance. To make matters worse, they thought it was funny that they had this little game going that involved flipping people off under the table.

"Oh, I don't like that one's pants," one would point out. "He gets a finger." Or, "Check that queen out. She needs to lay off the steroids big time. You know what that means—finger."

Listening to these guys one would think that everyone else was dog shit in comparison. I focused on my fusili pasta and vegetables as they went on directing insulting quips toward every other person in the Abbey.

I went from happy to be sitting with a minor sitcom star to wondering why Kyle thought he was such hot shit. As he sat on his invisible throne, it was imperative for him to avoid contact with anyone. God forbid someone noticed him.

Never mind we were in an environment completely designed for interaction. In actuality none of the guys around, many of whom were quite attractive, seemed to notice him and if they did, didn't give a rat's ass.

When not looking like he was afraid to be approached, he wore an expression of perpetual boredom.

I kept thinking about how whenever I caught his show on the tube I never bought for a minute the fact his character was interested in the female lead. I wonder if the other people watching at home felt the same? I mean, he was so obviously gay. But then I thought about it some more and decided that there were people out there in places like Kansas where the idea never crossed their minds. Candy tried to keep a conversation going, but it was useless.

"Okay, let's find someone else. Next victim," Kyle said while darting his head around. His eyes were like scanners, darting back and forth and back and forth.

Finally Candy couldn't take it any more and after being interrupted for the hundredth time, said sweetly, "You know, Kyle, if you want someone you find interesting to flip off you can always go home, look in the mirror, and give yourself the finger."

A sly smile came across Kyle's face and he laughed, "Touché!"

After getting the hint that everyone, including Collin, thought his game was tired and lame, he grew bored and asked Collin if he was ready to leave.

"So give me a call sometime. We'll hang out or something. If you talk to Gary tell him I said hi," Kyle said before disappearing into the crowd.

"Nice meeting you both." Collin smiled, then turned to me, winked, and said, "Good luck!"

"Whatever. I'll never hear from them again," Candy said through sips of her apple martini, apparently the trendy drink of the moment. Every other person in the place also had a bright green martini in hand with a sliver of apple hanging off the side.

"Could you believe how stuck on himself he was? Everyone else is fly shit 'cause they're not on some sitcom. Give me a fucking break," she said disinterestedly.

"Do most people out here behave like that?" I asked.

"Some of them," Candy shrugged. Then stopping to reconsider, admitted, "Well, a lot of them. But you'll get used to it."

We sat gazing at the meticulously groomed and manicured crowd, some of which stood in clusters while others weaved their way among them, checking out the bodies as they went.

"Well," she sighed, breaking me out of my trance, "do you want dessert?"

"That's all I've thought about the whole time Mr. Finger was sitting here," I replied.

The Abbey boasted a really great dessert case at their coffee bar, a plethora of cakes, pies, brownies, and more sinful treats to taunt the body-obsessed patrons. I could just visualize scores of gym queens feeling guilt ridden when they sprang up the next morning and raced to spin class. Candy got up to get a piece of the Oreo cookie cheesecake confection we had spotted earlier.

Staying seated to save our table, I took a moment to observe the crowd. It seemed to me that there was a lot more posing and less interaction going on. I didn't remember it being quite so bad in New York.

My first evening didn't shed a favorable light on the prospects of meeting a great guy at a place like this. But this was only my first night in town, so I wouldn't be too quick to judge.

As we ate our dessert, we both agreed it looked better in the case than it tasted in our mouths. It most definitely looked better in the case than it would look on our asses. Nevertheless, we finished the overly sweet dish and got up to leave.

"Are you leaving?" asked a prissy voice from behind. I looked over to find a massively overbuilt and overly tanned dude with craggy skin and an attitude looking at our table.

"Be my guest," I replied, always finding it amusing when these steroid-pumped guys opened their mouths and still sounded as gay as a May Day Parade. All that effort for a tough, masculine appearance was blown away by the slightest movement of the vocal chords.

We made our way back to the Benz. I was eager to get some sleep and call it a night. An unsure feeling gripped me. Looking around at the unfamiliar landscape, perhaps I made a rash decision in coming here. Maybe I let the shit in the foyer get the best of me. If I needed some space for a while and an escape from New York, perhaps I should have taken a summer job in Provincetown, basically something less permanent than picking up and moving straight across the country.

So far LA didn't seem that much more relaxed than New York. The people just appeared less responsive and outgoing, not as energetic, and if tonight was any example, more judgmental. But I would hardly describe that as "laid back."

The crowd at the Abbey struck me as having a feeling of being impenetrable. If tonight was any example of how it was going to be meeting people and trying to get my foot in the door in terms of a career, maybe I should have bought a round-trip ticket. Something told me I'd better gear up and prepare myself for more than a few superficial experiences in La-La Land.

"Adam, hellooo? Are you listening to me?" Candy's annoyed voice called out to me, breaking me out of the manic thoughts swimming in my head.

"Sorry," I smiled. "I completely zoned out for a minute. It's been such a long day."

I turned my churning brain off, listened to her list of the things I should do to get settled, and felt the cool air blowing against my face as I stared at the taillights of the car ahead.

Gym Cliques

"Adam, what side of the street did you park your car on?" Candy bellowed into my room early one morning a week later, almost giving me a heart attack.

"Same side as your building. Why?" I mumbled groggily.

"Remember, Tuesdays and Thursdays are street cleaning. Thursdays are my side of the street. You don't want to get another ticket," she scolded.

Shit. It wasn't even 8 a.m. But I had no choice but to drag my ass out of bed to search high and low for a new spot.

"Want me to pour you a bowl of Kashi?" she asked as I walked groggily to the front door.

"Okay," I croaked.

After one week in town, I had already collected two parking tickets. It seemed as if the parking-enforcement Nazis were everywhere you went. They drove around in these hideous, generic white cars that resembled giant marshmallows with orange lights on top. This wasn't exactly the Welcome Wagon I had wished for.

The second ticket really pissed me off. It happened when I looked up a high school friend and we decided to get coffee together in West Hollywood.

After finding metered parking, we discovered that between the two of us we possessed a grand total of change worth fifteen cents. This bought us about ten minutes of parking time, so we figured we would run in, get change from our coffee, then I'd run back out to feed the meter.

When we walked inside the Coffee Bean there was a line of gym bodies in uniform tank tops, workout pants, and Abercrombie & Fitch baseball caps. Abercrombie & Fitch was pasted on bodies everywhere in West Hollywood.

It figured, being pressed for time there were six or seven people in front of us who insisted on the most complicated coffee concoctions imaginable. All with skim milk, of course. By the time my friend and I reached the front of the line almost ten minutes had gone by. As soon as we were rung up and had change in hand I darted back to the car in the public parking lot.

"Fuck!" I yelled at the top of my lungs as soon my windshield was in clear view. It couldn't have been more than a few minutes after the meter ran out and a nice white ticket with a mailing envelope greeted me, tucked neatly under my wiper.

Now, I'm not one to rush to conspiracy theories, but I was really starting to get paranoid. Did these people wait in the bushes or something, count the meter to the exact second, attack with a ticket as fast as possible, and disappear again?

It was like a cruel joke. At this rate, living in Manhattan seemed like a bargain when compared to the twenty dollars a day it cost me just to park in LA. From that moment forward I was compulsive about parking correctly, though I didn't always succeed, and the LA parking Gestapo would prove to be the bane (actually one of many) of my existence in La-La Land.

So with Candy waking me up this morning, I wasn't about to collect a third ticket and owe the City of Los Angeles close to a hundred bucks. After successfully moving my car and enjoying a bowl of Kashi, I spent the day as I had for the past week, dividing my time between job seeking through the trades and newspapers, and getting familiar with my new surroundings. Candy was busy with her classes and appointments. Besides, I didn't want to overwhelm her by constantly hanging around her or the apartment. So, in order to be shown around town even more, I looked up the sister of my best friend from home.

A few years older than me, Sarah worked in high-end retail. Because she worked in retail, almost all of her friends were gay men. She was always outgoing and a very pretty girl. She told me over the phone she wasn't dating anybody at the moment and had a bitter breakup with her long-term boyfriend in Las Vegas, the catalyst for her decision to move to LA.

We decided to meet in the parking lot of Pavilions supermarket on the corner of Robertson and Santa Monica. She came rolling up in a Ford Explorer driven by a cute blond guy with perfect spiky hair that flipped up in the front.

I was excited to see a familiar face. They smiled wide and waved through the tinted windows, both of them wearing expensive designer shades. Sarah put her window down and stuck her head out.

"Hey sistah! What up?" she said in a slick manner, sounding very changed since the last time I had seen her.

"Hey you! You look great!" I said, sticking my head through the window and planting a kiss on her cheek.

"Adam, this is Stephen," Sarah gestured.

"Hi, Stephen," I said, reaching my hand across the front of the SUV and trying to make out his eyes behind the dark shades.

"Hi," he smiled back, revealing a perfect set of white teeth. "Hop in. We have someplace cool planned for lunch."

Stephen was a former co-worker and now Sarah's best friend. He was currently "between jobs." It turned out Sarah was also unemployed, having lost her job in a dispute over ruining her nails after putting up a window display. But you wouldn't know they were out of work by hanging out with them.

Stephen was friendly but flashy and pretentious. I hadn't been in the car but a few minutes when he started going over his list of do's and don'ts.

"We don't go east of Fairfax when it comes to apartments," he began. "That is way too east. It gets too trashy. We stay in the core of WeHo."

They were horrified to learn I didn't have a cell phone.

"Adam, you are in LA now. You definitely have to get a cell phone! I'll give you one of mine. I have five of them. Then find yourself a service right away!" Stephen declared.

They insisted we go to a fabulous spot for lunch called Red on Beverly Boulevard. I immediately gathered that the words of choice for Sarah and her friends were "fabulous" and "sister."

Actually, it was pronounced "sistah."

On the way to Red, one of their cell phones rang every other minute, making it difficult to carry on even the most mundane conversation. This continued at the restaurant. And, to make matters worse, Stephen was a bit snippy with the waitress, who he made feel like an inconvenience. It was apparent Stephen never had to wait tables before.

After rudely barking out his order to the waitress while simultaneously speaking on his cell phone, he became more demanding.

"Can I get more ice than this?" he asked, while holding his glass up to the sun-drenched sky and peering at it through his shades.

The harried waitress looked down at the sidewalk, breathed in heavily, and raised her eyebrows in exasperation, obviously trying hard to bite her tongue.

"Everything is great so far," I piped up, embarrassed by his behavior. Our eyes met and she knew I was horrified.

"Thanks," she said sweetly, then took Stephen's glass and shot him daggers from her eyes before spinning around in irritation.

"You better be nicer to waiters in the future or you might find more in your drink than just ice!" I jested, but was really serious.

He failed to see the humor in it. Needless to say, if this was how he always behaved while dining I'm sure he swallowed some spit here and there.

After lunch, Stephen drove us to a shopping mall called the Beverly Connection, where we went into a store called the Sports Chalet. It was absolutely imperative Sarah purchase the right shoes for spin class.

"Sarah, you have to have that outfit! It looks fabulous on you!" Stephen proclaimed loudly in the store, relishing the attention his loud mouth brought upon him.

"Adam, are you getting anything?" he turned and asked me.

I completely lied, not wanting to admit, "No, Stephen. I can't shop! I'm a poor motherfucker," for fear that this revelation might repel him to such a degree that they would both ditch me right then and there, leaving me stranded in the Sports Chalet. Instead I said, "No, I'm waiting until I move into a place of my own before I get more stuff that I have to lug around."

"Oh, that's smart. Moving around is such a pain in the ass," he mumbled back, focusing on a rack of tank tops in front of him and not showing much interest either way.

Watching Stephen and Sarah tear through the racks of marked-up nylon-blend gym gear, I had a moment of sadness and melancholy. These weren't my college friends living in the Williamsburg section of Brooklyn with clothes proudly bought secondhand at Canal Jeans that I could joke with about being flat broke. I snapped myself out of it. A mere week was way too soon to start feeling melancholy.

The three of us went in the same fitting room, the two of them to try crap on while I stood there to give my opinion on the clothes.

I wasn't interested in the gym outfits, but I did have a different opinion—that opinion being Stephen had a large basket and a tight ass that caught my eye. Maybe that's where the attitude came from, though it didn't make up for his personality. But then again, I'm sure the guys he dated thought personality didn't matter as much as a big dick and bubble butt.

He must think he is such hot shit because he has buns of steel and big cock, I thought, gazing in the mirror. *Well, I have way better cheekbones,* my thoughts continued to drift, before scolding myself for letting myself sink so shallow.

"Ohmigod! Stephen, that looks fabulous! You've got to get it!" Sarah shrieked, breaking me out of my warped daze.

Ugh! There went that word again. It brought me back to when I first moved into the dorms in New York, when every other word used was "Fierce!" "Fierce this" and "Fierce that." "Honey, you look fierce!" Months of hearing that left me wanting to stick every club kid and art fag through the heart with a giant skewer.

Finally the trendy twosome decided on their new gym wardrobe and we went up front to pay. While they were charging a few hundred bucks, I wondered what kind of unemployment checks they were getting to be making shopping excursions for such superfluous possessions.

After leaving the Beverly Connection we headed to Crunch Gym on Sunset. This was where Sarah's whole gang worked out. Candy had just gotten a membership there as well.

I was familiar with Crunch, having been a receptionist at their location on Christopher Street in New York, one of my countless part-time jobs. I remembered when the first one was just some hole in the wall aerobic studio on Thirteenth Street with brightly painted walls and a bohemian membership that almost wore black to work out in. These original members always seemed more inclined to attack a canvas with brushes rather than jump on a treadmill.

This wasn't the case in LA. The hip workout spot was located in a shopping plaza complete with a Virgin Megastore and a Wolfgang Puck restaurant. It appeared that everything of importance in LA came attached to a shopping plaza or strip mall.

While at the gym I got the complete tour required of every guest by a nicely built salesman with wide blue eyes and wavy blond hair, who Sarah told me was an aging surfer. I was more interested in looking at this aging sexpot of a beach boy than the equipment.

As he walked me around, I kept my eyes open for any big celebrities but failed to spot or recognize any. After the tour I met the rest of Sarah's gaggle of gay men, one by one. It seemed like their names were all either Scott or Brett and I couldn't keep up. They were all cute and pumped up, and seemed to gravitate toward one another due to their common interest in looking good and hanging out at the right places.

It quickly became apparent Sarah had become the ultimate fag hag of West Hollywood. It seemed as though people in LA ran around in packs, and she was the star of this one. She was almost like their mascot in a way. I thought it was a little creepy how they cooed over her, and somewhat of a waste since nothing would ever become of it in terms of an intimate relationship. Shit, I was a relatively attractive gay man, come hang over me for chrissakes!

Before leaving the gym, Sarah and Stephen convinced me to join, telling me it was *the* place to work out in LA, one of the "do's" on Stephen's list.

"It's the best gym in town. Everything else is tired and lame," he said, urging me to sign on.

I reasoned success in my new surroundings was all about getting out there and meeting people for me at this point.

"Connections baby. Get those connections and work them." The words sailed through my mind. Damn it, I was here to make a success of myself and determined to do it. I needed to be around the right people, no matter how obnoxious they might be.

Besides, the only people I really knew well all came here. I sat down with the faded sun-kissed salesman, signed the paperwork, and gave Crunch my credit card number, which until this point I swore would be for emergencies only.

So much for sticking to that promise I thought while whipping the plastic out a week after my arrival. I tried to tell myself what a great business move I was making as Mr. Buff Surfer filled out my membership contract. But I knew I was lying to myself.

A few days later, I really started to wonder what I had been thinking. The parking lot was always full. The street parking around the complex was by permit only. Sarah even warned me not to park at the strip mall across the street.

"Sistah, one night McDonald's had my car towed. I was like, freaking out. Ohmigod, I was so pissed off," she went on between breaths at the treadmill, further traumatizing me about the parking situation.

I was already paying a small fortune to work out at a gym that was proving an obstacle course to get to. When driving into the lot you had to grab a ticket, which in turn you had to have stamped, or "validated," before leaving.

My second time there I had already forgotten to get my ticket stamped, and the parking attendant actually made me park my car again and go all the way back up.

"Either you go back up or pay me twenty dollars," she ordered flatly, leaving me feeling quite humiliated and annoyed. It felt like I was caught walking the halls in grade school without a bathroom pass. I also found out that after two hours passed, you could expect to start paying for parking, on top of the small fortune you had already paid for membership.

Getting to this fucking gym was a bigger workout than my actual workout. Whoever planned this place must have been smoking some serious crack. It was a functional disaster, a nightmare of architectural planning.

On the plus side, there were plenty of attractive guys there. A little bit of locker room cruising, but not too much. I wasn't about to start any funny business in the steam room. If they put George Michael in handcuffs here they sure as hell could do the same to me. I could just see myself being led out of the place in front of everyone, all my prospective connections down the drain. The shame of it! I would be fodder for Stephen and his gang. I could just imagine their talk.

"Oh sistah, he didn't waste any time getting busy!"

Besides, nothing came close to the cruising at American Fitness gym in Chelsea, back in Manhattan. That place was an ongoing orgy, and most of the guys partaking in the festivities were very yummy. Everyone knew monkey business went on, but nobody cared. All the members were cool about it. Either you participated or ignored it. And yes, I had more than my share of additional workouts there. I even went so far as to plan my workouts around a hot blond guy from Baltimore who worked for Amtrak and frequented the gym on his daily route to the city. God, he was so fun. At the time I figured a little hanky-panky never hurt anyone just so long as it was safe.

About my third or fourth time at Crunch, I went to work out with Candy. We finished at the same time and both went in the locker rooms to change. I finished first and waited out by the lobby, talking it up with the aging surfer. I was beginning to get more infatuated with him after each visit. All of a sudden I heard Candy call out in an urgent and excited tone, "Adam! Adam! Come here!"

"What is it?" I walked over and asked, wondering what could be so important to pull me away from my new blond obsession.

"Look!" She pointed down the hall to the sides of the locker rooms, laughing hysterically.

"What?" I snapped impatiently, seeing nothing and getting annoyed.

"Oh . . . shit," I murmured. To my dismay I found myself staring at the silhouettes of men and women showering. The glass was opaque, but I never really noticed it before. And you could see it all—members soaping up their privates, douching out their assholes with water, everything.

"Adam!" Candy sputtered, now beet red and gasping for air between convulsions of laughter. A model-type girl walked past us and laughed, getting a kick out of the fuss Candy made.

"You guys never noticed that?" she asked.

"Uh . . . no," I answered, gazing at the figures in front of me in dismay.

Candy just shook her head, her hands over her mouth and tears coming out of her eyes. Was this Crunch's way of trying to be titillating and promote a sexy image? No wonder those sides of the showers were always empty. I was actually a little pissed. I had used one of those stalls and could imagine how stupid I looked yanking away at my penis with soap and water, no idea that what I was doing was completely visible from the other side.

It was a good thing I didn't have the nerve to invite someone else in my stall here. What a show that would be. I swear, if Candy hadn't pointed out this discovery I'm sure I wouldn't have noticed it for weeks.

After we got ourselves together and left for home, I sat in Candy's car having rather paranoid thoughts. The shower stalls just defined LA—one big fucking tease for the eyes and senses. They probably designed the showers like that so they could catch people doing something dirty. I mean, this town went gaga for catching people with their pants down, just look at Heidi Fleiss or Hugh Grant.

Central Casting

My other big purchase that week besides my new gym membership was the *Thomas Guide,* a massive book of maps that illustrated the countless street grids of the Los Angeles Metropolitan area. Candy had kept pestering me to buy it, and so far I had gotten lost more than once.

"You're going to need it if you want to find anyplace on your own," she said in a scolding tone when I told her for the tenth time I still hadn't grabbed a copy.

When I finally broke down and bought the *Thomas Guide* I was horrified. It looked like it weighed a ton and was hundreds of pages long.

Shit, I thought. I hadn't even read the whole Bible from front to back, but I was sure it was less of a challenge than this monstrosity.

At the end of the week I decided to make the trip to Central Casting in Burbank. Central Casting was the largest service for extras in town and had been around forever. It was in the depths of the valley, and getting there would be a challenge for me. I was still terrified of freeways.

"Can't I just take the boulevards?" I asked Candy meekly.

"No, you can't just take the boulevards!" Candy responded in a baby voice clearly meant to mock my freeway phobia. "It will take you way too long," she continued in a no-nonsense tone. "I really want you to stop being such a pussy about this. You lived in the toughest city in the world and you're scared to merge?"

I guess it was something I would have to learn to get over fast if I ever needed to be anywhere in Los Angeles other than Hollywood and Beverly Hills. As a New Yorker, my vision of LA freeways was miles of endless, crisscrossing vessels of aggression and road rage with shootings and televised car chases thrown in for good measure.

I would come to find that I wasn't too far off. And, not being great at multitasking to begin with, having the *Thomas Guide* was of no use whatsoever. For starters you needed a magnifying glass to read the print. Then you had to keep glancing at it to keep up with where you were going while driving, not an easy thing in LA traffic. I could just picture myself veering off the road and colliding into a palm tree. I was a *Thomas Guide* disaster.

I found Central Casting in the core of Burbank, and it took forever to get there as I abandoned the freeways altogether and took the scenic route over Laurel Canyon to the boulevards that never seemed to end. The San Fernando Valley was miles of endless sprawl and the worst architecture I'd ever seen, a lot of stuff straight out of a *Brady Bunch* episode. Actually a lot of buildings looked as if Mike Brady had proudly designed them himself, complete with avocado exterior tile and faux Tudor stucco.

Central Casting was located in a nondescript two-story building. Parking was a bitch, and I left my car around the corner and a few blocks down.

There were already dozens of people when I arrived, and a form with a number waiting by the door. The form asked the usual crap, such as measurements, wardrobe, skills, and talents. After filling it out, I sat with the other hungry actors in a room with tables and mismatched furniture.

I hadn't seen a sadder cast of idiots in some time, actually not since the filming of *Sect of Lucifer*. It was just plain depressing looking at the hopefuls who had obviously passed their prime in Hollywood and hadn't much of a prayer of going further than having their back to a camera in some restaurant scene. One deluded girl with runs in her stockings was going on about how the people at Spelling Television always called for her, and kept throwing the term "Spelling" around as if she were a cast member of *Beverly Hills, 90210*.

"The people at Spelling told me I should keep my hair this length, even though I'm dying to cut it," I overheard her telling someone across the foldout table.

At the same time a guy in his forties with glasses and bad skin loudly shelled out acting advice to his moronic cohorts sitting nearby.

"Make sure not to get too tan," he ordered to a blank-looking beach dude. "The camera doesn't like it."

Many people were here to reregister and had probably been doing this for years. I had heard about people in LA who did this for a living. They were just professional extras living on union wages and driving around with twenty different changes of clothing in the trunk of their cars. After almost an hour of waiting, I had begun to really hate myself for failing to bring a good book. An older and somewhat haggard bleached-blonde woman with a helium voice came through with a basket of apples and cookies for the casting people upstairs, jarring me from my thoughts.

"I just had to give them something," she gushed to someone nearby me. "They kept me working two months straight!"

Obviously, job security was not a priority with these people.

Finally it got closer to my number being called and I was allowed to go upstairs and wait in a smaller line to have my picture taken. Then it was up to a window to pay the twenty-dollar fee to register. The frumpy girls behind the windows barked orders at me.

"Stand behind the strip of tape at the floor! Look straight at the camera! Now turn to the wall and give us your profile!"

It was like getting arrested and having your mug shot taken. I should have known they were all a bunch of raging bitches. When listening to their phone recording for directions I remembered the hostile voice on the other end exclaiming in disdain, "If you are sick, please do not come to the office. We do not want the whole office to get sick!"

When the whole thing was over I felt like I had been at the DMV, only a strange, surreal DMV full of drivers with stars in their eyes.

It was almost evening by the time I made it back to Candy's. Dean wasn't there because Frank was coming into town the next day. I was glad it was just the two of us. Before long we were laughing hysterically as I went on in detail about my day.

"That's why I refuse to do extra work," Candy rambled on while munching chocolate chips. "You sit there for hours feeling like a piece of dirt."

Neither of us felt like going out, so we settled for baking chocolate chip cookies instead. Candy climbed onto the counter to search the cupboard for vanilla, her blonde ponytail bouncing behind her. Her cats, Goldie and Frosty, watched in wonder as we danced around the kitchen to ABBA *Gold*.

"Take a chance on me . . . take a chance, take a chance, take a chance," I sang to the cats while jumping up and down. Used to being around erratic behavior, the cats didn't flinch.

After eating half the batch between us, she went to bed and I scanned the papers for work. I had picked up some local gay papers at the Abbey that first night. Maybe there was something in there.

Before hitting the sack I prayed to God that I would have an easy work search. My thoughts drifted back to the few times I had done extra work in New York, besides the Woody Allen project. The worst experiences that stuck out in my mind were the films *The Mirror Has Two Faces* and *54*.

The first was shot on location at Columbia University and consisted of a slew of college-age extras crammed into a huge lecture hall while Barbra Streisand paraded around as our supposed professor, in the ugliest Donna Karan dress I've ever seen. It looked like she was wearing a black potato sack. We were subjected to early-morning calls and being kept all day until the following morning while Ms. Streisand did take after take. The scene consisted of her playing a professor and giving a lecture that her students are just mesmerized by. Then, as her admirers, we applauded in sheer admiration and adulation at the end.

I guess it's hard for her to lose the diva personification, even playing a teacher.

By the time the whole thing was done and over I hated Barbra Streisand's guts. Talk about the walking, breathing, and living definition of neurotic. That and the fact she was addressing us like we were a herd of simpletons and providing the most unrealistic college scenarios in order to direct us.

"So you're just in awe of this professor," she gestured wildly with her hands.

In reality most of the people there were college students anyway, but the way she spoke to us made it clear she had never stepped into a lecture hall in her life. I ran out of there screaming. This was before I joined the union, so one could say I ran screaming with nothing but peanuts for pay.

In contrast, the 54 set was a complete circus in freezing subzero temperatures. The film, which turned out to be a huge bomb, was based on the legendary club and shot at the actual location of the former nightspot in the middle of the winter. The problem was, the geniuses behind the project decided to film exterior summer shots outside the front of the building in unbearable, freezing cold weather. They even had contraptions to blow hot air at the masses outside, which dissipated immediately and didn't do shit to keep us warm. Even more bizarre was the number of elderly people there dressed in disco outfits, people who never would have thought of venturing into the actual club in its heyday. After being herded out a few times in the frigid air, I told myself there was no way in hell I was going to contract pneumonia for the slim chance of being glimpsed on camera for a split second. Freezing to death while waving my hand around like a maniac and posing as some stupid loser unable to get into Liza and Halston's playground just wasn't worth it.

Lucky for me and twenty other smart people, we found a stairwell in the corner of the club that led to a few locker rooms and a boiler room that you could squeeze through a narrow opening to get into. We hid out for hours, sipping hot tea and coffee, basically talking crap. When the production assistant went on his search for us we ran like the most frightened refugees you've ever seen.

"Here they come! Everybody run!" the person on lookout would urge, and we'd scatter faster than mice.

We stood silent, ignoring the impending doom that threatened us. Stifling laughs, we kept still as the exasperated production assistant yelled.

"Come on you guys! I know you're down here! Just a few more shots and then we're done!"

With the other few hundred suckers freezing their asses off outside, they got along fine without us. We spent the rest of the time playing with old hats we found in the basement, and laughing as we wondered when we'd creep upon one of Steve Rubell's old cocaine vials or condoms. That night when the set was wrapped, we filtered into the rest of the crowd and got our waivers signed with no problem. A few months later, when the weather warmed, I was coerced back to the 54 set with the promise I'd get a bit on camera as one of the fabled and legendary bartenders. Sure enough, I was given a short scene on camera counting cash from the bar till, only to discover I had been cut and all you could see were my hands in the actual film. Not that it was a big loss. Nobody saw the big box office stinker anyway, and I got paid.

Those memories coupled with today's experience at Central Casting almost gave me a panic attack as I lay back in bed staring up at the ceiling. This was one of the many times I wished I had turned out to be a normal person with normal ambitions. Why couldn't I have just decided on becoming a pharmacist, an architect, or an engineer? Anything with some degree of safety and order would do. Today's events were the perfect example of the ongoing struggle between the side of me that desired creative freedom, artistic freedom, and fame and fortune, versus the side of me that desperately craved stability and order in my life.

I guess many artists possess this inner conflict, almost a schizophrenic battle between the two. The bottom line in life is you can't have your cake and eat it too. It's either one or the other. I had made a choice in what path I had to follow, and these were the obstacles in my way. Whether I picked the right path to begin with, I wasn't sure. And that's what bothered me the most. I didn't have the strong attitude that it was all or nothing. I wasn't prepared to eat out of garbage cans like Madonna supposedly did before hitting it big. Somehow the vision of a nervous six-foot-tall gay man eating out of garbage cans is considerably less of a charming tale than that of a sexy street urchin from Michigan.

Oh, the life of a tortured artist!

Good Lord, talk about envisioning worst-case scenarios. I wasn't going to worry any more about it tonight. Tomorrow I would start afresh and begin pounding the pavement for a job waiting tables. But one thing was for sure: after today I was pretty sure my future didn't lay in being a professional extra.

Circuit Disaster

The job hunt wasn't going so well. The hot bars and restaurants on Santa Monica were less than receptive. I was so burned out from hitting up every other restaurant in town I couldn't keep track of where I'd gone or how many applications I filled out. It was the same story everywhere. "The manager is in tomorrow" or "We'll keep your resumé on file and if anything happens let you know."

The worst moment was when I hit one popular and well-known restaurant on Santa Monica and the aging sexpot of a waiter, pushing into his late thirties, sized me up and down and said coldly, "We haven't hired a new waiter in over three years. There is no turnover here."

"Thanks anyway. Keep reaching for the stars," I said to the career waiter before leaving in frustration.

With half the people in town aspiring actors and all them vying for a server position, I might as well be auditioning for the role of a waiter in real life.

The temp agencies weren't much better.

"I can schedule you for an appointment a week from today," a tired-sounding woman said on the other end of the line.

"Can't I just come in during open interviews?" I asked.

"No. We do scheduled interviews only," she replied.

So much for accessibility. I always did horribly on those typing and computer skills tests anyway. Back in New York I was always assigned to the phones.

To ease my worries I attended my first big social event in LA, the "Labor Day LA" celebration. This was the end-of-summer circuit party in town and was being held in a space called The Palace located in the heart of Hollywood. I wasn't a huge circuit party fan. I did enjoy them every once in a while but didn't plan my whole existence around them like countless other gay guys. Besides, I didn't have the money or energy to organize weekend drug binges that enabled me to stay up endless hours packed into a crowded space with a bunch of gym queens strung out on crystal. But I appreciated the energy, the music, and checking out the hot bodies every once in a blue moon.

I was glad when Sarah had invited me to go out with her and her cohorts. They were obnoxious but other than Candy were the only people I knew in town.

"You're coming to Labor Day LA with us, right? Stephen is getting the whole crew customized tank tops," she went on.

I had gathered by now that these people considered themselves an exclusive group. When they walked in a place they acted like they owned it, all of them gravitating toward one another. And many of the other people gravitated to them, stopping to chitchat and make idle talk. I even heard a few of the guys jokingly refer to themselves as "the A-list," but they sounded half serious. And I'm sure they really believed it. Strangely enough, other people around them seemed to buy into the idea as well, which I found even more disturbing.

The night of the party I planned on picking up Sarah at her place and then driving over to her friend Fred's apartment, where we'd meet up with the rest of the group.

Fred was the uber-stud of the clique, with a perfectly chiseled body, a face that was almost too pretty, and the ideal job and apartment to go along with his looks. I actually liked him better than any of the other guys in this conceited convergence of queers that was the A-list. He seemed much more genuine than the others. The rest of the guys were well aware of Fred's physical appeal, and I had even heard a few of them make sniping remarks suggesting he might have had plastic surgery. But when I was first introduced to him he asked me plenty of questions about my interests and seemed genuinely interested in getting to know me as a person.

He was definitely not afraid to show his gay side, having an extended conversation with me about who our all-time favorite actresses were, a sure sign of two gay men hitting it off.

"And I love all those luscious women from Fellini flicks, you know, like Anita Ekberg and Claudia Cardinale!" I gushed, going on and on.

"Mmmm. And what about Lana Turner?" Fred would reply, pursuing the subject further.

This guy wasn't concerned about appearing macho, or maybe it was that he just wasn't trying to impress me in particular. Either way it was cool. Nothing irritates me more than a gay guy who tries to maintain a rigidly straight and heterosexual image in public, just for the sake of attracting other men, then goes home at the end of the day to dance around to his Diana Ross CD collection.

The night of the party I thought I'd be a little funky and have some fun. The East Village boy came out of me and I got inspired to smear my whole upper body, including my hair and tank top, with Jerome Russell gold body glitter.

When I got to Sarah's place she was more than taken aback at my glittery look.

"Check you out, sistahhh!"

The guys she hung out with were very uniform. They dressed to conform, not stick out. But as the new guy in town I wanted to grab some attention and be a little different. I suppose in a way I was already beginning to rebel against the A-list. That was the bohemian misfit stuck inside me, the one I have trouble suppressing and who is most likely responsible for my life becoming one twisted situation after another.

The tank top I was given had the number 9 on it, my random number in the group that night. Stephen decided to print "Tank bottom" on the front, in reference to my occasional proclivity for wearing vintage 1970s' tank tops with Bo Derek or Pink Panther transfers that were cut off at the bottom. I thought it was a stupid name, but he thought it was really funny, so I just humored him when he gave it to me at the gym earlier that week.

"Oh, how funny. That is so brilliant!" I lied, wishing he had come up with something a little more clever.

Fred's apartment was truly amazing, located on the corner of San Vicente and Fountain in a beautiful old Hollywood building, complete with high ceilings and a marble lobby. It looked like the kind of place a silent movie star would have lived.

The rest of the crowd was there when Sarah and I arrived, and while my glitter drew a few compliments and quite a bit of comments, I could tell that more than a few in the clique were put off by my attempt to have fun with my look.

Screw them, I thought, and gave myself a little tour of the apartment while they socialized in the other room. When I came back it was time to pass out the drugs. Earlier in the week at the gym Sarah had asked me if I wanted to front her money for some X. Her friend Ryan, a cute graduate student, was getting some great stuff from this dealer he knew.

Ryan was one of those people who liked to act like they never met you before and didn't remember who you were, when in fact they had seen you enough times that they had to. I never knew what motivated people to do this, outright cruelty or the need to feel self-important. It was probably both.

I seldom did recreational drugs, but I figured in order to loosen up and have a good time with this group I would have to. So I agreed and gave her the money that day.

Sarah passed me my X. It was like sorting out treats on Halloween night, as people passed shit around and swallowed.

"Can I get some ginger ale to mix this G with?" someone asked to no one in particular.

I had no idea what half the stuff was. I put mine in my pocket, figuring I had a hard enough time driving to begin with. And as I had never been to this place before, I'd better have it together on the drive over.

Before leaving, we all posed for a group photo in our matching tank tops, and then it was off to The Palace.

There was already a long line by the time we arrived. On our way to the back I received a few appreciative comments, the name "glitter boy" being bestowed upon me more than once. One of Sarah's friends managed to work his way to the front and beckoned with his finger for the rest of us to follow, leaving all the other poor suckers that had been waiting for minutes in the dust.

Once inside I heard the music pumping and saw the floor filling up fast.

"Should I take my X now?" I asked Sarah.

"Of course! You mean you haven't taken it yet?" she exclaimed, giving me an amazed look. "Let's go get you some water."

After getting water and swallowing my little pill, we met up with the rest of the A-list, who had formed a little circle on the dance floor.

Within minutes I started to feel a buzz coming on, and all of a sudden really began to appreciate the men around me. I mean, I was really admiring the men around me, to the point I couldn't keep my hands to myself. I waved my arms around in the air, and every time I made a sudden movement glitter sprinkled everywhere like fairy dust.

It wasn't long before I was gyrating and squishing my pelvis against the groin of any available man within reaching distance. Every few minutes I'd get near another one, this time pressing up against him from behind. Usually more tense and anxiety prone, X did wonders for my disposition. I probably should be on it regularly, along with some Xanax for good measure.

The Palace was getting overwhelmingly hot and steamy, so I decided to take a walk and get some fresh air. I went up the stairs to the balcony, walking in a slow, stupid swagger and sticking my ass out a bit more than was normal, as if inviting someone to tear my pants off and ram their meat up me.

I traced my fingers along the railing like some Hollywood actress of the 1930s making a dramatic entrance into a room.

I must have looked incredibly stupid, but I didn't give a shit. I was having a purely enjoyable and amusing time. Even the A-list was getting a kick out of me. As I looked out into the crowd of sweaty, muscular bodies, I wondered if I was gonna get laid.

I was interrupted from my thoughts of lustful abandon when I spotted Sarah at a couch in the corner of the room. Seated next to her was Fred, who had his head slumped between his legs while Sarah rubbed his back with a look of concern on her face.

Sauntering over in my drug-induced state I asked emphatically, "What happened? Is everything okay?" as if I would have been any help at that point whatsoever.

"He took too much shit," Sarah informed me, looking up with dilated eyes for a moment and then proceeding to rub Fred's shoulders.

Supposedly he had swallowed a shitload of G to go with whatever else he had taken and was a total wreck. A couple was staying with him from Canada, and one of the guys volunteered to take him home.

The best guy of the bunch, and he doesn't even get to enjoy the night, I thought as the Canadian placed Fred's arm around the back of his neck, wrapped his arm around Fred's waist, and walked him out the door.

After this turn of events, the party got uglier. A half-hour after Fred was helped out, I saw a bunch of men in red fire hats standing near the door.

Cool, I thought, figuring it was just some sexy guys in fetish getup, and went back to dancing around like a maniac.

That is, until the music suddenly stopped and an announcement was made that the fire department was shutting the place down. With too many people above maximum capacity, the party was in violation of local fire codes. Looking around I could understand the concern. If a fire ever did break out you'd have a bunch of messed up queens killing each other to get out of the place.

I could just see the news headlines the next day: "Hundreds of Gay Men Trampled to Death at All-Night Drug Fest."

A loud, instantaneous groan sounded from the crowd of dazed party dwellers. The crowd looked considerably less attractive as the indoor lights were suddenly turned on. My eyes squinted in discomfort as I half expected everyone to scurry under the woodwork like a bunch of roaches startled by the flick of a light switch.

"Figures a good party gets shut down in Lame Angeles," one guy next to me muttered as we shuffled our way toward the door with the rest of the masses.

Outside the scene was even worse. The night was unseasonably chilly and everyone was a sticky and sweaty mess. The poor, overwhelmed valets were trying desperately to keep up with the mob of screaming gay men trying to retrieve their SUVs and sports cars all at once. It felt as if a riot were coming on.

"They put the keys underneath the seats!" someone hollered out.

By now people were scrambling to find their cars and drive off themselves. If your car was blocked on all sides you were screwed and had to wait for the mess to clear up. I spotted my red Honda and made a run for it, seeing there was no car in front. Sarah decided to drive off with another friend to a bar.

"Are you okay to drive?" she managed to ask amid all the madness.

"Yeah, I'll be fine," I said, already making my way to the car.

With the stress of all the chaos around me, my buzz had worn off long ago.

"Call me on my cell phone!" Sarah yelled over her shoulder as one of her gaggle of gay men grabbed her hand with a muscular arm and dragged her away into the night.

After much screeching of brakes, I finally broke out of the pandemonium and drove back to Candy's. I was in no mood to go anywhere else. All I could think about was bed, and washing off what was left of the sticky Jerome Russell body glitter.

Two days later I joined the group again, this time at Will Rogers beach in Santa Monica, or "Ginger Rogers beach" as the guys liked to call it. Stephen drove, swiping a parking spot from some poor oblivious lady, who unrolled her window to tell him she'd been waiting for a spot for ten minutes.

"Sistah, relax," Sarah muttered out loud.

It didn't seem to concern him one bit, instead saying to her from his window, "Whatever, bee-ah-itchh!"

If this behavior was typical of Stephen, I was surprised his car hadn't been keyed up ten times over. I had been hanging out with these people because they were generous in showing me around. They probably thought I felt privileged instead of embarrassed.

The day was sunny and hot, with streams of people blading and biking on the pavement, and teams of volleyball players across the walk at the nets. We set up our spot and stripped down to our suits.

Because I swam in high school, I always wore a Speedo. Not exactly popular out here, with long, California trunks being the standard. But I felt a Speedo looked good on me, whereas trunks made me look like a beanpole.

Within seconds guys were coming by our blanket to talk crap and flirt. After a while some of the boys decided to be brave and go into the water.

"I'll come with you!" I wasted no time in tagging along, finding just laying on the sand an immensely boring thing to do after awhile.

My enthusiasm left when I put my foot into the freezing, dark water. Miami Beach this was not. Outside it was hot as an oven, but the water was completely frigid. I even remembered the water off Fire Island being warmer than this. The rest of the guys worked their way in like it was no big deal, so I followed suit.

"Be sure to keep your mouth shut under the water!" Fred hollered over at me. He had recuperated enough from the other night to spend the day with us.

"Why?" I shouted back, jumping up against the waves.

"People get intestinal infections all the time from the sewage and pollution. Especially after it rains," he explained.

"Sounds great!" I shot back. So much for California dreaming. Vomiting and diarrhea didn't exactly sound like a peppy version of a Frankie Avalon and Annette Funicello beach flick to me.

After bobbing around with the boys for a while I stumbled out of the water, pretty far from where we went in. Apparently there was a strong current to go along with whatever else was in that water.

"It looked like a movie, the way you just emerged out of the water," some guy said to me as I jogged back onto the sand.

"I should be so lucky," I smiled back, thinking about my favorite Bond film, *Dr. No.* Maybe next time I came to the beach I'd wear a dagger around my thigh like Ursula Andress. I wonder how that would go over with the A-list.

The day ended when we all went to a Mexican restaurant across the beach for a late lunch. There Ryan, the Ecstasy supplier who always behaved as if he'd met me for the first time, asked me where I was from for what must have been the fifth time.

I just looked at him point-blank and replied, "Has anyone ever told you that you have the brain retention of a two-year-old?"

The whole table went quiet.

"Ohmigod. That was so rude," one of Ryan's pals finally said.

"You're a tough crowd, you can handle it," I replied.

"You know some charming people, Sarah," Ryan said.

For the rest of the meal the crowd ignored me. Stephen and Sarah barely said a word to me on the way home.

"Thanks guys," I said as they dropped me off.

Not one for confrontation, Sarah told me to take care and she'd give me a call. Stephen didn't say a word, and as soon as I got out of the car the SUV whizzed around the corner.

It was for the best. I needed to concentrate on getting a job, not familiarizing myself with the city by hanging around a bunch of people who for the most part I found loathsome.

That evening I sat with my highlighter in hand and shut myself in my room. No ABBA music tonight or baking cookies. Candy had copies of both *Variety* and *The Hollywood Reporter* to scan through the help-wanted sections of. She poked her head in for a bit to show me what Frank had bought for her at the Pasadena Flea Market. He had come in town for the weekend and she spent all day with him.

"And check out these earrings. Bling bling!" she laughed, flicking at them with her lacquered nail.

"If you keep it up you're going to have to go to Spenders Anonymous, or Debtors Anonymous, or whatever the fuck support group is right for you." I rolled my eyes.

Candy laughed out loud when I shared the events of the day at the beach and restaurant with her.

"Good for you! At the gym they seem so obnoxious. I don't know how you stood being around them as much as you did."

"I don't know either," I replied. Putting on a pretentious voice, I stuck my nose in the air, snapped my fingers, and announced "Sistah, I'm just glad they didn't leave me stranded at that Mexican restaurant, or you would have had to haul ass to Santa Monica to come and get me, okay?"

"You would have found yourself on the bus," she laughed. "I'm going to have a cigarette on the balcony. You want to join me?" she asked, picking her latest luxury goods off my bed. One of her white Persian cats, Frosty, flopped on top of the *Variety* that was opened to the help-wanted section, looked up at me, and purred, waiting for me to rub his belly.

"Maybe later. I need to finish faxing out my resumé."

Turning my focus back to the want ads, I circled away with the dried-out highlighter. I was determined to find a job in the next few days and get to work as soon as possible. Then I could start building and really get my shit together. I went to bed that night thinking about good things to come in the near future, and a more mellow, laid-back life than I had back in New York.

Wading with the Sharks

I landed a job answering phones at Acclaimed Talent Agency, one of the biggest agencies in town. They counted such big-name stars as Jim Carrey and Jennifer Lopez as some of their clients, among others. I went to the interview all dressed up, having borrowed a tie from Candy's husband, Frank. The agency was located on the edge of Beverly Hills, right near the intersection of Doheny and Wilshire.

"Go ahead and valet your car," Whitman, the operations manager, instructed me when scheduling the interview.

Whitman informed me there were four receptionists altogether. Since I was the last one hired, my shift started last and I was the last to leave at night. All the parking was filled by the time my shift started, so if I took the job I'd have no choice but to valet.

I spotted the want ad in a local magazine called *Frontiers,* a gay rag that one picked up in bars, coffee shops, gyms, etc. The fact that I came across the want ad in such a publication clued me off that there was some major gayness going on at Acclaimed Talent Agency.

Whitman turned out to be a hunk of a gay man who I would have loved to be supervised by in bed. My interview turned out to be very amusing.

"Basically our past receptionists were more interested in dating and marrying an agent than doing their job," Whitman said with a wry manner, cutting to the chase.

"Every week the necklines got lower and the skirts shorter, while the phones were increasingly put on hold. It got to the point where it became a competition, and things got a wee bit catty. The agency can't become an episode of *The Bachelor.* We've had a better track record with gay men, and most of the administration staff is gay themselves."

Whitman also stressed that he was not looking for an actor to fill the job.

"If you want to be an actor you can go sell star maps on Hollywood Boulevard," he said.

"The only thing that has brought me to LA is the warm weather," I answered in a boldface lie, proceeding to tell him I was just looking to get settled and had no interest in acting whatsoever.

Good thing I was smart enough not to mention "Screen Actors Guild member" on my application where it asked for professional organizations.

There were two floors in the agency and two receptionists to each floor. The other receptionists consisted of an unusual-looking woman named Kim, a sweet gay guy named Toby who had been hired a few weeks earlier, and an ex-alcoholic gay man in his forties named Matthew who was head receptionist and took his duties way too seriously. I knew this Matthew guy was trouble from day one. He had the most irritating Texas drawl. There is no worse accent in my mind than a Texas drawl.

"Well, we'll make sure you have everything down and right in no time at all," he told me the first day on the job, asserting his authority and coming off like a complete prick.

Kim, the lone female receptionist, appeared to be thirty but was actually thirty-nine. She was odd looking, resembling a younger version of Endora from *Bewitched,* and ironically enough had jade green feline eyes, one that was noticeably smaller than the other. Apparently she was not one of the receptionists vying for the affections of an agent. She was too involved in a torrid romance with a guy in the copier room.

Right away she had begun to fill me in on the office gossip.

"Matthew, the head receptionist, had his alcohol rehab paid for by the company. That is why he is loyal to the point of ridiculousness," she confided to me in a sly whisper, her feline eyes gleaming with mischievousness.

Within a few days I found out who was dating whom, which agents were gay or in the closet, and which ones were on antidepressants.

"See that one over there?" She discreetly pointed out some guy waiting at the elevator. "He sent his assistant out to pick up his herpes medication, so the whole office knew he had VD the next day. Can you believe anybody would be that stupid?"

Such a large talent agency was a huge microcosm. What was most fascinating was that Ivy League graduates, some with law degrees, started out working for $8.50 an hour in the mail room. From there they moved up to being an assistant, and then with luck and years of hard work and putting up with all sorts of bullshit they became agents. That's where they hit pay dirt and started making the big bucks. Of course, the guys above you had to like you as well. Otherwise, you were screwed. Every white-collar job in America comes along with ass kissing and backstabbing, and in entertainment the amount is ten times so.

Now, anybody who could take a job paying $8.50 an hour in Los Angeles either came from money or already had connections from within. So of course nepotism played a huge part in the whole thing.

"Yeah, that one and so and so are cousins," Kim commented on a few agents who shared the same surname. "And there are a number of married couples too."

It seemed to me that many of the agents were nerds in high school or just ugly guys who never got a date. As a big Hollywood agent they could finally get a chick with big tits and have aspiring starlets blowing them every night, something they could only dream of before.

As for the women agents, especially the older ones, they looked like harried shrews with glasses falling of their faces and frizzy hair, ready to snap at you if you glanced at them the wrong way.

All in all, the whole operation was something to see. Why anybody would want to deal with a self-absorbed and temperamental actor or actress when they could work in a top-notch law firm making just as much money was beyond my imagination.

Stars came in and out of the place all the time. Alyssa Milano with her latest fling, smiling perfect white teeth and placing her parking ticket ever so softly on the desk to get validated. Dean Cain came in regularly to goof off with his rep, racing by the front desk without a word. Helena Bonham Carter dressed like a bag lady when bringing birthday flowers for her guy. George Clooney came in for a meeting once, and Toby the young receptionist nearly passed out when he asked him to validate his parking.

Being completely out of tune with the likes of the general public, I wasn't impressed or blown away by any one of them.

I thought it was cool that Cyndi Lauper was a client, but since she wasn't exactly a mainstream Hollywood actress, I didn't expect her to come through the elevator doors anytime soon greeting me in her squeaky Brooklyn voice. There was, however, one name in the building that really grabbed my interest. But she wasn't a client of Acclaimed Talent Agency.

On the lobby directory and in the elevators the top floor of the building was listed as Pia Zadora's offices. At this point in time, most people probably have no idea who the former Golden Globe–winning, scandal-ridden, multimillionaire-marrying singer-actress is. But being a John Waters fan and an oddball, I found her kitsch image and scandalous past fascinating. Now this was a large-sized building with an investment company and a large talent agency taking up four of the five floors. Why Pia Zadora, who as far as I knew hadn't done anything in years, needed an office was a mystery to me.

Every day I kept my eyes open for Pia Zadora, but to no avail. And no one ever seemed to go up to the fifth floor. Finally one day I noticed an average, everyday-looking blonde girl going up to the fifth floor. I couldn't resist.

"Excuse me. Does Pia Zadora come by her office very much?" There were a few other people in the elevator with us. Until that point it had been pretty quiet, so all focus shifted to the demure blonde.

"Umm, she comes in every now and then," she answered very slowly and very cautiously, as though she was really thinking about how to answer my question without her answer sounding bad.

Translation—no, she never comes in, and just keeps expensive offices in Beverly Hills for the hell of it. Damn. After that I knew I'd never catch a glimpse of Pia Zadora. Now working at this place held even less promise than it had a minute before, if that was at all possible.

After a few weeks Acclaimed Talent Agency was beginning to wear on my nerves big time. At the end of each day my butt felt as if it had been flattened by a skillet from sitting so long. My throat was hoarse from constantly answering the phones and having to say the same words over and over and over again.

"Thank you for calling Acclaimed Talent Agency, how can I direct your call?"

Also, because I was the last of the four receptionists hired, that left me stuck with a 10:30 to 6:30 shift, right smack in the middle of the day. With Los Angeles traffic and a schedule like that you could forget about getting anything done. I nearly killed myself trying to get to a hip-hop class at Crunch Gym every Tuesday and Thursday.

On top of it, I had been chewed out by a few of the boob-chasing prick agents for no reason whatsoever.

"When I tell you to hold a call you don't have to remind me twice, got it!" one particularly hirsute and sweaty guy yelled at me with foam at the corners of his mouth.

There had to be something better than this, if only I could get off the phones for a split second to look for it.

I worked closely with Kim, who was still being driven mad with love for the copier boy. They would call each other from the front desk to the copy room over the phone and have passionate, conflicted conversations in hushed voices.

"Why are you acting like this to me?" Kim would plead into her headset, as I sat less than a foot away trying to ignore what I was hearing. I didn't care to hear the details. Every once in a while she'd lose it and her voice would rise.

"No, that's not true!" she yelped into the line at her defense one afternoon right as Whitman was walking by. He glanced at her, furled his eyebrows, and just shook his head in comical exasperation.

Kim took the bus every day back and forth from Echo Park on the other side of town, and she did performance art on the side. She was definitely the kind of person that could be described as a fringe dweller, which was saying a lot coming from me.

"I'm throwing a barbeque with friends this weekend," she would tell me. "And we're going to read poetry, have body paints, and do Reiki. Want to come?"

I never made it out to Echo Park. Yet she was nice and entertaining, which made the days pass by easier.

On the other hand, Matthew was slowly becoming my nemesis on the job. For some reason the guy had it out for me from the get-go. He was just a complete wart on my ass and obsessed with every call that came in and out of the place, and every visitor that stopped by the front desk.

I rarely had to sit with him answering phones, but when I did it was like having teeth pulled.

"You and Kim have the calls backed up to eight or ten at a time. When the four of us are here they should never be backed up more than three at a time!" he accused in his irritating Texas drawl.

One of the more excruciating aspects of the job was blowing off aspiring hopefuls and dreamers who called or came by the place. Acclaimed Talent Agency strictly took on talent by referral only with no exceptions. In other words, if you were not the kid or relative of somebody important or already known, forget about it. Don't bother calling or sending your picture, because it just ends up going in the trash.

To say we got some sad cases on the phone is putting it mildly. Some people called saying they were actors looking for an agent, but you could hardly understand their speech. "Hi. I'm an actor and was calling to see if y'all can find me some jobs," I'd hear on the other end of the line.

I doubted some of them could even read a script. More than half of the time I had to give an explanation of what "by referral only" meant since they didn't get it.

"So what does that mean?" some pathetic soul with bad diction would ask.

"It means you have to be sent in from somebody they know," I tried to explain patiently and politely.

Of course, it was somewhat agonizing for me being an actor and in the union to be surrounded by so many people who had the potential to start a career. But if I dared mention it to anyone, Whitman would have me out the door in a minute flat. I was here to answer phones, period.

Security was tight and kept people from walking in, but on occasion someone slipped by with a script or a head shot and tried to give it to me. which was basically pointless since nobody but administration and the other receptionists knew that I even existed. To the agents I might as well be invisible. It was like the Boulevard of Broken Dreams came through the phone every day.

Every once in a while something interesting would happen in the office. When I was working there a scandal occurred that involved a supposed teen writing sensation named Kaylee Reston. Hollywood's creepy obsession with youth was getting out of control at this time, with programs on the WB Network such as *Dawson's Creek* and *Buffy the Vampire Slayer* the happening thing.

Kaylee Reston was supposedly nineteen years old and had just landed a two-year half-million-dollar contract to develop and produce shows for television. That fact in itself was disturbing enough for me, who after four years of college was answering phones for peanuts while a nineteen-year-old gets to write fun scripts for half a million dollars. Was there no justice in the world?

What rocked the agency was when a story broke in one of the trades and on *Entertainment Tonight* that Kaylee Reston was really a thirty-two-year-old who had been in Hollywood for years working under a different name.

For a week everyone made jokes about it, and it was the main conversation by the elevator bank.

"Dude, I can't believe she pulled that off!" junior agents would joke in amazement.

The gay guys in administration took particular pleasure in the episode, walking around the office and pronouncing with glee, "Tomorrow I turn sixteen!"

They thought it was just hilarious. As if lying about one's age was something new in Hollywood. Christ, even Nancy Reagan lied about her age. What the hell did people expect in a town where at age twenty-eight a person is considered the equivalent of a geriatric patient?

It was like coexisting in a town full of pedophiles.

From my perspective Kaylee Reston was a hero that duped the business. And the business deserved it. She should have gotten a gold medal. She was just giving Hollywood what it wanted—youth, youth, and more youth. I hoped that Acclaimed Talent Agency was thoroughly humiliated, but I doubted it. They probably enjoyed the publicity.

I also hoped, at the very least, that Kaylee Reston was able to keep the money from her development deal, or at least some of it.

It was also amusing to observe the behavior of some of the agents when it came time to meet with clients or potential clients. One day a flashy black girl came through the elevator doors with a few huge thugs trailing behind her. She asked to see Ben Fassas, one of the egotistical pricks who had reamed me out for nothing.

Ben Fassas was the worst stereotype of a sleazy Hollywood shark, fat and ugly with an inflated ego. He handled all the rappers and hip-hop people, so I knew the moment she walked in she was probably going to ask for him before she even opened her mouth.

"Hello. Tasty Jones here to see Ben Fassas," she said sweetly. I thought she was a pretty girl as well. After complimenting her on her very noticeable diamond watch, I asked if she and her friends (homeboys, really) would like a bottled water. Taking me up on the offer, she grabbed a seat while I called up the asshole and let him know she was there.

"Tell her I'll be right out!" he barked over the phone, as usual sounding like I had inconvenienced him by letting him know his appointment had arrived.

"I'll be right out," meant let them sit there for ten minutes before coming to get them.

When their meeting was over and she'd left the office he lingered at the front for a minute or so to talk crap with a few of the other agents who had seen her come in.

"Man! Her face was wrecked!" he exclaimed, laughing like a jerk with his cohorts.

I thought this was ironic coming from a fat, hairy, greasy-looking eyesore with such a heavy beard that he could shave and have a five o'clock shadow ten minutes later.

Since I have canine hearing I heard a lot of dish while sitting with my ass glued to the front desk chairs. Which client was difficult, which one was demanding, and so forth. Some clients hung around way too much.

One child actor, who had been chosen for the role of a lifetime in a big-budget thriller over hundreds of other hopefuls, was always in the office. He ran around the place like a bull in a china shop, pestering basically everybody and behaving out of control.

"Yo! What up dude?" he'd yell down the hallways.

With a grandma in some faraway state, the agency seemed to be his daycare while he was in LA. Now well into puberty and entering his teen years, this kid was on his way to having an impressive arrest record to go along with his acting career. Not that the agency cared; as long as he was bringing in money they'd put up with his antics.

The cocky, aspiring actress who wore an annoyingly trendy choppy haircut and spoke with a squawky voice was almost as bad. She constantly hung around the office walking in and out of the place like it was her home, and it almost was.

"Hey baby!" she'd coo to the male agents, hugging them and smothering her breasts against them.

"Somebody get that girl a part on a location far away," I told Kim after she passed by us the twentieth time in one day.

By the third month of my being there Acclaimed Talent Agency was beginning to be the ninth circle of hell. Even in bed the words "Thank you for calling Acclaimed Talent Agency, how can I direct your call?" raced though my head like a reoccurring nightmare.

What did I get myself into? I thought. The phones never stopped there. The headsets we receptionists wore seemed to congeal to your head. Was this what I went to four years of college for?

"Adam, can't you at least try to become friendly with clients in the waiting room? Maybe you can get a job as an assistant or something," Candy asked between puffs of her cigarette one evening when we were sitting out on her balcony.

I had just finished my latest tirade about how intolerable life at Acclaimed Talent Agency had become.

"Are you kidding? I'm just a parking stamp or bottle of Pellegrino as far as they're concerned. Besides, even if they cared to speak to me to begin with, we'd be continuously interrupted by my answering and connecting calls. Or getting rid of them, depending on what kind of freak is on the other end," I said flatly while picking wax out of one of tens of cast iron candleholders placed around the terrace.

"I can see how that would be a problem," she pondered, flicking her ashes over the railing. "What we really need are some mentors."

Candy was forever going on about mentors, and how it was really important to have an important role model in life. Her idea of an important role model was Sharon Stone or Cathy Moriarty, both of whom she was always thinking of trying to contact.

Personally, what I felt I really needed was a few thousand dollars saved to give me a decent start on an apartment and time to buy to find a decent job.

But coming to LA with less than $500 in my pocket hardly provided the luxury of time to seek out a rewarding job that actually led to a career. And with a one-hour lunch break that was strictly enforced, looking for something better seemed a near-impossible task.

The temp agencies I called still made appointments for a week or two ahead. In New York I usually walked in or even went out for an assignment the same day I called. Everything in LA was a big production, even if it wasn't showbiz related.

In fact, any temp agency that took me would probably just send me out on a job like the one I had now, answering phones. Besides, some of the temping experiences I had in New York were just as scary as Acclaimed Talent Agency. And doing extra work seemed hardly in the cards for me either, as I called that stupid hotline at Central Casting all the time and they never had any work for my look or age range.

As a matter of fact, Central Casting had only called me once in three months.

"Is this Adam Zeller?" a snappy voice called one day.

"This is him," I answered.

"We submitted your profile to some show producers and they want to know if you are available for an audition in Santa Monica this Wednesday between three p.m. and six p.m."

"Is it for a speaking part?" I asked.

"No," the woman answered impatiently, "just background."

"Well, didn't he see the photos you took? Isn't that enough?" I asked. It was a bit much to want someone to drive out to Santa Monica during a workday to be an extra.

"He still wants to see everybody in person. Can you do it?" she pressed.

"Not this time."

That was the last I'd ever hear from Central Casting.

It amazed me that people were willing to drive miles to audition for an extra job that wasn't even guaranteed. Was everyone out here on crack? Wasn't it enough that Central Casting already had a picture of me that I had waited around for half a day to take? Not to mention all the frustrated and deluded professional extras I had to wait around with. What a waste of time, gas, and mileage. Not to mention the fifty bucks they charged to register with them.

There had to be something else I could do other than answer phones and stick bright orange validation stamps on parking tickets.

I thought about modeling, but the reality was that I just wasn't that stunning. An attractive guy, maybe, but no stunner. While in college I had given it a try. My modeling career had lasted a mere few months and consisted of a page in *Details Magazine* and a hack runway show at a downtown nightclub named NV Bar where the biggest name in attendance was Grace Jones. I didn't have money to sink into pictures, but if you looked that great you shouldn't have to, an agency took care of that. That should have clued me in at the beginning that modeling wasn't in the cards for me.

Always being strapped for cash, however, I was not above doing another kind of modeling. And LA was the capital for this sort of modeling. I had done nude modeling before in New York, when Candy gave me the number of her hung-like-a-horse photographer friend. If I did it back there, I could do it again here.

After getting out of Acclaimed one night, I drove to the nearest magazine stand and grabbed *XXX Showcase Magazine*. In the back it had the *Adam Gay Video Directory* which listed all the gay adult film companies. I was sure I could call some numbers out of the back of this and find some jobs that would help me out with some extra funds to pay my bills.

I even recalled the name of a company that an aspiring independent director I met in New York told me about. His name was Perry Bristol, and he supported himself and his mainstream film aspirations by moonlighting as a director of porn.

The company was ingeniously titled HUNG Video. Perhaps if I told the people there that I knew Bristol, their star director, they'd come up with some gigs for me right away.

In the meantime, life at Acclaimed Talent Agency continued. Surely I could find a better job in a week or so; it couldn't be that hard. After all, I found a job at this shit hole after only a few weeks in town. I had shot myself in the foot before, quitting a job without having another one lined up, but this place was just making me miserable, with no time to interview for anything else. And my misery must have really showed.

"You might think you are too good for this job, but we all have a job to do and you need to do yours too," Matthew the head receptionist said one day in a sharp tone that basically conveyed all the venom and contempt he had for me.

Management had begun to split up Kim and me, for fear that we were getting along too well and not paying enough attention to the phones. The consensus was we were not behaving stoic and serving enough to visitors.

Which was kind of the truth.

Still, it didn't feel any better to be treated as though you were kindergartners who had to take their mats to opposite corners of the room during nap time.

And to top it all off, I knew the Mexican valet guys were reckless with my new car, noticing some dings on it already and hearing them come around the corner like Speed Racer. One valet in particular liked to fart in it before I got in, so it stunk to high heaven. And man, could he ever break some foul wind. I could just see them laughing at me as I drove off, joking in Spanish about stinking up the gringo's car. That was a real slap in the face, or rather an assault on the nostrils, after working a demeaning job.

The farts in my car were the final straw. Patience had never been a strong virtue for me; if anything, I am way too impulsive. And it got the best of me again. One morning when I really didn't feel like being there I walked into the administration's office and gave my notice.

"Oh no," Whitman cooed, tilting his head to one side and doing his best to sound surprised and disappointed, despite having gone through dozens of receptionists during his tenure there.

"Where will be you going?"

"I got a job working on a friend's film," I lied.

It sounded a lot better than "I don't have shit to go to, but if I stay here one more day I'll throw myself out the window."

Less than two weeks later *I* was out of there for good, marking my end on the phones at Acclaimed Talent Agency forever. It also marked the beginning of my slide into the seedy underbelly of La-La Land.

HUNG Video

Where the interaction, social hierarchy, and manic personalities at the talent agency were unbearable, the porn industry was just plain mind-boggling. I would come to find out both environments had plenty of larger-than-life characters. The difference was in the porn world people actually treated each other better and lacked the big egos. Those involved were realistic about the kind of work they did, and that they were considered the bottom of the barrel by the rest of Tinseltown. Yet at least they were honest and up front about being money-grubbing pigs and users, which was more than I could say for the suits at the agency. It was sad but true, the dirty world of porn was nicer than the legit business world, whether it be a television network or Wall Street.

As far as taking my clothes off, I had no problem with it. I always said that if it came back to haunt me, I would tell the truth.

"I was poor, broke, and needed the cash," I would fantasize myself crying to an interviewer upon getting famous someday, my past being found out. Boo hoo, boo hoo.

Everyone has to pay the bills somehow. And if you are an artist of any kind, be it actor, writer, painter, or whatever, at times you had to be very creative to make ends meet.

I figured I could just be in some solo videos and pose for some naked pics. Perhaps HUNG Video had production work I could do as well. I wouldn't have actual sex on camera though. What if someday I did come to a position where it came back to haunt me? Jerking off in front of the camera alone was one thing; fucking another guy was something entirely different.

I was still paranoid about sex anyway and never fully relaxed when it came to it. I have always practiced safe sex (or safer sex, as it is called now) but still suffered from a bad case of nerves after every time I fucked a guy I didn't know well. Hypochondria and prostitution don't mix very well.

I spoke to the man in charge at HUNG Video, a guy named Ron. He sounded very Middle America, almost like an insurance agent from Missouri.

"Hey, Ron. I'm Adam," I introduced myself on the phone with some trepidation. "I'm looking for some work, and thought I'd give you a call. I got your name from Perry Bristol; we met a few months back in New York."

"What do you look like?" Ron cut to the chase.

"Well . . . I'm six-one, dark brown hair, hazel eyes, swimmers build, and I've been told I'm a good-looking guy," I answered honestly, not wanting to overexaggerate.

"Can you come by this afternoon?"

"Sure," I answered. That was quick. Good thing, since I needed some bucks badly.

Ron gave me directions. HUNG Video's offices were located on Hollywood Boulevard, just a few blocks east of La Brea in an old high-rise that had obviously been constructed in the 1960s. The cavernous garage smelled like piss and the lobby of the building was in bad need of repairs. The directory had those white, blocky letters straight from the 1970s, very retro. I took the elevator up. A guy at the front of the office steered me along while checking me out.

"Go down the hall and make a right at the last door."

On my way down the hall I passed a room that was obviously where the graphics must have been designed. Porno cases were scattered everywhere. Images of men with oiled-up bodies and tan lines stared at me from every direction.

I stepped into the right office and found Ron sitting behind his desk. He looked like a high school football coach. Actually, he looked exactly like Dave from the Wendy's hamburger chain—same white hair, dopey blue eyes behind glasses, and lumpy build.

"Yeah, that's right," he spoke loudly into the phone. "And make sure he gets that invoice paid for . . ."

He even spoke with the same slow, flat accent. Not exactly what I was expecting. More or less I pictured the owner of a porn company to have a few gold chains, chest hair coming out of his shirt, a diamond pinkie ring, maybe frosted hair—that kind of thing.

Ron continued speaking on the phone as I sat down. He motioned he would be a minute with a wink of an eye and point of a finger. As I waited I looked through the windows. The office was on a corner and everything below was a massive grid with cars moving like ants across a picnic blanket.

"Sorry about that!" he said as he hung up the phone with a smile. I sensed that he was pleased with what he saw.

"So let me ask you, what exactly do you want to do, both in front of the camera and off the camera?"

"Well, right now I'm looking to make some extra money since I just moved here," I answered, unsure of what to say. "I thought maybe you could use some help on shoots and stuff."

"Cause if you want, we can get you in front of the camera in some upcoming scenes," he answered back, getting right to the point. "I've got a gang bang shoot scheduled in a week."

"I don't know if I'm ready for something like that at this point," I answered cautiously, not wanting to insult him or sound like I was too good for that kind of thing.

"You sure? I got a cute blond kid with an ass like two volleyballs stuck together flying in from Denver for a gang bang. And the other guys are mighty hot too," he persisted.

It wasn't that I saw anything morally wrong with it in my mind. In fact, I found the idea arousing and a turn-on and almost wanted to say yes. But it just seemed that once you crossed that line, there was no going back, kind of like entering Hades. Tragic thoughts of people who became caught up in the world of porn with nothing to fall back on after they were dried up and burned out came to mind. Like that chick Savannah who fucked all the rock-and-roll stars and then blew her head off one night after crashing her Porsche in front of her home. Not that I was expecting to sleep with Slash from Guns N' Roses or own a Porsche anytime soon.

Still, this was just dabbling for me, just something crazy and out of the ordinary to do until I found a permanent job, something better than the phones at Acclaimed Talent Agency. I hoped that would be in a few weeks.

"Well then, would you be interested in doing a solo jerk-off video?" he pressed.

"Sure." That seemed harmless enough, and I was perfectly comfortable with that.

"How does this coming Saturday look for you?" he asked.

"Great."

"I'll call you with a time. And I'd like it if you could go to a tanning bed for some color. Your body would look even better. I'll reimburse you for it; just save the receipt. And if you change your mind about the group shoot next week let me know. Otherwise we can use you as a production assistant, have you pick up the boys at the airport, help set up the equipment, that sort of thing," he rambled on.

"Sounds good," I said.

My first starring role in LA, and the plot was jerking off. My right hand was to be my costar.

The solo video took place a week later, in a one-story building on Santa Monica Boulevard. These were facilities used by HUNG Video, where they duped their tapes, kept equipment, and also did much of their filming. Before I shot the video I had to have some still photos taken of me with a full erection.

As I sat on some folding chair in the cold cement studio I was interrupted by a voice.

"Hey, I'm Brian."

I turned around to see a cute dark-haired guy in his mid to late twenties with both arms full of photography equipment.

My day just got a whole lot better.

Brian was a cute ex-UCLA student who was now an aspiring photographer/filmmaker/actor/model/whatever. I couldn't get his story straight. What I did understand is that he worked on the side for HUNG Video, under a different name.

"All right," Brian said when we got down to business. "Let's start with some shots of you taking off your shirt."

"No problem," I said. "So how'd you get involved with HUNG Video?" I asked, eager to keep the conversation going. The camera clicked and whirled.

"Word of mouth. I approached some other companies first and one thing led to another. Helps out with the bills. And I always hit it off with the guys," he added.

"I bet," I said, and Brian smiled sheepishly.

I didn't know if he was this flirtatious with every model, but he and I were hitting it off like hotcakes. I could sense he was attracted to me. We talked college lingo, spoke about classes, that sort of thing. As we spoke I hoped he thought I was out of the ordinary from your average models.

When he finished with the tame series of shots it was time to get to the nitty-gritty, full-out, in-your-face hard-on shots with my butt stuck up in the air, ass pouting, and winking in the camera.

"I gotta go next door and pick up the lights and reflectors," Brain said while placing his camera down.

"Let me help you," I offered, eager to oblige.

"Cool. Thanks." He smiled again boyishly.

After we set up the lights it was time to get naked and grow some wood. The room where we shot the pictures was large and empty with cold cement floors, making it difficult to get aroused. The reason it was empty was so when they needed to film some scenes, they could bring in some cheap props for whatever kind of set they wanted to create. Not that the set was all that important to them. There were some mats stuck in the corner of the room and that was about it.

"Do you need some magazines?" Brian offered when he saw me close my eyes, turn around, and vigorously start yanking at my cock.

"Brian . . ." my voice trailed off, eyes still shut tight.

"Yeah?"

"Do you think I could . . ." my voice trailed off again.

"To hell with it," I moaned, and opening my eyes up I walked across the mats to where Brain was standing and unbuttoned his fly, pulling a beautiful, plump dick out of his jocks and enclosing it in my mouth.

He didn't resist.

The warmth of his flesh in my mouth was a relief from the damp cold of the cement block room. The friction of his trimmed body hair and firm flesh against my face helped even more. His hands gripped my head firmly as he moaned gently.

Now I was as hard as the concrete walls around us.

I released his cock with a slurp and let it slap back against his belly. Then I gasped, "Okay! Let's do this."

The clicking and whirring of the camera started again. Bulbs flashed furiously as I thrust my pelvis forward and flexed my muscles.

"Great! Now turn you torso a little to the left," Brain gave orders. "Stop there! Perfect!" The camera snapped some more.

When I felt my hard-on faltering, I went back on my knees and took his dick back in my mouth, pulling it in and out, slapping it across my cheeks.

"Okay, good to go again!" I'd wait until my cock grew to its fullest size once more, and we went back to shooting again. This went on a few times until Brain got all his shots.

"You did that like a pro," Brian said while peering across at me with mischievous eyes.

"Thanks," I said and stretched across the mat. "I was glad for your help."

"Glad to oblige," he answered, and began walking toward me when the metal door of the hallway crashed open, startling us both.

"Yo!" a booming voice shouted in the air. A tall and beefy fellow with a happy-go-lucky disposition came sauntering into the room.

"Hey, Dale!" Brian greeted him while retreating from me.

"What up, Bri?" he bellowed then turned to look my way.

"You must be Adam," he said, walking toward me. As he got closer I noticed his cheerful, sexily slanted eyes and boyish face. Even his haircut was schoolboy, with straight short bangs cutting clear across his forehead.

"That would be me," I said with a bit of a snotty edge to my voice. I was annoyed at being interrupted with Brian, and this guy acted like he owned the place.

"Dale Warren," he said, sticking a strong hand out toward me. "You ready to do this thing? Don't mean to rush you, but I got a lot of editing yet to do today." As he spoke he walked away to pick up some bags he left by the door.

"Well, I should go," Brian said. "I have some business to do with Ron. Adam, it was great meeting you."

"Same here," I smiled.

"Brian, I'll see you at the shoot!" Dale pointed at him.

"Shoot?" Brian looked perplexed.

"Yeah, the army gang bang. You're doing stills, right?"

"Oh, right, right . . . yeah, I'll be there," Brian said. Cute he was, but a bit of an airhead.

My spirits rose when I heard Brian would be at the shoot. That was the one Ron wanted me to make my sex debut on, but the one I was planning on just helping out with behind the scenes.

"You can just leave the equipment here since it is in a few days, Bri," Dale said. "No sense in trucking it back and forth. I'll make sure everything is locked up good."

Brian expressed his thanks and was gone.

Dale and I were left alone. He had a rough kind of demeanor that sort of reminded me of the guys you'd expect to see in shop class. Nothing about him struck me as giving the impression he was gay until we started to speak and he made comments about his attraction toward the same sex.

"Yeah, the guy a few weeks ago had a sweet ass," he said while getting things together. "But you! You look like you could be a model!"

"Thanks," I said. A lot of people told me that. If they only knew what a colossal failure my actual attempt at modeling was.

Thankfully, a solo jerk-off scene was a quick and easy way to earn cash. I was set up with my legs lying on the floor, my back leaning against the wall. Dale threw some large pillows behind me and placed a large potted plant on the side to add whatever atmosphere he could to the place.

During the filming Dale talked me through it. He took on the role of a dirty narrator, asking me questions off camera.

"So," he'd start in a gruff voice. "How many times a day do you play with yourself?"

"At least twice a day," I breathed back heavily. "Once in the morning and before bed at night."

Then Dale began telling me what piece of clothing to take off. The whole thing was so narcissistic and silly to me that I decided to have fun with it. I already had blue ball from wanting to nut all over with Brian. Now after playing with myself for minutes on end I was ready to spray the ceiling. My cock looked like a bright red torpedo about to soar. It was slick and glossy from the big pump of WET lubricant a few feet away.

"Ah . . ." I moaned in earnest as a searing sensation traveled to the tip of my penis.

"Yeah!" Dale yelled gruffly. "Let me see it rip, you hot cocksucker!"

"Here it comes!" I yelled. Before I knew it I was staring at white ooze flying from the slit of my dick to my face, hitting me on the bottom lip and chin.

"Oh yeah! Shoot it!" Dale hollered as my body jerked convulsively like an epileptic.

After I climaxed, I looked straight into the camera and moaned out loud, "I love me!" as though I had just bestowed upon myself the best orgasm ever.

Having a sense of humor, Dale clearly appreciated my improvisation.

"That, my friend," he paused for dramatic effect, then said, "was priceless."

He grinned at me like a proud parent, and I looked back with petulant pride. He was really kind of cute in his own way.

"Here ya go." He tossed a roll of paper towels at me, and with that we wrapped things up.

"Great!" Dale said as he snapped his camera lens shut. I got my check from Ron and called it a day.

The Human Sponge

The group shoot was basically a large gang bang set in an army barrack. The day before the shoot Ron asked me to pick up two of the models at LAX. I drove to the arrival flight level and sat in my car trying to spot two young guys from Denver who I had never seen before and wasn't even shown a picture of. I was just given a brief description.

The traffic to LAX was a bumper-to-bumper nightmare. When I finally got to the arrival level nobody in sight fit the description. *Shit,* I thought. There was no fucking way I was going to drive into the parking structure, park my car, start searching, and go through all that trouble to find these morons. It was bad enough I had to make the drive to the airport; I would have refused if I didn't need the money so badly. I put my emergency signals on and jumped out of the car.

I went upstairs to departures, thinking maybe that these guys were confused. There was no sign of them up there either. By now I was starting to get really irritated when I finally saw two scrappy blond dudes standing on the sidewalk in baggy jeans and sweatshirts.

This had to be them. I went ahead and approached them, and sure enough it was this weekend's talent. They looked relieved to see me. I threw their stuff in the trunk and drove off. They appeared to be just over nineteen years old. Neither looked older than twenty, and if I thought *I* was misguided, seeing these two left me feeling I could be much worse off.

The first guy was a self-proclaimed skateboarder who wore a baseball hat that hung so low over his forehead you couldn't see his eyes, and he enjoyed listening to annoying techno music. He sat in the back and kicked his shoes up against the front seat, fueling my bitterness and resentment over my current job responsibility.

The other kid was a pudgy-faced blond with wide blue eyes who informed me that he was the bottom of the scene.

"So how'd you two get involved with HUNG Video?" I asked.

"Our agent sent in our pictures," the bottom told me.

"Can I put in one of my tapes?" the skater leaned over and interrupted.

His music sounded like something you'd hear in a bad disco in Berlin, or perhaps Eva Braun's bedroom.

"Sorry, dude. It's broken," I lied. Not that it mattered much. I could still hear his awful music blaring from his headphones.

We had just gotten on La Cienega and had a long ways to go, and I was already sick of them. Sitting in the LA traffic, I listened to the blond bottom blab on about his life in Denver, which sounded warped and disturbing. He proceeded to prattle on and ask me what I thought they should do that night in Hollywood.

"Not much without a car," I replied.

I wondered if either of them had the slightest idea of what they were getting into as I waited at a traffic light. Eventually I reached the Holiday Inn on La Brea, right around the corner from Hollywood Boulevard. A bunch of Pakistanis ran the place, and they looked at me suspiciously when I approached the front desk. They then informed me that in order to check dumb and dumber in I had to have the actual credit card with me, even if reservations had been made prior. Now I was visibly pissed and just wanted to get out of there.

I called HUNG Video. Ron bitched endlessly about it over the phone and told me he was sending Dale Warren over. Dale arrived with the credit card.

"I'll take over from here," he grumbled. He looked frazzled and pissed.

I took off, glad my driver gig was over.

The next day was the big shoot. I headed to the Santa Monica location in the morning to help Dale set up. Brian was there, along with Ron and a small camera guy who was very serious, made no conversation, and looked like he really didn't want to be there. In the same large room where I filmed my solo video we set up cots and flagpoles, re-creating a half-assed looking army barrack. After helping set up the equipment I was sent off to pick up a giant sub at Blimpie for the cast and crew.

By the time I came back with the food the cast was beginning to arrive. They included a very handsome Eastern European guy. Maybe he was Armenian or Turkish. I wasn't sure. Two well-built blond guys came in together, looking as if they had just been picked up from a farm in Nebraska. Then I spotted a gorgeous dude making conversation with Dale Warren. He had an amazingly solid and buff body, thick brown hair, and green eyes. I later found out he was a pharmaceutical salesman who did porn on the side for money. I was introduced to him and we spoke a little. He told me that he lived in Redondo Beach. I imagined that Ron paid him well, because this guy was a knockout. His only drawback was that he had bad skin, but not bad enough to take away from what was otherwise an outstanding package.

Two more guys came in together. They struck me as rough and working class, the kind of guys you'd see at a pool hall in San Bernardino or someplace like that. Unlike the others, these two actually did resemble real army guys. For all I know, maybe they were in the military. But I wasn't going to ask.

One was a bit too red. I'm sure Ron told everyone to go in a tanning bed, including him. But this guy had stayed in for way, way too long. It looked painful to me.

The two twits from Denver rounded out the illustrious cast. Dale had picked them up at the Holiday Inn while I went to grab the giant sandwich, which now looked totally unappetizing as it sat on a fold-out table in the corner. A cooler of soda and bottled water was shoved underneath.

Before the cameras rolled Ron took me aside.

"Now," he began in his flat, lazy accent, "if you want to jump in I'll throw you a couple hundred extra bucks for the day." He wore a satisfied expression on his face, as though he had made me the offer of a lifetime.

I rejected his offer. I almost wanted to join in just to have sex with the pharmaceutical salesman. But making my porn debut with eight other people on camera would have been a bit too much.

I noticed the baby-faced blond from Denver sitting in the corner staring at the floor with his eyes glazed, fear written in his expression.

"What's wrong?" I went over and asked him.

"I'm going to have to get gangbanged by eight guys," he murmured, looking completely petrified.

"Didn't they tell you before the fact?" I asked awkwardly.

"No, they just said it would be a few," he answered.

"Wow," I replied, a little speechless.

I was at a loss for words. What do you tell someone who is about to get the shit fucked out of them by eight other guys, gangbanged six ways since Sunday?

Brian had started taking still shots of the guys, all of whom were in the room now. They were all well hung; nobody was lacking in that department. But the most endowed of them were one of the farm-fed-looking guys and my favorite, the pharmaceutical sales guy. With a long and thick member, he must have been very popular with the girls (and boys) in Redondo Beach.

The shooting began with the European guy laying on one of the bunks, looking at a girlie magazine, and the wide-eyed Denver boy coming in to get nailed. My job was to stand by with lube in one hand and paper towels in the other. Today I was the official lube man. Evidently, instead of having a makeup person running on set in between takes to powder the actors' noses, a porno set had a lubricant person standing by to squirt some grease into their hands. I also had to make sure that condoms were unwrapped and available nearby.

As I stood there waiting for the action to begin I wondered if they taught a class for this at The New School.

As the blond twink sat on the European's dick, immediately it became evident something wasn't right. A foul smell arose and the condom the European had on looked darker than normal, with a cloudy grayish-brown hue.

"I thought you said you douched yourself," Dale said, clearly annoyed.

"I thought I did," the blond responded, blushing red from embarrassment.

"Go back in the bathroom and do it again," Dale ordered.

The humiliated baby-faced bottom sprang up and darted into the bathroom.

The European lay there with a disgusted look on his face. I grabbed some paper towels for him, beginning to fulfill my professional duties on the set. Ron glanced at me with a grossed-out expression. "This side of the business does not appeal to me at all," he sneered.

That comment left me confused, as anal sex was the bottom line of this business and what it was all about, so maybe he was in the wrong business altogether. Perhaps he should try something else to suit his sleazy personality, like used car salesman.

Soon the blond returned with everyone hoping he had cleaned himself out completely.

Evidently he had, as the next scene called for him to be on the bed and get it from both ends. First he started with the pharmaceuticals guy, who seemed completely at ease, not minding sticking his huge shaft in another guy's mouth or rear end if the price was right. Then the two big blond corn-fed-looking guys came in and began playing around with each other.

"Oh yeah. Take that dick," they ordered in bored voices.

"Can you guys make it look at least halfway believable?" Dale complained.

Brian and I glanced at each other, trying our best to keep from laughing.

They were followed by the marine guy without the sunburn and the skater. Now they all surrounded the baby-faced blond, a few keeping him occupied while others played around with each other, switching around places every once in a while.

"Yeah. Fuck him!" they ordered one another comically in gruff tones.

If the kid had any reservations about getting gangbanged earlier, by now he lost them. It was especially apparent when he demanded out loud, "Can I get a dick in my mouth?"

Someone was turning into a little gay porn prima donna diva in front of our very eyes.

Dale turned around and jokingly said, "I like this kid," while Brian and I just looked at each other and rolled our eyes.

The models kept calling me over for more lube, a few giving me suggestive looks when I stepped forward. One of the stocky blond guys was jerking off with extreme vigor as I approached. The next thing I knew he made a little groaning noise and then gave me an expression of guilt and surprise, as though he had done something wrong. Looking down I saw he had ejaculated in his hand.

"Oh shit. I came," he said.

Dale overheard and barked, "Don't anybody come yet!"

The stocky ejaculator turned back to me, smiled, and said quietly, "It's cool. I can do it again."

The whole situation was surreal. Me running around with a bottle of lubricant for a bunch of naked men, all busy slapping their salamis. I could just imagine telling my friends about this one, or better yet, my mother.

"How was your day?" she'd ask.

"Well, I have a new skill to put on my resumé, Mom! Lube dispenser and condom overseer!"

I'd have to write this experience down in some journal to believe it years from now.

The other marine with the sunburn was the last to step in. This guy actually had lines. He was the angry drill sergeant who finds his men having gay sex and decides to punish them by joining in on the action. Wearing a uniform supplied by HUNG Video, he did his best drill sergeant à la *An Officer and a Gentleman* or *Stripes*.

"What in God's name is going on in here!" he spat hoarsely at the top of his lungs.

He was surprisingly convincing, and now I was 99 percent sure he and his buddy were really in the army. God only knows how HUNG Video found them. He joined in the circle and starting humping the blond like the rest of them.

After that they all ejaculated over him in a circle jerk. Dale and the camera guy moved in for close-up shots, and I put aside the lube and readied myself with a big wad of loose paper towels.

At this point, I was really sick of the smell and feel of lube, to the point where I felt like I was about to puke. One by one they came all over Mr. Denver.

"He's like a sponge!" one of them cracked.

The other actors thought that was really funny and laughed about it, telling Denver it was his new nickname—"The human sponge."

With the jizz having popped from almost everyone, we were all ready to get paid and scram. Dale was just waiting on the skater guy, who tried and tried to come but with no success. Finally the human sponge, still lying there all covered in what by now must have been very cold sperm, snapped, "Let's just finish. He's never going to be able to do it!"

In a few hours he had made the transition from nervous bottom to snappy star, almost like some fucked-up gay-porn version of *A Star is Born*. Dale gave up on waiting for his last money shot and called it a day. The models grabbed their pay and took off. I stayed behind with the others to take the equipment down and clean up a little. Not having been in LA six months, I had been given an explicit view into the world of gay porn, up close and personal.

Beer and the Billionaire

Before long, my first brushes with porn led to the first trick I turned in Los Angeles. Ever since I became involved with HUNG Video, Ron had been telling me of possible tricks he could arrange with important men in town. It turned out that besides being an expert porn producer he was an expert pimp as well. All in a good day's work for him. He kept mentioning how he knew "major" clients and emphasizing that I must never reveal their identities and must keep them in complete confidence.

As if prostitutes signed honor codes like students at Columbia University or some other Ivy League school, or their work was right up there with FBI agents. I could just see the male hustlers who serviced Hollywood bigwigs going out for a drink afterward and blabbing about it to their friends, exchanging secrets like "He had a dick smaller than a peanut" or "This time he threw in a few extra hundred."

But I just kept reassuring Ron I'd always keep my mouth shut. Besides, who did I have to tell but Candy and my school friends back in New York? Other than Candy, they couldn't care less and probably didn't know who any of these people were anyway.

"Would you be interested in seeing these clients for the right price?" Ron asked me a few days after our initial meeting.

"Sure," I told him.

I was now paying Candy $450 a month in rent for her guestroom. She charged me less rent than the place was worth because she used half the room to store her excessive wardrobe. But still, I had gas, food, car insurance, and other expenses. And though I was looking for a job on the Internet and in publications like *The Hollywood Reporter* and *LA Times,* I still hadn't found something decent.

Yeah, I could have gotten something at Starbucks. But if I could stand turning a few tricks for a while, I'd rather hold out for some-

thing better and have more time to look. That and the fact I was sick
of low-paying jobs in the service industry.

It was a few weeks before Ron would become more specific about
who his very important clients were. Then he divulged the names,
emphasizing both a famous manager and a billionaire producer. At
first I thought he was bullshitting. Ron was such a sleaze, and a bit of
an idiot on top of it, that I could not believe such accomplished people
would speak two words to someone like him, even for the freshest
piece of ass off the farm. Ron nonchalantly went on to explain that the
billionaire had been out of town for a while but was back in LA. He
had just been sent nude pictures of me taken the day of my jerk-off
scene.

I wondered why someone so successful couldn't find a gorgeous
boyfriend to satisfy himself with. I reasoned the bigger the bank account, the bigger the appetite.

Supposedly that was how it worked. Ron sent him pictures of guys
and the billionaire decided if they were worth his time or money. I
thought of myself as attractive but hardly an Adonis, therefore putting any thought of ever meeting the billionaire out of my mind. A
few nights after Ron mentioned the whole thing, I got a phone call at
home.

"The billionaire wants to see you tonight. How soon can you be
ready?" he asked in a serious tone.

"Umm . . . fifteen minutes," I stammered, caught completely off-
guard.

"Where are you again?"

"Right near Robertson and Olympic."

Ron figured it would take me an hour to get there.

"Just so you know, I told him you love to swallow dick and can suck
the metal off a tailpipe, so be prepared to do just that. Sometimes he'll
have guys stay over depending on how much he likes them or what
mood he is in. And the pay is at least five hundred dollars."

He gave me directions and told me to call him when I got there.
The address was in Malibu, right on the Pacific Coast Highway.

I showered quickly. After getting out of the shower I stared at myself in the mirror, immediately focusing on the first feature I always looked at, my hairline.

At age twenty-three I was convinced my hairline was already beginning to recede. I was continually paranoid about it. Every morning I worried about how someday I was going to have to go to the Boseley hair transplant institute. I was so neurotic about losing my hair I would work my mind into frenzy about how I'd better get some acting roles very soon, while I still had a full head of hair.

I got dressed and headed for my car. I remembered reading an article about the billionaire in *Vanity Fair* years ago. My mother used to subscribe to *Vanity Fair,* and it was always on the living room coffee table. In this particular issue there was a photo of the billionaire at his colossal mansion in Beverly Hills. His name was Wayne Hanley. I guessed his place in Malibu was where he met all his tricks, a more casual environment. *No hustlers allowed in the big place,* I thought while driving down the Santa Monica Freeway toward the coast.

Excited thoughts raced through my mind the whole drive there.

I can't believe I'm going to this powerful man's house to sleep with him. Should I have brought a resumé? Nah, I don't think "gym receptionist" would impress him very much. Maybe he'll want to see me again, even for a few weeks. Then I'd have a lot of money. He might even notice I'm reasonably intelligent and offer me a great job, who knows?

Eventually I passed the restaurant on my left that Ron had told me to look for when giving me directions.

It was an excruciating task to make out the numbers of the buildings while driving, as it was so dark and each number was placed somewhere different on every home or apartment, some barely visible at all, others nonexistent.

That was one thing I noticed about LA, especially when driving up in the hills. It was as if no one wanted to be found. Some street signs where hidden behind trees, and many homes didn't display numbers at all. And if the numbers were on a curb chances were that a car was parked in front blocking it. That always drove me nuts, and I consequently got lost in those twisting roads in the hills.

Anyhow, eventually the numbers I could see grew too big and I knew I passed the correct address, so I swung around and drove south again. Maybe this time it would be easier driving on the same side of the road as the house, the beach side. Finally I spotted the right number on the gate of a two-story home. I parked on the side of the road and walked up to the buzzer. The place had a tall wooden fence and hedges in the front, obscuring it from the street. I pressed on the intercom. A voice answered, asking my name and then telling me to come in. The gate buzzed open and I nervously went in. It was like I had just made it to the Emerald City and was finally seeing the wizard.

Here we go, I thought, and braced myself for the unknown.

I could see now that the place was a pretty Cape Cod–style beach home, with a perfectly manicured lawn and a brick path that led to the door. The door opened as I approached it. A short man in a plain white T-shirt, jeans, and sneakers appeared. He introduced himself.

"Adam?"

"Yes."

"I'm Wayne."

We shook hands and he motioned me inside. The place was immaculate, furnished expensively but tastefully. Casual but chic, as one would expect a weekend beach home to look. There was a kitchen on the left after the door, a large room in the front, and a smaller room with a television also on the left, around the kitchen. Wayne told me to have a seat in the room with the television and asked me if I'd like a beer. I could hear him clanking around in the kitchen. It seemed that there had been somebody else, probably a housekeeper, in there when I entered; now they were gone. I assumed they had been sent away. Eventually Wayne came back from the kitchen with a beer.

"Do you want anything else?" he asked.

"No, thanks. I'm good."

"Are you sure? You don't want any pot? I have other stuff too," he pressed.

"No. That's cool," I answered.

"You're sure?"

"Yeah. I'm fine."

I supposed most everyone else who came over for this purpose took up his offers like kids grabbing for sweets in a candy store. Maybe it was the only way they could get comfortable. I didn't want to risk becoming a total mess.

Let's just do it and get it over with. I tried to make small talk but wasn't very successful. Wayne just sat there nodding his head with a superior expression on his face. What did you say to someone who had a billion dollars and was close to some of the most fascinating and famous people on the planet that he could possibly find interesting?

"I wish the weather were warmer; it's freezing tonight," I blurted out.

Wayne Hanley looked at me straight in the face, his heavy-lidded eyes gazing at mine steadily, and said, "I wish a lot of things, Adam. I wish I were a foot taller. But there is no point in wishing on things I can't control, is there? It's just a waste of time. It doesn't get me anywhere to focus on it, wouldn't you agree?" he said in an authoritative and somewhat demeaning tone.

"Umm . . . sure," I stammered, somewhat taken aback. So much for discussing the weather. God forbid I ever bring up something of substance, such as politics. I could only guess how I'd get cut down in a discussion pertaining to that.

I sat there a little taken aback as Hanley flipped the channels with the remote, frequently stopping at CNN and bypassing the other programming. We continued to make small talk. Then he stopped in the middle of conversation, looked at me, and laughed.

"You're funny," he said.

"How so?" I asked, fearing I had said or done something really wrong, and might have messed the whole thing up.

"I don't know. You just are," he responded.

We kept making small talk, and it was as if Hanley had some little quip or comeback to whatever I had to say.

"Are you being facetious?" I asked at one point, by this time more irritated than intimidated. Hanley looked a little caught off guard.

"Am I being facetious? No. Just making conversation," he replied in amusement.

You could bet that few of the tricks, if any, used words like facetious. Obviously it wasn't the kind of vocabulary Hanley was used to hearing from the hustlers that frequented his place. He told me to come over to the couch closer to where he was sitting, and stretched his legs across my lap. I started clumsily taking off his shoes.

"We should do this somewhere more comfortable," he ordered.

With that we stood up and went upstairs, bringing our beer with us. The staircase and walls were a beautiful polished wood. The steps led straight to the bedroom where floor-to-ceiling blinds covered what must have been a spectacular view of the ocean. At the end of the room there was a large bed and a bathroom to the left.

We went near the bed and undressed. I was glad I washed well, and that my ass felt fresh. I was also thanking God I didn't feel any bowel movements coming on. This was the most inopportune time for feeling the need to take a dump.

I was shocked at what I saw next.

This little man had one of the largest cocks I had ever seen on anyone, and I had seen plenty at this point.

The gigantic penis in front of me was made even more apparent by the fact he was wearing a snug cock ring around the base of the shaft, obviously well prepared for the night ahead.

Hanley propped some pillows in front of the headboard and motioned for me to go down on him. Before I knew it I was choking on the tycoon's enormous dick. This went on for minutes, with him grabbing the back of my head and shoving it facedown forcefully. Drool was spilling out of my mouth everywhere. I took it out of my mouth and started slapping it against my face, just to give my throat a break and give myself time to breathe.

During this whole time Hanley was being very forceful and asking me repeatedly what other sex acts I liked, but not giving me any time to answer.

"So what else do you like, huh?" he seethed with a clenched jaw. "What else turns you on?" All the time he jammed his freakishly huge schlong down my throat.

The man apparently had a sadistic side in bed. If he was this ruthless and brutal in business no wonder he was one of Hollywood's most powerful men. I tried to break away and make my way up, attempting to suck on his nipples a bit and give myself a rest. But it was evident Hanley did not want to be bothered with above the waist, and even told me so after a few attempts.

"I don't care for that, Adam, and don't try to kiss me," he ordered.

I went back down and Hanley again kept asking me what else I liked.

"So tell me what you like to do," his now sinister voice rang from above.

Did I like toys? Did I like to get fucked? I tried to ignore him, afraid of what would happen if I said yes to any of these questions. There was no way that thing of his was going up my ass. I finally told him I didn't do it up the ass without knowing my partner well.

Big mistake. Hanley stopped shoving his anaconda in my mouth, paused to look at me, and calmly stated, "I'm in perfect health."

I wanted to tell him it wasn't that I was worried about as much as my ass being torn in half, but I restrained myself.

Luckily he didn't push the issue.

I brought my head up for a sip of beer and then got an idea. Wouldn't it be sexy if I dribbled some of it on Hanley's crotch and then licked it off? Maybe he would think that was hot and even throw in an extra couple hundred bucks.

This was not one of my more brilliant ideas. I went a bit overboard and some beer spilled between his short legs and onto the sheets. Hanley squirmed and bolted upright.

"Adam, why did you do that?!" he snapped in an annoyed, scolding tone.

"I'm sorry," I sputtered. "I thought you might like it."

"I don't want this to seep into my mattress," he went on angrily. "Some people do not care if their homes smell like beer. I prefer to have my house not smell like beer."

Hanley went on about it at length. I felt bad enough for my failed attempt at being kinky and creative in the sack. Why did he have to rub it in further?

Son of a bitch, I thought. *Like he couldn't afford to buy every goddamn mattress in the whole country.*

We continued to go at it despite the beer incident. Finally Hanley came. I got a little in my mouth but most of it on my chin and the side of my face. Then I lay back and came over myself. He got up and went into the bathroom, bringing towels with him. He went on for a bit babbling about cock rings.

"They have to be leather," he babbled on. "The rubber ones just pinch and are far inferior."

We made some more small talk, and Hanley continued with the snotty comments.

"You know, you're not really facetious—just condescending," I finally said.

He looked at me for a moment and then grinned like the Cheshire cat. This he definitely wasn't used to hearing.

"You like to use big words, don't you?"

Well, I might as well put what has so far proven to be a worthless college degree to some use, I thought to myself.

Hanley brought up the beer again. Apparently he wasn't over the incident yet.

"I think it's time for me to turn in," he said a few minutes later.

"Do you want me leave?" I asked.

Hanley looked at me as though he had insulted me and asked, "Is that okay?"

"Sure. That's cool," I replied.

I was only mildly insulted he didn't ask me to stay. It would have been nice to wake up to an ocean view instead of Candy clattering in the kitchen, or arguing with Dean over the phone, or worse, fighting with her estranged husband Frank when he occasionally dropped into town. Things had gotten so bad between them that a few nights earlier he came home in a drunken stupor and she dumped a bottle of Merlot on his head and threw him out the door. He had even called *my* name in a stupor, pleading for help, but there was no way I was coming out of my room to intervene.

Yet hearing about the beer one more time would have been torture, even compared to the drama at Candy's.

I got up from the bed where I'd been laying naked the whole while. The room was still dark, and my body was just a silhouette. I knew my broad-shouldered swimmer's build and narrow waist must have looked good, even to someone like Hanley who had seen the best bodies out there, and I was proud of that. I felt confident and cocky walking around the room, picking up my flung pieces of clothing and putting them back on again. I had accomplished my mission and was proud of myself for that.

We walked down the stairs together, and Hanley asked me how I got connected with a sleaze bucket like Ron, only he used the word "gentleman" to describe Ron for the sake of throwing more sarcasm out there.

"Of course, using the word gentleman and Ron in the same sentence is an . . ."

The word escaped him.

"Oxymoron," I answered for him. *Hooray! Yet another big word out of the male whore!*

I hope he's not looking at the top of my head and noticing my thinning hairline, I thought as we walked down the stairs. I walked at a brisker pace to prevent him from noticing it.

Downstairs I put on my fleece jacket and sat down to tie my shoes. Hanley stood nearby and thanked me for coming over, much to my surprise. Our conversation coupled with the fact that I actually told Hanley what I thought of his personality during the course of the evening must have caught his attention. That and I used a few big words.

He seemed nicer now that we had finished having sex, letting his big shot guard down a bit and actually showing a softer, human side. I got up the nerve to suggest we do it again, and Hanley had me write his number down. Then he went into a drawer and pulled some cash out and handed me an even five hundred. I had hoped for more and was disappointed, but relieved to have some cash in my fingers.

He walked me to the door, and before he shut it I turned around and said, "Thanks for everything." Then I sarcastically added, "My Visa bill thanks you too."

He shut the door and that was that. I don't know what in God's name possessed me to say something so goofy. I guess I was pissed he didn't give me more, especially after being so rough. Not that saying something stupid every now and then was anything new for me. But chances were I might have had a better hope of hearing back from him if I had played it cooler. Then again, maybe not. He probably preferred fresh meat each time.

Candy was in disbelief when we sat on the balcony later that night and I told her I had just had sex with one of the most powerful people in show business.

"You're kidding me" were the first words out of her mouth, to be exact.

For the next twenty minutes I filled her in on the details of how the event unfolded while she grilled me with questions.

"Do you think he's going to want to see you again?" she asked pressingly.

"I have no idea," I sighed. "No, I don't think so. I made a crack about my Visa bill. It's been on my mind because it has gotten so run up from moving out here and not having a steady job. I don't think he appreciated it."

"Well, that's too bad," she said bluntly. "Having a sugar daddy like that, even for a little while, could solve a lot of your problems." Candy had my interests in mind, and this was her way of showing that she cared.

"Yeah. I know."

"There is a rumor he takes care of that pretty boy at the gym," she went on. "The one I pointed out to you, from the music video. They say it was Hanley who bought him a Jaguar. I mean, all the guy does is go to acting classes and the gym, kind of like yours truly. And all he's done is that one music video. And he is always hanging with a few pretty girls, but none of them are his girlfriends."

"Well, if that's the case, I can kiss my chances good-bye. Comparing me with him is like comparing Divine Brown and Liz Hurley. I was the cheap trick for the night. And that's it," I murmured while petting one of the cats as it purred loudly below.

"Come on. You don't know that for sure."

"Look, its not like I'm broken up about it," I spoke up, coming to my senses. "The guy almost put a hole through the back of my neck!"

"Eww, I guess you're right," Candy laughed, scooping up one of the cats and placing him on her lap. "Who needs that?"

I knew better than to think I'd hear from Hanley again. I didn't just fall off the turnip truck. Sure enough, a few days went by, then a few weeks. Soon I chalked Hanley up as another life experience and laid him to rest with all the others.

Lights! Camera! Coffin!

The old metal shelves around me were covered in a thick layer of dust, drawn through with lines where videocassettes had been stacked. Due to boredom I found myself fixating on the gray dust and cruddy smears on the paint of the walls.

For the past few weeks I'd been toiling around the offices of HUNG Video, doing shipping work and whatever else needed to be done. It wasn't so bad. I was getting $10 an hour for mindless work. But I'd tired of focusing on trying to perfect my shrink-wrapping. For some reason I just couldn't get it right. Invariably the plastic at one corner of the cassette box came out bubbled and fried.

"You're holding the blow-dryer too close to the box," a voice boomed from behind, startling me. I turned around and saw Dale Warner looking my way with a smile on his face, a combination of amusement and mockery. It irritated me.

"And you're holding it in the same spot for too long. That's why you're getting holes. Here, learn from an expert," he said while grabbing the dryer out of my hands. Ripping a length of shrink-wrap from the roll, he proceeded to heat up the plastic, sealing it perfectly smooth.

"Voila!" he said, holding up the shiny tape cassette. The title *Jungle Gangbang* was blazed across the front, two naked and oiled models wearing forced smoldering expressions staring from the photo with tropical foliage behind them.

I stood unimpressed with my arms folded across my chest.

"Wow. That was great," I said in monotone. "I have a hundred more. Why don't you keep that for the rest of the day?" I added, nodding toward the blow-dryer.

"Sorry. No can do," Dale smiled back smugly. "I'm afraid I've graduated from the shrink-wrap department."

"Gee, did you wear a cap and gown?" I asked, grabbing the blow-dryer back.

"Well, we're sure in smart-ass mode today, aren't we, Mary?" he said in his finest church lady voice.

"Whatever," I murmured as he walked away. Although he was not the perfect pinup of a guy, there was a cockiness about him that was sexy. Maybe it was his skater clothes, gruff voice, and stocky lumbering body. I tried to visualize what he looked like naked. He probably had a thick, fat dick, like his meaty forearms.

He's trouble anyway, so quit thinking about it, I told myself.

While my days taping up packages at the warehouse were often boring, evenings at home with Candy were always eventful, especially when she had a new project or endeavor, which was more than half the time.

Later that evening was one such occasion. Candy ran a racy, yet not explicit pinup site of herself to promote her lagging acting and modeling career. Every night she clicked away at her computer e-mailing various "fans."

One visitor to her Web site saw a photo of her from *Sect of Lucifer* dressed in character as Morgana Sateen. This guy had a vampire fetish and e-mailed her a request. He would pay her $500 to make a ten-minute video of herself dressed as vampire in a French maid outfit. In the video she would have to crawl out of a cardboard coffin that he would supply in the mail. He would pay her half up front and the other half when he received the tape.

When Candy asked for my help I imagined what a fiasco the whole event would be. The fact I hadn't held a camcorder in my life didn't further my enthusiasm for getting involved in this latest project. When I arrived at home to help her out she was just as eager to get it over with as I was.

"Okay, Adam, let's knock this thing out. I just want to get this shit done so we're not up all night like a couple of idiots," she said while running around getting stuff together.

She was already wearing a cheap French maid outfit, the kind you bought prepackaged around Halloween. The clicking of the black patent leather pumps she wore against the hardwood floors sent the cats scurrying under the furniture.

Dean the useless ex-boyfriend was over that night and seemed doped out as usual, more interested in watching television in the other room than helping me assemble the cardboard coffin. Somehow I managed to get the thing together even though I am notorious for being the worst handyman to hit the planet. Too bad I wasn't this good with home electronics or furniture from IKEA.

Candy was wondering how she was going to keep her fangs in, with toothpaste the only thing on hand to glue them. We put candles all over her living room and they actually looked very good with her ornate baroque mirrors and overstuffed furniture. If you stretched your imagination a little you could think you were in some European palace that a vampire might haunt, albeit with a lot more cream and shabby chic accessories. After practicing on the camcorder a bit I got the hang of it. We leaned the cardboard coffin against the mirrored armoire and had Candy open it slowly and come out that way. It didn't look right on the floor, and besides the cats kept walking back and forth to see what all the fuss was about. Having a fluffy white Persian cat walking by in the frame took away from the dramatic effect to say the least.

Dean just sat on the couch the whole time like a lazy bum while Candy and I did all the work. Her fangs weren't staying in well and she had to continually keep sticking them to her teeth. The tape needed to be at least ten minutes long. We tried to do everything as slowly as possible, like have her take a long time to just step out of the coffin. She was so over the top I burst out laughing a few times and had to stop the camera.

"I adore the night!" Candy pronounced in an affected, thunderous boom that sounded like a cross between Joan Crawford and Mrs. Howell from *Gilligan's Island.* She continued babbling nonsense into the camera to kill time as I grew steadily sicker of holding the damn camcorder.

"Her name is Lilly," Candy purred into the lens out of the blue in a sultry, taunting voice. It was like a bad impersonation of Eartha Kitt.

This caused me to break into titters of laughter.

Lilly was the name of Candy's little sister, but not an actual little sister. Candy did volunteer work for the Big Brother and Big Sister program. She was forever keeping me entertained with tales about Lilly. Lilly was peculiar, like Candy and myself. She was an overweight child who happened to be a very talented young artist. Her favorite activity to do with Candy was go to Color Me Mine, this place where you bought ceramics and could paint them, and then have them bake it in a kiln for you.

Lilly once painted this really cool Elvis bust and even counted the exact amount of rhinestones needed to glue around his collar. How many nine-year-olds out there would choose an Elvis bust to paint to perfection?

I had a soft spot in my heart for Lilly because like her I had been an eccentric child, and we are both Capricorns. Lilly was obsessed with astrology and the zodiac. One day Candy and Lilly were crossing the street and the light turned in the middle and Lilly ran and screamed like a lunatic. When Candy told her to calm down Lilly's response in her baby voice was "I worry a lot because I'm a Capricorn."

Lilly had an obese mother who met men on the Internet, putting her picture up on sites for men who love fat women. Their house was always in filth and disarray. The carpets were crusted with crud, the walls were dingy, and there were ketchup stains on the ceiling. Toys were strewn all over the house and the backyard. Her grandmother lived with them as well.

Every week Lilly would tell Candy and me, "And guess what? Grandma says if we clean the house we can get a puppy!"

And on the next visit: "Guess what? Grandma says if I have a good report card, we can get a puppy!"

And the following week: "Guess what? Grandma says if we pick up the yard, we can get a puppy!"

"Talk about hope," Candy told me one night. "With her tenacity this girl should be a fucking actress."

So needless to say, with all I knew and had heard of Lilly, I lost it at the mere mention of her name.

"Knock it off, Adam!" Candy groaned, barely able to stifle her own laughter as I tried to get my composure back together.

"That was a bit over the top, Candy," Dean commented with a dumb laugh from the couch behind us, where he was sprawled out with a can of beer.

"Shut up, Dean!" Candy snapped in exasperation. "Look, you guys, I want to get this stupid thing over with. These fangs keep falling out and I'm really getting over it," she went on, indicating how tired and impatient she'd become.

"Okay, okay. I'm sorry. I promise I won't laugh any more," I said in earnest.

I'm guessing it was hard work improvising and trying to be a convincing vampire woman for ten minutes. Therefore, she had to draw inspiration from whatever peculiar ideas crossed her mind.

"Where is my beautiful Lilly, she was supposed to be here!" Candy roared, sounding like a sex-crazed lesbian awaiting the arrival of her lover.

Though it was difficult, I kept my mouth shut through the remainder of her performance, and signaled to her when ten minutes were up, finally able to put the camcorder down. Candy sent out the video to her quirky admirer a few days later. He wasn't very appreciative after viewing it, complaining he would have rather had her lay the coffin on the floor and climb out of it that way. And instead of Candy lifting her skirt up for the camera, he wanted the camera to actually travel up her skirt.

I took his complaints very personally since as the cameraman I was somewhat proud of my last-minute work. After all, the video was in part an artistic vision of mine.

"The poor guy," I said sarcastically. "Some people just can't be pleased. Everybody's a critic."

After filming the vampire video we caught camcorder fever for the next few days. Candy wanted to audition as one of the "clue crew" on *Jeopardy*. I thought the tape we made of Candy was cute, especially when she gave a clue about the Eiffel Tower while speaking some French and tossing a beret in the air. She would have been great giving clues on TV alongside Alex Trebek. Unfortunately she never heard back.

We videotaped each other for *Survivor,* setting up her house plants to create a faux jungle and stating how far we'd go to win.

"*Survivor* is nothing compared to opening day at Barney's Warehouse sale!" Candy roared into the camera lens. "If I can come out of there alive with four pair of Jimmy Choo heels and a choice Gucci wrap dress, then I can survive anything!" And with that she stabbed her umbrella as though it were a spear at her silk oriental rug.

I don't know that either of us would have lasted long on a deserted island or in the Australian Outback. Not that we weren't physically tough enough, but the other contestants most likely would have conspired together to vote off two eccentric nutcases like ourselves before the plane even landed.

"I still don't know why you are not doing stand-up," I said after putting the camera down.

"You know, Adam, other people wouldn't get my humor," she sighed. "I'm funny when I'm going off to you, when I'm not thinking about it. If I tried to do it on stage, I'd bomb and make a jackass of myself."

Then after a sudden jump where she sprang up on her toes and spun around ballerina style, Candy pronounced in a singsong voice, "Only you can appreciate my humor, Adam!"

"That's what frightens me," I muttered under my breath.

Bobby Steelhard's Hollywood Garage

Given the state of my financial affairs and my work environment, it was bound to happen sooner or later. The time for me to copulate with another man in front of the camera was looming.

"You talk to Ron?" Dale asked me one afternoon while passing through the warehouse.

I shook my head no. Ron was trying to hook me up with more "clients," but I was trying not to appear overly desperate. Ron just wasn't the kind of guy you wanted to appear in a vulnerable spot with. He'd take advantage of it any which way he could.

"You know we're shooting another video in a week, right?"

I knew where this was going. Ron had been hinting at wanting me in his new production for days now. I just didn't want to go that far. Everything I had done to this point had been me alone, solo. That was bad enough. But others had moved beyond it. Even that kid Simon Rex made a solo jerk-off video and managed to go on to an acting career. Yet sex on film with another guy, or two guys, or three guys, or more—I had never heard of anybody going on to do something in the public eye after that.

"You've got gorgeous model looks, why let them go to waste?" Dale joked, trying to lighten things up.

"No thanks," I answered curtly. "I plan on performing in front of cameras again, but not that kind of performing and not in front of HUNG Video's cameras."

"Yeah you and a million others," Dale shot back sarcastically. "Look, Adam, I don't mean to burst your bubble, but I'm sure you've heard Dionne Warwick sing it, *all the stars that never were are parking cars*. And for a gay guy, you've got to get real. The odds of you breaking into acting are nil to nothing. As far as this ever coming back to haunt you, take it from me, there is so much fucking porn out there.

Not just zillions of videos, but Web sites, magazines, you name it. So what if somebody sees you? You tell them the truth—you were on your last cent and needed the money, pure and simple."

Those had been my thoughts exactly regarding the solo stuff.

"Ain't that the truth," I mumbled.

"Besides," Dale was now heated and worked up, "I don't understand the fucking stigma anyway. It's not like we're robbing people or hurting people; we are all adults doing what all adults do. At least you'll look damn good doing it, which is more than most people! Fuck, most people couldn't do this even if they wanted to, unless it was some amateur or fat fetish thing. And nothing's forever anyway. Traci Lords was doing this before she was eighteen, and she got out of it and is doing fabulous. And whatever happens, you'll do fabulous too!"

I took a deep breath and smiled. The perspective he put it in made it sound okay, like it wasn't the end of the world and I wasn't slipping into oblivion.

"Well," I said gently, "if I do it, and I'm only saying if, I'm sure I'll feel better about it with you directing."

"And I take that as quite a compliment coming from big talking, smart-aleck Adam," he laughed, then playfully picked up the blow-dryer and turned it on my face.

"Watch it!" I laughed, grabbing the end. He turned it off and we both held it for a minute, gazing at each other again and smiling.

That same day Ron had approached me in the stockroom and asked me in his flat Dave of Wendy's voice, "Dale tells me you've changed your mind about being in our next video. Is that true?"

"Yeah," I answered. "He did a little convincing."

"Great!" Ron yelped, slapping me on the back.

"What better way to make money?" he winked. "I can't think of any!" he chortled and walked off.

A lot of better ways to make money came to mind, but not with my useless degree and pathetic resumé.

The next day Ron came into the warehouse more excited than the day before.

"We've secured Missy to direct our film!" Ron said excitedly. "This is the big time. No better way for you to start out."

I had no idea who he was talking about. It sounded like the name of someone's pet cat.

"Missy?" I asked.

"Yeah, Missy Manhandler!" Ron repeated, expecting the name to register with me. I just looked at him blankly. "Come on, you've had to have heard of Missy."

I picked up the phone and called Dale in a panic.

"Why didn't you tell me a girl was directing the shoot? How do you expect me to fuck a guy in front of a girl and not feel funny about it? I thought you would direct me!" I asked angrily.

"What the *hell* are you talking about bud?" Dale asked, bewildered.

"Ron said that the shoot is going to be directed by some bitch named Missy is what I'm talking about!" I snapped impatiently.

"Oh Lord," Dale snickered on the end of the phone.

"How is that so funny? I'd rather have you direct the first time!" I fumed.

"Babe, Missy is no woman. Missy is an enormous drag queen," Dale explained.

"Oh. All right," I answered entirely confused.

"But don't worry. She won't be in drag during the shoot," Dale laughed.

"I assumed you would be directing," I said.

"Nope. Not this time, as much as I'd love to. When Ron secures a big name like Missy, it's a real coup. It's a compliment toward you, being that Missy is the top director in gay porn right now and wants you in her movie. Besides, I have my hands full with editing work. Don't worry though. I'll get to directing you soon enough. Look, I gotta go now. Everything will be fine. You'll have a lot of fun. Just relax. Later."

And with that he hung up the phone.

Things were just getting weirder and weirder.

Eventually the day for my all-out porn debut arrived. I decided to go by the name Adam Zee. I felt that if someone recognized me, it was better to own up to it than have an entirely bogus name like Sam Strong or something like that. For me that was almost like owning up to being embarrassed or having something to hide.

The video was titled *Bobby Steelhard's Hollywood Garage,* Bobby Steelhard being the big star of the video. The shoot was to take place in the San Fernando Valley, the porn capital of the country, at an address in North Hollywood to be exact. The call time was 10 a.m., and when I arrived I made extra sure to read every freaking street sign in sight, not wanting to add yet another parking ticket to my extensive collection. The building itself was an actual garage, complete with a car on a lift and tools strewn all over the place. A few guys were milling around, getting things prepared. After introducing myself to them they directed me to the back of the place, where there was an office, kitchen, bathroom, and a makeup room. My guess was that this place had been used as a set many times before.

Sitting down at what looked like a kitchen table was a heavyset man. He had really beautiful shiny chestnut hair, on the longer side, cut in feathery layers. He wore glasses and had an attractive face, showing a nice smile with great teeth.

"You must be Adam," he said in a chipper voice.

"That would be me," I smiled.

"I'm Missy. But you can call me Tommy on the set!" He winked.

I immediately felt comfortable with him and we began making small talk and joking with each other.

From there it was on to the makeup artist, a skinny guy with bleached locks and lots of tattoos. *Wow,* I thought. *This shoot has a makeup artist. At least I'm not doing low-budget gay porn.*

The makeup guy looked like he partied way, way too hard for much too long. But like Tommy, he was cool as well.

While working on me the makeup maestro proudly showed off pictures of himself dressed up in bizarre drag-meets-bondage getups for some weird fetish magazine that I could hardly believe someone actually printed, or that people actually paid for.

"And don't you love that shot? Hot, isn't it?" he asked enthusiastically.

"Yeah, it's great," I lied, staring at a picture of him in a black latex bustier, safety pins clipped to his flesh, and his head pulled back and gagged with a huge knot.

We continued to talk about idle crap while he worked on cleaning up my pubic area. Having someone shave your pubes all nice and neat was something that didn't happen every day. The guy just kept carrying on conversation like he had done this hundreds of times, which was very possible.

"Okay, let's take a look at your asshole!" he announced nonchalantly, as though he were ordering coffee at Dunkin' Donuts.

I guess my chute didn't look too swell, as he had to do a little bit of extra trimming down there.

When that was all over I left the makeup room and went back to the garage to have some still shots taken. Along the way I met my costar, Paul Powers. This was the one thing I was a little nervous about; I was so hoping he wouldn't be a jerk, have bad breath, or something that might make this experience really unpleasant. Having one bad thing to brood about could make this event a lot worse, and how I chose to look at it was a matter of perception. I could perceive my porn debut as fun and money or that I had hit a new low in life. And I was going to think the former rather than latter as I was in no state of mind to delve further into depression.

I had seen Paul Powers before, on some video boxes. I remembered what he looked like when asking for details about the shoot, so I knew ahead of time that I wouldn't have to have sex with someone revolting.

Actually I found him pretty damn hot and was looking forward to getting dirty with him. Paul was good-looking with sandy blond hair and eyes a gorgeous color of blue green. His body was well built and tan. Somehow it made it better being paid to have sex in front of the camera with someone I would have slept with for nothing.

Although Paul certainly didn't come across as the sharpest tack, he was friendly and very complimentary, obviously looking forward to fornicating with me as well. Now I was completely at ease with my surroundings and able to come up with a big boner for the photographer.

When we were finished I walked to the back displaying my raging hard-on, feeling a little cocky.

"Look at you, all raring and ready to go!" Tommy's jolly voice boomed.

He brought me back down to earth though when he told me not to tan in the bathing suit I had been wearing.

"Wear some Calvins instead, honey. That tan line makes your ass look funny, like it's not there at all," he said with the brutal honesty only a drag queen possesses.

Soon it was time to get the show on the road. This first scene was strictly oral, no anal intercourse. It was set up in the bathroom at the front of the garage. In reality one place I would never have sex in real life would be a public restroom. The concept of wanting to fornicate where strangers piss and shit was foreign to me. But in pornos it seemed to be a popular spot to get it on, so whatever.

Before the scene Tommy pulled me aside and asked spastically, "Do you like to eat ass? If not, no problem. Paul loves doing it. He can chow down for hours."

"Uh, it's not really my thing," I stammered, trying to word it lightly. I was glad we had cleared that up ahead of time.

My directions were to read the filthy words scribbled on the walls and then to start playing with myself, at which point Paul would enter and then the action gets started. I felt like a real moron as I traced my finger along the wall and read out loud "Suck my dick!" and "Lick my balls!"

I tried to do it in a manner that sounded really erotic, but I'm sure I came off as idiotic instead. When that was done, and not a moment too soon, Paul came in dressed as a mechanic complete with grease stains on his hands, arms, and face. Within seconds my dick was in his mouth, and Tommy's voice was in the background fervently coaching us on, instructions fluttering out of his mouth.

"Okay, now go faster! Nibble on the end a little bit! Slap it across your face some! Now spit on it!" he yelled out in his hyper voice.

Before long all the clothes came off. Paul lived up to his reputation for eating ass, and while he was doing it I was amazed at how thorough he was.

"Oh!" I yelped out a few times, squirming my butt around the wet, ticklish sensation. I'm sure my eyes were captured on camera almost rolling to the back of my head.

We switched positions around and it was my turn to go down on Paul. His body was nice and smooth, and his dick a nice size. It was large, but still possible to take the whole thing in one's mouth, not monstrously gigantic like the billionaire's.

"Good job, Adam!" Tommy cheered.

At this point I was having fun and really getting into it. It wasn't so bad having sex in front of people I had just met, and there was not a moment when I was not aroused. Toward the end, while the camera was being reloaded, I got really horny and said to Paul, "You know what I would really love? Is if you could blow your wad all over my chest and the side of my face. Just don't nut in my eye, okay?"

"You got it," Paul smiled.

Tommy turned his attention back to us and began giving Paul instructions on what to do when it came time to come.

"Uh, he wants me to come all over his chest and face," Paul offered.

"Great. Go to it!" Tommy agreed.

In minutes I was covered in jizz from my chin to my belly.

Now it was my turn to film my money shot. Tommy had Paul turn his back to me and lean against the sink. He instructed me to place my cock against the crack of his ass.

"Can you come without touching your dick?" Tommy asked.

"Sure," I answered, feeling pretty confident and as horny as possible.

Sliding my dick up and down his crack, from Paul's lower back to his hole, I prepared to explode. "Move your arm, it's blocking the view!" Tommy screamed out, not wanting to miss the climax and most important part of a scene. About thirty seconds later I shot a straight stream of semen up Paul's back, hitting the nape of his neck where a little glob attached to his hair.

Tommy shouted in glee, very pleased with the outcome. It was a wrap!

Afterward I headed back to clean myself up. By this time a few more models had arrived and were hanging around waiting for their turn in front of the camera. At some point I spotted a huge body-builder with a pretty-boy face. He had on jeans, a white T-shirt, and black leather jacket, and he carried a motorcycle helmet. Basically he was every gay man's fantasy, straight out of *Playgirl.* If they had asked me to stay and do another scene with him for free, I probably would have said yes. But I was too proud to volunteer.

Shit. This town was turning me into a bigger male whore than I ever thought possible.

I gathered that this was Bobby Steelhard, the star of the production. He said hello to me and sounded a bit like a moose. Not that it mattered. He was making more money with his buff body than anything I could do with my English literature degree. At this point in life, who was I to judge? I stepped into the bathroom and Bobby followed, checking himself out in the mirror and making a crack about the place. He seemed to be paying me some attention, perhaps because he thought his scene was with me. Or, dare I say, because he wanted to have his scene with me. After all, I was a pretty good-looking find, and feeling cocky after my successful debut! It came as a surprise he was being so chummy, since a lot of the perfect-looking guys, especially the gay-for-pay ones, had plenty of attitude and made it clear they were there for the bucks, not for socializing.

"Adam, you did great," Tommy's voice boomed as he stuck his head in the bathroom. "I see you've met Bobby," he smiled.

"I sure did," I smiled back.

"Why don't you guys come join us in the kitchen? We ordered a ton of food from Koo Koo Roo," Tommy said.

Comparing the sizes of Tommy and Bobby, not to mention the other people there, I was sure that they had in fact ordered a ton of poultry. Following Tommy and Bobby out to the table, the crew and other guys were already grabbing pieces of chicken and scooping bright orange macaroni on their plates. Lunch conversation revolved around the banal, such as recent movies seen or somebody's move into a new apartment. Later, when most of the people had wandered off to

set up or get ready or whatever it was they needed to do, I was left
with Tommy.

"You know, Adam, you were really terrific earlier. With your looks
and attitude you can go a long way in this business," Tommy said
while smearing grease off his hands with a napkin. He stopped short
of saying "looks and talent." Tommy was a realist, and that's what I
liked most about him. This job might require a certain attitude and
ability, but talent, no way. Mostly what it required was either a big
dick or a great body, preferably both.

"What do you mean by long way?" I asked.

"Top billing, travel, money from a Web site, escorting, stripping,"
he said matter-of-factly.

"Higher fees for shoots?" I asked wryly.

Tommy put on his best Missy Manhandler smile and said, "Yes,
higher rates."

"Cool," I answered.

Tommy "Missy Manhandler" then proceeded to write me out a
check for $800, and we said our good-byes.

I walked out of the garage and back to my car, which thankfully
was ticket free. As I drove home I pondered my further leap into the
porn world. Prior to this I had only jerked off for the camera and
posed nude, which didn't seem as severe in my mind. Today I suppose
I really crossed the line into taboo terrain. Not exactly the kind of
Hollywood production I had dreamed about being in for as long as I
could remember.

I wasn't as ashamed as I was just plain numb. That and relieved to
have money in my pocket. I was living my life one day at a time, waiting for the moment when a better opportunity or a way out from my
current desperation opened up. I felt like I had no direction in my life,
and was more misguided than ever. I was just striving to pay my bills
and get through each week.

I couldn't even remember how I got to this point. I suppose there
are millions out there in the same circumstances, just in a different environment. Like the countless single moms working at Wal-Mart and
wondering how they are going to get through the month. At least I
didn't have a few kids to feed.

So I was immortalized copulating on film. I was closer to being Jeff Stryker than Jeff Goldblum, or any other legit actor for that matter. There was nothing I could do about it now. One thing was for sure, I wasn't going to beat myself up when I was already down, and that was one revelation I could take from this whole experience.

When I confided to Candy about what I'd done, she was concerned but realized all had been done, no use crying over spilled milk. So her concern quickly turned to reassuring me.

"I wouldn't worry about it. Do you know how much of that porno shit is out there? There are millions of videos and Web sites and magazines. Nobody will ever notice," Candy said reassuringly when I told her about this latest event.

In fact, she sounded exactly like Dale had that day in the warehouse.

"At least you can be grateful you were able to make a few bucks doing that," she went on. "You could be ugly and fat and flat broke with even less options."

That was Candy for you, always listening, always looking at the glass as half full, always trying to make you feel better. You could inadvertently run over a sweet old lady and she'd find a way to make you feel better about it.

She would joke constantly about how she was so good at giving advice, despite the disarray of her own personal and professional life.

"I'd rather manage other people's shit," she'd laugh. "It's like their lives are more manageable. Give your shit to me."

Getting back to the matter at hand, I sighed, "Well, either way it's done. You can't put an egg back together once it's been broken."

"Exactly. So don't beat yourself up," Candy ordered. "It's not the end of the world. You know what you need to stop turning this over in your mind? A little Mae West!"

Popping in a Mae West flick was what Candy and I did to unwind. Her famous one-liners were right up our alley. We loved the way she strutted around with her overt sexuality, wrote all her own material, and was revolutionary as a sex symbol, surrounding herself with bodybuilders and playing the game by her own rules. Even when the plots reached ridiculous heights, her films were still genius.

It comforted me to think that just as Mae broke down sexual barriers in the early part of the century, I did the same today, although in a far less hilarious and creative manner. Perhaps I was thinking a bit too highly of myself.

As Candy put a movie in I flopped on the couch and thought about our conversation. She was right. It wasn't the end of the world, just a drastic turn in *my* world.

If indeed I was spiraling out of control, I had too many distractions to think about it. I was caught up in a series of surreal events, living my life one day to the next without much of a long-term plan. Almost a week had gone by since my porn debut, and in the meantime I had done a few more nude layouts to promote my new career as a full-fledged gay porn star.

"Missy really took a liking to you!" Ron gushed to me. "She plans on using you again very soon. You were born to do this, Adam."

Dale was slightly more tactful, and even seemed to be looking out for me.

"So how was it?" he asked. "Did everyone treat you okay?"

"Yeah," I answered in a no-big-deal voice, putting up a tough front. "It was fine. They were all really cool."

"Good. If you ever have any questions or concerns, or feel that something's not right, you're being taken advantage of, whatever, give me a call," he said with a genuine look on his face.

"You got it," I said. "Thanks."

"No problem. I got you covered," Dale answered, then winked and gave me a pat on the ass. Now I was sure his intentions went beyond just business.

One night after a long day shipping out pornos from here to Timbuktu, Candy greeted me at the door with a mischievous gleam in her eye. I could already tell she was up to no good.

A night on the town with Candy was never an ordinary event. Invariably something strange or unusual happened to make the evening stand apart from the usual dinner and a few drinks. Therefore, I always prepared myself to expect anything, no matter how freaky a turn our circumstances took. Sometimes we made plans at the last minute.

Candy had been trying to meet quality men in LA for some time with no luck whatsoever. Things with her and Frank were coming to an end. He came into town only occasionally, and when he did he got as drunk as a skunk. Dean was still a no-good loser not even worth calling when suffering from crippling boredom.

So Candy took out an ad in *LA Weekly,* looking for men. In the ad she stressed she was looking for a man that would help support her, so it was a weird hybrid of a singles ad mixed with that of an escort. Basically, she was looking to be a kept woman, now that Frank was soon to be out of the picture. In addition to her ad in *LA Weekly,* she figured she would give the Internet a try, like so many other folks nowadays. After all, the men she met on AOL couldn't be any worse than the guys out at clubs and bars.

And it was on AOL that she was first introduced to the slave who wrote her an e-mail stating he would cater to her every need. The slave was a middle-aged man who got thrills out of being dominated and ordered around by beautiful women. When he kept pestering Candy to let him clean her house for her, take out the garbage, do various chores, and whatever else she asked of him, she eventually permitted this guy to come over to her place and do exactly all of the above.

"Are you out of your fucking mind?" I asked in disbelief when she first told me about the guy.

"Relax, Adam," Candy said with a flip of her manicured hand. She made it sound as though she were ordering pizza or some other routine thing. "I'll only have him over when you or Dean are here."

"Great," I shot back in irritation, "so we can all be hacked up into little pieces together."

But it was Candy's place, and she was going to do what she wanted to do. And I was so involved with my new career in gay porn that I didn't have time to dissuade her. She thought about it and decided it would be cool to have a maid/cook/slave. Not to mention he was willing to pay her, by the way. And no sex was involved. All in all, to Candy it sounded like a pretty good deal.

Sure enough, when he came over Dean or I was always there, thankfully usually Dean. He was an olive-skinned middle-aged man on the short side with permanent dark circles underneath his eyes. While the slave walked around in an apron Candy would call him names like worm, dirty dog, and, my personal favorite, sissy slut. I got a particular kick whenever she called him that.

"Get on your knees, you sissy slut!" Candy ordered in her best dominatrix voice.

Candy's encounters with the so-called slave were entertaining. Unfortunately the guy turned out to have less money than he put on, which wasn't a good thing to begin with but probably the worst possible quality in Candy's mind. He was a terrible cleaner and cook to top things off. She was constantly on his ass to clean properly. The food he prepared was so bad that even Dean told Candy not to use him anymore, because it just plain sucked.

All the time the slave would whine, "I just followed the recipes, Mistress!"

Candy knew he would in fact replace some ingredients with others if he couldn't find them or just leave them out altogether.

She even bitched that he couldn't buy himself a rhinestone collar, which she really wanted him to wear around her apartment.

On the plus side, it was amusing how he liked to be a footstool for her and crawl around on all fours like a dog. She even had him licking milk out of the cat's bowl. The maid outfit left over from our vampire video was what she made him wear while he did his lousy cooking. He loved wearing the maid's uniform.

"Looking good," I commented awkwardly upon seeing him in it for the first time, then immediately retreated to my room.

She always wore a skirt and some high stripper shoes when he came over, and since he had a shoe and foot fetish he would kiss her feet first thing after coming through the door. The slave also spoke French, something Candy appreciated since she is fluent from years of it in high school and college. And it's always a good thing to practice a second language.

"Adam, what are you doing tonight?" Candy asked one evening.

"The same as usual. Going to the gym," I answered.

"Have you had dinner yet?" she inquired.

"No."

"Would you like to come to dinner with slave and me?" Candy offered.

"No thanks," was my immediate response, sensing such an event would lead to trouble. Besides, what the hell was I going to say to her slave for Chrissakes? Tell him to polish my shoes while I ate my appetizer? I could see how strange the whole scenario would be.

"Oh come on! It will be fun!" Candy tried convincing me.

"He's driving us to Dar Maghreb and paying! It's that Moroccan restaurant with belly dancers on Sunset. Don't you feel like seeing the belly dancers spinning around?" she pressed.

Actually I was more interested in the free meal than the belly dancers.

That sounded so much better than the frozen pizza I was about to pop into the oven. I think that would have made the third frozen pizza for the week, and it was only Wednesday.

I was still reluctant, but with a little more prodding and pushing I agreed to go. Candy and I inevitably had a good time and never lacked for conversation, which was why she must have wanted me to come along so badly. I guess bossing around your slave in a public restaurant all alone wasn't her idea of a good time. That and the fact Candy didn't want anybody to think she was dating him.

Forty-five minutes later I threw on my best Armani Exchange shirt and a furry black cap from Urban Outfitters because it was a chilly night, and waited for Candy to get ready. Candy came out of her room wearing the most outrageous outfit I'd seen her put on in a long time. And that was saying a lot. You'd think we were going to the Playboy mansion, her frequent haunt.

She wore a black beret with white rhinestones on it from Dolce & Gabbana, a fur scarf, Dolce & Gabbana jacket and barely existent skirt, and thigh-high zip-up boots.

"Looking to upstage the belly dancers?" I asked. "You better be careful or the customers will be handing you dollar bills instead."

Candy just laughed it off.

Downstairs the slave greeted us in the indecipherable moderate accent he spoke in. For the life of me I could not figure out where the man was from, and didn't care enough to ask. I climbed into the back with Candy and off we went.

The slave said nothing the whole ride there, and Candy spoke to him only to give him directions. I thought the whole thing was so weird, and uncomfortable, to say the least. All I kept thinking about was the delicious lemon chicken awaiting me.

When we arrived at the restaurant he said he would go look for parking and dropped us off at the front. We stood outside the door for a minute or so, and I had a feeling something was wrong right then and there. Parking wasn't too much of a nightmare in this neighborhood, a rare thing in LA. The air was turning really cold, so Candy suggested we wait inside.

It wasn't so much better inside, as the waiting area had an open ceiling with a fountain underneath. There were two dining areas, one to the left and one to the right, and a private dining room in the front. Quite a few people were already waiting for a table when we came in.

Immediately I sensed the focus of the room shift toward us. I could imagine that we made quite a pair, the voluptuous blonde with her outlandish outfit and the chiseled tall guy next to her with pronounced cheekbones and a furry black cap. I sat down on a little stool while Candy stood up, starting to look a bit concerned after a few more minutes of waiting.

"Adam," her voice was hesitant, "this is weird. It couldn't be taking him that long to get here. Do you think he took off?"

Actually I had been thinking that since before walking through the door. He had just been too detached and distant, even for a slave.

"It's never taken me this long to park around here, and I have the worst luck finding parking," I answered gravely.

Candy went out to the street again to check, but still no sign of the slave. She went on about it in disbelief, but I was too distracted by the obnoxious drunken party seated in the private room across from us. They had been laughing loudly and were staring and laughing in our direction, at Candy in particular, the second we stepped in. I had said something about it, and Candy made some remark back about them not knowing fashion if it hit them in the face. Candy was used to getting reactions from her outfits.

When she first moved to LA, she wore a gorgeous Chanel suit and hat to a restaurant and some guy cracked to his girlfriend "Where's the parade?" I never forgot that story. That hat had probably cost his whole week's salary. But in LA the idea of fashionable was dirty-looking hair, a tank top, workout pants, and cell phone. But you had to drive a really nice car that was meticulously washed at all times. I swear people would carry about or wear their fucking cars around their necks in LA if they could.

The final straw was when some stupid middle-aged woman with one of those ugly short haircuts like the kind Angela Lansbury wore on *Murder She Wrote* or some suburban moms in the Midwest still sport pulled her friend into view and pointed our way. She was blatantly poking fun at Candy's appearance, not even bothering to be discreet about it.

After being deserted by the slave I was not in the mood. I felt like a mother lion defending her cub, immediately springing into attack. I was always protective of Candy, like two misfits sticking together in a world that was hard enough as it was.

When I get angry, I take on the behavior of a deranged person who can do major harm. Think Jack Nicholson in *The Shining*.

"What!" I screamed at the top of my lungs. "What the fuck are you looking at!?" I screamed, staring straight at the bitch and almost foaming at the mouth.

Around me it got quiet. It was a good thing this was a Moroccan restaurant with belly dancers, musicians, and lots of noise or I'm sure the whole restaurant would have stopped. The woman in the ugly haircut and dated baggy sweater wiped the goofy smirk off her face and immediately looked away. Her stupid friend sat back down, and a few seconds later someone slid the doors to their dining room shut.

"Who wears baggy sweaters like that anymore?" I screamed as the door shut.

Candy was surprised and taken aback, and it took a lot for me to surprise Candy.

"Jesus, Adam," she murmured, "you really went off on those people."

"Good," I grumbled. "We don't have to hear their annoying mouths or avoid their ugly faces."

We didn't discuss it for long as a nearby voice interrupted our conversation.

"Hello. Can I take your picture?" I heard someone say. It sounded like he was deaf. I turned around to see a retarded young man sitting down next to me with a digital camera in his hand.

"Sure," I said in an overly friendly voice.

One thing I have to say about myself is that I always go out of my way to be considerate and kind to retarded and handicapped people, as I think most people should.

Candy and I went on to speak to the retarded guy at length. He let us know that *Chitty Chitty Bang Bang* and *Bedknobs and Broomsticks* were his favorite movies

"Do you know this one?" Candy asked him in a cooing voice one would use for a toddler, and blurted out "Supercalifragilisticexpialidocious!"

The retarded guy twisted his face up in glee and laughed loudly. The men that were with him smiled at us, showing their appreciation for humoring the guy.

"You are my new friend," he said to each of us, which we reaffirmed with a profound "Of course!" and "Absolutely!"

After the retarded guy and his party left to be seated we looked at each other in expressions that said what we were thinking. Namely, *Can you believe this night? Is there a full moon out or what?*

By the time two of us got a table it was obvious the slave was long gone. Across from us sat a group of people in their twenties and thirties. Next to us was a large table of retired men and their wives. Again everyone looked at Candy and me as we sat on our cushions next to the low table. Candy was pissed but took on the attitude that we were here and might as well enjoy it. I was a little more peeved, and I don't know why. She had more reason to be. After all, he wasn't my slave.

At one point I got all bitchy and said to her something to the effect of "Well, what did you expect!" I guess I was annoyed because I sensed trouble from the start.

Candy looked at me with a very serious and hurt voice, stared me in the face, and said slowly, "Adam, don't yell at me. It's not my fault."

A few of the young people across the way glanced at us. I don't know why I was so concerned with all the reaction going on around us the whole night. I guess this jumping Moroccan restaurant was sensory overload. I immediately felt terrible. It was a very rare occurrence for me to lose patience and Candy get serious with me in turn.

"I'm sorry, Candy. I didn't mean to flip out on you. It's just that your slave is a real shithead," I apologized.

"Well, we're here, Adam. So let's just enjoy the food and the belly dancers and have some fun, okay?"

When we finished dinner Candy put it on her charge card and asked the waiter to call us a cab. After waiting for what seemed forever we went to the front.

The hostess said she had never been asked to call a cab. Now I was getting pissed again. It didn't help that a bunch of middle-aged drunks, different ones from the ones I yelled at earlier, were coming up to Candy and petting her scarf. One woman asked what it was and I snapped, "It's the real thing! We're from New York and don't fake it!" in my nastiest voice possible.

I am a huge animal lover but was in no mood to hear the riot act from anyone. There was a taxi outside but other people were climbing into it. We had no idea if it was meant for us or not. Desperate and standing around like two idiots, we went around the corner to try to hail one from Sunset, a virtually impossible task in LA since the only way to get a cab was to call for it. Such moments made me wish I'd never left Manhattan.

I realize we must have looked like a very expensively dressed, very fashionable and high-class pimp and his whore walking up and down an empty stretch of sidewalk on Sunset Boulevard.

Finally we walked back to the front of the restaurant, saw a cab drive up and grabbed open the door before it came to a full stop, not giving anyone else a chance to take it.

"Where are you going?" the cabdriver asked us.

When we told him, he protested, "But that is not where I was called to drop off."

"Just go!" we yelled at him like two nut jobs waiting to be taken to Bellevue for evaluation.

He drove off, and we relaxed a bit on the way back home, happy that the whole evening was behind us. Candy had lost her good humor, and vented about how the fucking prick would pay for taking off and leaving us there, using every expletive in existence to make her point clear. When we got home she called his machine and went off on it.

"You asshole! Don't you ever fucking contact me again or I will cut your balls off!"

I went in my room and shut my door so I didn't have to hear anymore.

It wasn't long before he started calling, pleading with Candy, "Please, mistress, I beg you, forgive me!"

She would just hang up.

"I figure not even answering him is more torturous for him rather than calling him every name in the book, since he gets his kicks out of being abused to begin with, the sick fuck," laughed Candy.

E-mails came as well that started out by stating, "Mistress, it's your worm."

Finally we got the answer why he ditched us in the first place. He eventually wrote to her that his last mistress made him suck off her boyfriend's dick, and he was afraid Candy would make him have sex with me that night because she invited me along for dinner. That one had me on the floor, I was laughing so hard.

"That toad couldn't pay me enough to let him even touch my dick!" I laughed in tears.

Yet he kept e-mailing, messages that read, "Please, mistress, there is no one as classy as you, or as good of a mistress!"

"Guess the asshole should have thought of that before he hightailed it down Sunset leaving us stranded," Candy told me.

The slave was just one more example of depravity I was encountering in Hollywood. Between home and work, it was like the *Twilight Zone*.

But in a way it was fun and exciting to feel wanted for once. It was a real change, rather than searching for the right opportunity or big break. And whereas no mainstream agents or casting directors responded to my head shot mailings, I was a rising and wanted star at HUNG Video. I was just riding the wave; soon I'd find something else and come up with a long-term plan. But this is where I was now, and I was going to try and enjoy it and use it for all it was worth.

Who Says Not to Shit Where You Eat?

By now I had become an expert in shrink-wrapping. I could fold that plastic over DVDs and videos like gangbusters, and hold the blow-dryer so that the plastic melted over the surfaces and corners like wet glass. I had become quite proud of myself. In fact, I took more pride in my shrink-wrapping than I did in the fact that I was appearing on the covers of both *Men* and *Unzipped* magazines. *Bobby Steelhard's Hollywood Garage* was a hit, and Ron told me I was garnering some great fan response.

But I didn't take any of that too seriously. I had plans of my own. And they included getting my resumé together so I could land a job with a production company or a movie studio. An employment agency I contacted back when I was answering phones at Acclaimed Talent was offering free courses in Word, Excel, and PowerPoint, and my intention was to sharpen up my computer skills for an administrative job. All this X-rated business was just a stepping stone, an amusing diversion I could think back to years from now and laugh about. I was just having fun until the point when I could find a real job.

"Keep that shrink-wrap rolling!" a loud voice boomed behind me, startling the wits out of me and causing me to knock over a tall stack that had accumulated near my elbow.

I turned around to find Dale Warner laughing at me.

"Don't do that shit," I said in annoyed voice. "I hate it when people sneak up like that."

My irritation just seemed to give him more satisfaction.

"I knew you'd get the hang of this in no time flat," he cracked good-naturedly, picking up one of the fallen VHS cases.

"I had a very good teacher. Your shrink-wrapping surpasses all. Maybe you'll direct as well someday," I joked back.

"And I take that as quite a compliment coming from big talking, smart-ass Adam," he laughed, then playfully picked up the blow-dryer and turned it on my face.

"Watch it!" I laughed, grabbing the end. He turned it off and we both held it for a minute, gazing at each other again and smiling.

"You know," he said finally. "Why don't we go out for a drink tonight? It's on me. I am very curious to see what Mr. Adam is like in a change of scenery."

"Well now that I'm hot shit in front of the camera, my calendar is really full. But since you're paying, why not? Who am I to kick the gift horse in its mouth?"

"Spoken like a true hustler," Dale joked. "I see LA is teaching you well. How does seven sound?"

"Seven thirty sounds better," I said.

"Call you later," he said and walked off.

I turned around and bent over to pick up the videos I had knocked over. I heard behind me, "By the way, nice ass!"

Later that night Dale called me a few minutes before half past seven.

"You ready to hit the town?" he asked.

"Absolutely," I answered.

"How does Mexican sound?"

"Great."

"Then afterwards I have a favorite place I'll take you for drinks in Silver Lake. It's called Akbar. Have you been there before?"

"I haven't been to Silver Lake at all."

"This place is funky, has a great jukebox. You'll love it," Dale assured me.

We went to a popular joint in West Hollywood called Marix. With a bar that served one margarita after another and a retractable ceiling that revealed a night sky, the place was a mob scene.

We stood at the bar with frozen margaritas in hand while waiting for our table. Dale kept me entertained by filling me in on the gossip about Ron, Brian the photographer, and his other porn pals.

While we spoke, my eyes traveled on his body. I had to keep my thoughts from drifting about how sexy he actually was. I hadn't been that impressed when I first laid eyes on him, but his gruff looks were growing on me. He wasn't a pretty boy like Brian. But with his thick, tall, and stocky frame he was all man. His body was firm yet had just a bit of a belly, which I liked. I imagined what my dick would feel like against his abdomen. It must have had a bit of hair on it. His forearms had just the right amount of dark hair on them, sexy but not excessive. The farm-boy face was hiding under a baseball cap, and he wore baggy jeans and a T-shirt. He looked like he was about to go work on his car or get out of shop class.

A number of flashy WeHo guys came up to say hi to him. He seemed so different from the other guys in town. It was strange to think he lived in such a fast world.

"So how'd you get involved in porn anyways?" I asked after we had been seated.

"By accident, the same way a lot of people do I suppose," he began. "I moved out here from Ohio with a guy I was with at the time, who has since moved back to Cleveland. I started doing crew work on films, that and working as a delivery guy. Back home I had always been into building things, like sets for theater and stuff like that, and always huge projects in shop."

"So I was right!" I blurted out, happy at my early industrial arts assessment of Dale.

"Right about what?" he turned his head to the side with a suspicious smile and peered at me.

"You were an industrial arts dude. I'm sorry to interrupt. Finish your story," I said.

"Okay, we'll revisit that one later," he teased. "Soon one thing led to another and before I knew it I was doing what you've been doing, the grunt work on porn sets. I got along well with Ron and the other companies I work for, and saw the other idiots who were directing and didn't know what the fuck they we're doing." He stopped to take a sip of his frozen margarita.

"Anyways," he said after a long swallow, "I'd always been into filmmaking, you know, *Star Wars* and all that," he laughed. He was growing sexier by the minute.

"So one day I asked if I could pick up the camera at one of the cheaper companies, and they said sure. And using that as a springboard, I've doing it ever since. I taught myself how to edit, and now I edit my own shit and for other directors as well."

"And the rest is all history," I smiled.

"That's all she wrote!" he laughed.

"So you've become something of a tycoon," I said flippantly.

"Well, I don't know about *tycoon*," he emphasized, teasing me back. "But I'm doing all right. I'm not sure if it's something I want to do forever, but it's great for now. Some of the nicest, coolest people I have met are in porn. Most of them are much nicer than the mainstream industry people in town, who are just as sleazy behind closed doors. I mean, porn might not be for everybody, but it's been great for me."

"Right, not for everybody," I repeated, thinking out loud. Everything seemed to be happening so fast since I came to LA with no job and very little money. It seemed like a complete whirlwind. In just a few short months I found myself involved in a world I thought I'd never encounter, except perhaps during a few horny and lonely nights at my local video store. It wasn't even a case of whether it was good or bad anymore, it was just where I was in my life, trying to survive day by day. And for the time being the world of porn meant survival.

"Come on," Dale said, breaking me away from my thoughts. It must have been obvious I was thinking pretty deep. "Let's blow this joint."

Akbar was great—the first place I felt really comfortable at since coming to LA. It was definitely an eclectic crowd, totally mixed, straight and gay, guys and girls. Like Dale said, it had the best jukebox, from Tina Turner to David Bowie to Elvis to Nancy Sinatra, one great choice after another. The interior was lit with red Chinese lanterns and above a few banquet booths was a painting of a nude Asian woman reclining on cushions with an opium pipe next to her.

A pierced and tattooed girl bartender with a perfect Bettie Page hairdo and liquid eyeliner poured our drinks. We went and sat on a seat in the back near a few giggling girls and their boyfriends. The funky, artsy people reminded me of the East Village.

"So what do you think?" Dale asked loudly in a proud voice after sitting down. Dusty Springfield's "Son of a Preacher Man" was blaring from the jukebox. He could already tell I loved the place and he had impressed me.

"It's great," I said. "It reminds me of my old neighborhood in New York."

"You miss New York a lot, don't you?" he asked.

I looked up at an old autographed black and white head shot of legendary horror actress Karen Black and nodded. "Yeah. I do."

I looked at him solemnly. But I didn't want to turn the night into a downer, thinking I made a mistake moving to LA. "But this is really great," I repeated with a smile.

"Glad you like it." He smiled back sheepishly at me.

Then I grabbed his hand and gripped it tight.

"Thanks for the night out, Dale. It's really sweet of you," I said, gazing at his eyes.

He gazed back at me, and his expression changed from a sheepish grin to one of intense desire.

Then it happened. He leaned forward and pressed his lips against mine. I felt the tip of his tongue greet my own lips, but his tongue didn't have to wait long. I opened up my mouth and let it in, the warm wetness of our mouths melting into each other, tongues sliding around each other, taking breaks to nibble at each other's lips and tug back and forth. This went on for a few minutes until our eyes opened and we pulled back to look at each other.

"Come on," he said intently. "I'm taking you back to my place."

Saying nothing, I got up and followed.

He lived in a one-bedroom condo on Sweetzer, in the heart of West Hollywood. We said little on the way there. My hand rested on his thigh the whole way, and he rubbed his own hand up and down my thigh. When we got too close to each other's groins we stopped, saving anything more for when we reached our destination. The mood was feverish and intense for the duration of the ride. He drove like a madman, eager to get to his place as soon as possible.

We parked in his garage. After getting out of the car we leaned against the trunk and kissed under the fluorescent lighting, breathing heavily. In the quiet stillness of the garage and the shiny cars parked around us, all I could hear was our breathing.

"Come on. Let's go upstairs," he said, putting his arm around my waist and leading me to the elevator.

We made out some more waiting for the elevator, filling up our mouths and biting at each other's lips. The force he put on me made me struggle to stand up straight. When the elevator door opened we didn't stop right away. We kept making out, and Dale instinctively put his hand out to keep the doors open and pushed me inside.

When the doors closed our mouths were still on each other. Then, using his huge arms, Dale placed his hands under both my butt cheeks and picked me up, slamming me back against the elevator wall and shoving his tongue into my throat as deep as it could possibly go.

I let out a loud moan of delight. The little elevator shook at the force of our crashing bodies. My feet didn't touch the ground before we reached the third floor. Neither of us was aware of it when the doors opened. Dale was too busy straddling me up against the wall and I was too busy enjoying it.

Suddenly I opened my eyes to see a little old lady with a Yorkie. The old lady's mouth hung open in shock and the Yorkie stared at us with a quizzical expression.

"Oomph," I made a noise through our pressed mouths and pulled my face away from Dale's.

"Hello," I said in a barely audible, winded voice.

Dale turned around in disarray and panted, "Oh. . . . Hi, Mrs. Kaminski. How are you doing this evening?"

"Well," the woman said in a no-nonsense tone, "not as occupied as you and your friend!"

"I apologize, Mrs. Kaminski," Dale said while trying to catch his breath and put me down. I made my way out of the elevator as Mrs. Kaminski stepped back.

"Oh, what a cute dog," I managed to say, feeling completely embarrassed. I forgot the fact that Dale and I were two grown-ups. Instead I felt like a kid cutting class.

The dog barked furiously at me as I approached it.

"Come on, Cookie," Mrs. Kaminski said sharply. "Let's take you for your walk."

"Here, Mrs. Kaminski," Dale said, putting on the gentleman airs. "Let me hold the door open for you."

"Thank you," she said curtly and stepped in the elevator. Before the doors closed completely she ordered with authority, "And you two boys be careful! Use protection!"

Dale and I stood staring at each other, completely red faced. Then we both started laughing hysterically. Dale had one arm out holding himself up against the wall and the other on his stomach, bent over in convulsions.

"If she thought I was noisy and wild before with friends coming in and out," he said between chortles of laughter, "God knows what she thinks now. I'll never be able to redeem myself from that impression."

"Let's just go inside now before one of your other neighbors sees us acting like idiots in the hall," I laughed.

With that he shoved his hand in my back pocket again and dragged me down the hallway. Digging for his keys, we stopped at his door. After finding them he opened the door and pushed me inside. As he started kissing me he flicked the lights on.

"No," I said, flipping them back off. "Just take me to your bed now."

In a matter of seconds our lips were locked and our clothes were coming off. Rubbing his naked torso up and down, I kept stopping at his pecs, cupping them in my hands and squeezing at the nipples, which tended to pucker and droop a little, jutting out and making them easy to catch with my tongue and nibble on. His body had just the right amount of hair on it that grew beautifully toward the center of his chest and down his navel, leading a path to his cock.

I worked my way across his chest, stopping many times for his nipples and gnawing at them and kneading the fleshy tips between my teeth. Dale moaned and occasionally yelped or gasped with pleasure above me. When he let out a manly "Yeah!" in a deep, oversexed baritone it turned me on even further.

I peeled off his boxers and his cock popped out of them. Dale really had a beautiful cock. Although it wasn't very long, the length was perfect, at least seven inches. But it was girth that he boasted. Like his stocky build, his dick was fat and full, and I was thrilled at the sight of it. Grabbing it in my hand, it filled up my grasp entirely.

"Damn your dick is fat," I breathed.

"Yeah?" he breathed and licked my face. "You want me to fill you with that?" he growled.

"Mmmm," I just said, my sphincter muscles already beginning to tense up then loosen, then tense up and loosen some more. Just the sheer thought of that huge circumference of flesh inside me had my ass throbbing. I could feel it start to pucker around the edges.

The tips of my fingers traced around the tip of his dick. It was exaggerated to the point of caricature. Like a massive mushroom head, but more pointy and triangular.

I trailed the tip of my tongue down the middle of his torso and along the stream of body hair to his navel, stopping to bite at the flesh around the edge of his belly button. My lips gently blew air over where I had just traced his body with my tongue, giving him a tingle and sending shivers up his spine.

"Yes. Oh yes," he hissed, sucking in short breaths when his body racked with sensation.

I felt the oversized head of his throbbing cock meet my chin, then my cheek, and the next thing I knew the hot, wet flesh of my tongue was smothering the red tip of his beautiful dick. I sucked in my breath as my mouth enclosed itself over his enormous shaft, covering it like a blanket and submerging it in my hot saliva.

Dale was now lying on his back and I was breathing deeply, swallowing all his girth and gagging only slightly. Pretty soon my tongue was going even further, up and down the crevice of his ass. His legs flew up and I submerged my whole mouth into his ass, opening wide and gnawing away at it.

"Oh damn! Holy shit!" Dale was now yelling at the top of his lungs.

All hell broke loose when the tip of my tongue found his asshole and pointed at it dead on. I pushed a little, submerging it just a bit while opening up his pouting red flesh.

"Oh boy! Oh boy!" Dale trembled, tearing and pulling at the sheets like he was about to have a fit.

I pushed some more, my tongue was now well inside his anus, sliding against his hot, slick membrane. Finally I shoved my whole tongue up his ass so far that my face smashed up against the flesh between his legs.

"Oh, motherfucker!" Dale yelled out loud enough to wake the whole building.

After eating his ass for a while, he grabbed me underneath my arms and pulled me up so my face met his, tearing into my mouth with such a force I thought we would hurt each other. In a matter of seconds he had flipped over so that he was on top of me in a sixty-nine, taking my dick into his mouth, while he forced his into mine. He thrust his pelvis hard against my face, so that at every other second I was almost choking on the size of him. We continued exploring each other with our tongues, until he jerked himself upright and frantically reached for some lubricant and a rubber. Sprawled out and panting on the mattress, I tried desperately to catch my breath. Before I knew it, Dale had slid on the condom, grabbed hold of my legs, and pushed them apart, each calf gripped and held up by his hands.

Just the sensation of his penis head pressing against my ass made me flinch.

"Oh no. Oh no. Oh no," I chanted over and over like a mantra, gearing up for what was to come. I was about to be ravaged with a size of flesh I had never encountered before.

Then it began to happen. I felt my ass being penetrated and the muscles being forced open wide.

"Ahhh!" I yelped at the top of my lungs.

"Shh . . . baby," Dale whispered gently, putting his finger against my lips. It's all right. Just relax and take it easy. I'll try not to hurt you."

I threw my head back, closed my eyes, pointed my chin to the ceiling, and grabbed his hand with mine, squeezing tight. He hadn't even put the whole head in yet. I braced myself.

He inched it in closer. I felt like a well was being drilled into the center of my body.

"Ahhh . . . ahhh," I groaned loudly, trying to keep it down.

"That's it, baby, that's it. Open up for daddy," Dale ordered. My body quivered and I started breathing in and out deeply, trying with every bit of my will to relax my muscles and allow his massive cock to squeeze inside me.

Finally he gave it one last shove and he was all the way in, his flesh slapping against mine.

"Oh yeah!" I hollered louder than I've ever hollered before, wanting to crawl away from the splitting sensation but yet wanting him take my ass and use it.

"Yes!" Dale yelled, and abandoned all self-control. There was nothing he could do but break me in. I would have to shut up and get used to my ass and insides being pounded relentlessly.

At first it was excruciating and I wanted it to stop. The pain was too much. But slowly pain began to give way to pleasure. The sharp sensation around the entry of my ass gave way, my muscles giving in to his stiff cock. And the ecstasy I felt deeper within my anus where his dick massaged my prostate furiously took over.

My "oh no's" became "Oh yeahs" and "Fuck me harder!"

We carried on in endless positions, sideways, sitting, you name it— we did it. He was so strong he was able to lift me up and pound me with such force simultaneously that I gave myself over completely. I was his vehicle of pleasure, which in turn gave me a feeling of sexual abandon that was beyond what I'd ever imagined. I was so turned on my own stiff dick oozed and smeared glossy precum against my abdomen every time my body swung back and forth.

Eventually we both came within a minute of each other. When Dale pulled out of me, he peeled off the condom. His body was gleaming with sweat.

"I'm gonna come. I'm gonna come," he panted.

I turned around and scooted forward just in time to catch a large wad of hot jizz over my face, glazing over my mouth, cheeks, and eyes.

I heard Dale yell above as I splayed my body out on all fours, feeling the hot liquid begin to set on my face like paste. After gaining control Dale wiped off my eyes so I could open them up and see his still erect manhood in front of me.

That's when I took control and pushed him back on the bed, pinning his body down with my knees. I looked down at him and clenched my teeth, furled my brow, and squinted my eyes.

"Come on babe. Come all over me," he coaxed.

I could feel the heat start to work its way down my shaft and the slit of my dick start to feel pleasurable vibrations.

"Here it comes! Here it comes!" I repeated louder each time.

My body shook and waved like a tribesman doing a dance. While my eyes were closed I felt Dale take one of his fingers and shove it up my ass. That did it.

As I hollered I felt a load of come pop and explode from my cock, the sensation of release overwhelming me. One spurt after another, a few of them flying way over Dale's head and hitting the wall behind the bed. His body was streaked, the white liquid lying on top of his body hair.

"Holy shit. Did that just happen?" I mumbled in disbelief while collapsing onto Dale, my come mixing with our sweat and smearing between our two bodies.

It was the best orgasm that I could remember. Afterward we headed to the shower. He led me by my hand as I stumbled in a daze, my body settling back into itself. He washed me off with care, and I soaped him up in return.

"Thanks for coming over," he whispered in my ear as my chin rested on his shoulder. I was wiped out.

"Thanks for having me," I whispered back, while I made soapy swirls and patterns with his chest hair.

"Babe, you were made for doing this for the cameras," he said gently.

"Thanks," I mumbled, then added, "I think."

Dale smiled, kissed me gently, and said, "Let's get to sleep."

I turned over on the pillow, relaxed and ready for a good night's sleep. Before I closed my eyes, an object on Dale's bed stand glistened in the moonlight, catching my eye. Looking closer I noticed an almost empty glass vial tipped on its side, with white powder residue falling out.

So he likes to party once in a while, I reasoned. It was his business. Exhausted, I fell asleep.

The Mansion of Depravity

The weeks following I became immersed in a whole new world. I had appeared in two new films and my billing was rising. I posed for spreads in more magazines. My image was popping up all over Web sites. And I spent a lot of time hanging out with Dale, who directed one of my latest videos. We accompanied each other to a lot of parties all over town. Many of them got pretty wild, but I always ended up going home with Dale. Most of the time he was cool, though I began to notice that he was beginning to seem more and more wired.

After having sex, which was always at his place because I felt uncomfortable bringing men back to Candy's, he had more and more of a hard time going to sleep. He would stay up and play video games for hours straight. Then if he did hit the sack, it was just for a few hours and he would shoot out the door to do some editing work in the cutting room.

"You're doing way too much of that shit," I finally said to him.

"What are you talking about?" he asked.

"The green tea in the kitchen," I snapped in frustration. "What do you think I'm talking about? Let me think. Oh yeah, the tina you keep stocked up next to your bed."

"I know. I need to lay off it bit. It's just that I have so many projects piled up on me right now."

Dale did what he always did when I brought up his increasingly troublesome crystal habit. He changed the subject.

"So have you called Gary about getting your Web site up?" he asked. Dale had been pushing me to start my own Web site for a while now, where I could make some bucks on the side and even promote myself as a high-priced escort.

"No," I answered. "And I don't think I'm going to. I don't want it to swallow up my whole life, and become my whole identity."

"So then why are you doing it to begin with?" Dale snapped in irritation. "I mean you've already done it on camera three times, you're on the cover of magazines, and you're one of the hottest new faces in the biz. You might as well use it to your advantage and ride it as much as you can. Get the appearances, tour some clubs."

"And escort?" I cut in sharply.

"Yes, and escort. You've already done that too. So what's the big deal?" he asked callously.

I knew Dale was no knight in shining armor. But it still bothered me that he didn't care that I was with other guys, though it was part of both of our realities before we began sleeping with each other.

"Look, Adam," Dale continued to tell it like it was. "You want it both ways. You want to just dabble, skim the surface, and make some easy money, and then move on. But either you embrace it all the way, or you don't do it at all. It's like you're walking a wall between two worlds. If you have a problem with it, you should never have started to begin with. Get a job at Starbucks for chrissakes."

I didn't say anything. He had a point.

"Have you even started those computer classes?" he pressed.

"Not yet. I've had too many distractions," I mumbled. "Look, can we just not talk about it right now?"

"Sure. So then let's not talk about either of our issues right now, okay?" he said with resentment.

With that our conversation ended.

To my defense, I did have a lot of distractions. With all the parties we were going to and the attention I was getting, I was having some interesting encounters with some more Hollywood big shots. And then I was still going out on calls.

My most recent trick Ron hooked me up with was a legendary Hollywood photographer who loved munching on ass. It was appropriate that he liked to munch, because physically he reminded me of a munchkin. He was short, portly, with a round head and swollen nose. I saw him about four times, and it was the same routine each time.

I'd sit on his face as he greedily munched my hole like there was no tomorrow, chewing away until my ass was drenched with his slobber, which dripped down his face and trickled on the sheets. At the same time he wanted me to twist and tear at his sowlike nipples, which had been worked and pulled to a point where they looked mutilated. I always came first and waited impatiently for him to finish off. I couldn't wait to get off his nutcracker mouth.

There is nothing worse than waiting for someone you don't even find physically attractive to have an orgasm. Eventually his little dick would spout out a pathetic few drips of spunk, and when I looked back at him his little round head was bright red like a tomato.

At least he kept me entertained over expensive dinners with stories about celebrities he had worked with, which included Farrah Fawcett, Arnold Schwarzenegger, John Travolta, Richard Gere, and countless others, even good old Mae West in her later years. The fact that his long-time lover was a prolific film industry insider, who he met during his younger and more attractive years, didn't exactly hurt his career. As always, in Hollywood it was all about connections.

But my recent interactions with a composer named Owen Burger turned out to be even more interesting than my night with Wayne Hanley or the butt-munching photographer.

At one random party in the hills I met a slim, artsy-looking fellow named Vince. Vince was an assistant to the very successful composer. Mainly known for scoring some of the biggest box office bonanzas, Burger also dabbled in painting and photography.

You could say the Burger was a modern Hollywood renaissance man, sort of a gay Mozart meets Helmut Newton. Vince approached me about modeling for Burger and his boyfriend Diego, who was also a photographer.

"It could lead to something else, a job or the chance to work on a film," Vince suggested. "In the very least you'll get some extra bucks out of it."

I was invited to Burger's mansion off Beverly Glen, high up in the hills. I left late in the afternoon as planned and drove west on Sunset Boulevard, veering right where the Hamburger Hamlet was, just past Doheny.

The exterior and interior of the house had been built in a Spanish style. A few creepy-looking paintings hung in the hallway.

"Owen painted them," Vince said while leading me down the tiled hall.

If someone had shown them to me without my knowing who painted them and asked him my opinion, I would have said that I thought the person who created them must be disturbed, maybe someone who tortured and killed small animals or painted while undergoing psychiatric evaluation. They also brought to mind the doodles that a stoner in high school made on his desktop, the kind that listened to Metallica or something to that effect.

In the office I sat down at a table where Vince showed me a book of photos by Owen and Diego. Most of the photos were nudes and as disturbing as the paintings in the hall. The models, both men and women, had various body types and were covered in black paint from head to toe. It looked as if they had just stepped out of tar.

"These are all for a photo book Diego is looking to publish," Vince explained.

Such images were the last thing I would ever want to put on my coffee table. The view of the room, which overlooked a lush canyon, was more captivating to me than the garish photos.

Looking at that gorgeous vista only reaffirmed my theory that the only way to live in LA was in the hills or on the beach, and I could understand why many Los Angelinos loved it out here.

A few minutes later Diego the boyfriend came in. He was a large, strapping Hispanic man. The kind you'd expect to see at some inner-city boxing gym.

Outside the room other folks were shuffling about. When I inquired about who they were I was informed that Burger used this home as his offices and ran his production company, Ceremony Films, out of it. He owned the home next door as well and used that one as his residence.

I briefly met one of the people from the production company, a guy named Stuart. A paunchy blond geek with glasses, Stuart looked like the living definition of a nerd. But I imagined that he made a really good worker.

A disheveled, overweight woman with bad hair hanging in her face was the other full-timer at Ceremony Films, but she just ran around the whole time like a maniac and wasn't interested in saying hello. She was used to all kinds of colorful types coming in and out, I suppose.

Looking at her made me wonder what was up with all these poor, wretched looking, run-down females who come to LA to work as haggard production people. The hours are horrible, the demands immense, and the rewards few. It was a big mystery to me. But I had seen countless others of her type since being in Hollywood.

Then again, who was I to judge these people? A countless other myself, and one doing porn for a living. *Quit being such a bitch, Adam,* I finally told myself.

Eventually the big man himself came in. Everything up until this point had been "Owen this" or "Owen that." It was like the cult of Owen. *All that's needed is some poisoned Kool-Aid to go along with the ugly paintings hanging around this place,* I thought to myself.

Burger was actually an attractive man, pale skinned with puppy-dog-blue eyes. His hair was dark brown and he had a light mustache and goatee. He had a solid build, and the South African accent didn't hurt either.

I have always been a sucker for accents. I was a big-time Anglophile. *Mobil Masterpiece Theater* and *Mystery!* were regular viewing for me, and of course *Ab Fab.* There was something I found polished and superior about British accents. Take *The Osbournes* for example. The family wouldn't be nearly as endearing without their British accents, and Sharon Osbourne wouldn't come off as classy. Take away the British accents and the rock star digs and Ozzy and his family are nothing more than overpaid Jerry Springer material.

Owen Burger would have made a great catch if he didn't already have a great big, juicy Latino boyfriend. And if he was into big body builders it was pretty much pointless for me to wonder what he would be like as a lover.

We all got acquainted a little and Vince took me for a tour of the place. First I was taken to a huge open room with a tall ceiling that Burger used as his painting studio. This was where his atrocities, or rather, excuses for paintings, were created. There were easels, paints, and brushes, and a long table with magazines strewn on top. Most were pornographic, both straight and gay.

We proceeded on to the room where they shot their pictures. It looked more like a basement and was crammed with mismatched furniture. There was a cleared-out spot where a backdrop stood as well as some lighting equipment. The rest of the place was scattered with wigs, makeup, and other kinds of crap. Some of it I remembered seeing the models wearing in the grotesque photos I saw.

By now it was early evening and everyone else had left for the day leaving Vince, Diego, Burger, and myself by ourselves.

"So do you want to work out in our gym?" Diego asked. "That way you'll look more pumped up in the photos."

"Sounds good," I said.

"Why don't I show you the way while Diego sets up," Vince offered.

Vince led me outside and along a little walk that brought us to the back of the other house. On the exterior was a white spiral staircase that went up a few floors to a deck.

Vince switched on some lights when we reached the top and I could see behind the sliding glass door a fully equipped home gym. There was about six or seven machines, a full set of weights, stereo, magazine rack, and TV suspended from the ceiling. *Very nice,* I thought. When we went inside Vince clicked on the TV/VCR, producing noises not heard on regular programming. Sure enough a porno was being shown and had been left inside. In fact, there was a whole stack along with a few shelves of porno on the floor.

"They watch porn when they work out?" I asked incredulously.

"Yeah, they enjoy it," Vince answered nonchalantly, as if it were completely normal, not at all distracting.

Vince left me to pump some iron while he went to help Diego. At this point I went from thinking that Burger and his crew were eccentric to downright freaky. He had created a perverse playground in Beverly Hills, where anything went.

Good for him. He was probably one in a million.

Still, it had to be unwise, viewing porn while working out. If nothing else, it took away focus.

I was extra careful not to drop a dumbbell on my head while being distracted from my reps by the action on the television screen.

It wouldn't come as a surprise if Burger and Diego spent time working out a few muscles that didn't normally get exercised in a typical gym, except maybe in the steam room.

Finally I had to turn the TV sets off. I was surrounded by enough porn the rest of the day.

Soon it was time for the shoot to begin. I went down to the photo studio and I got undressed while Diego poured wine for everyone.

"All right, young Adam!" Burger pronounced in his exotic South African accent "Let's get started!"

"Would you care for some X?" Diego asked.

"No thanks," I smiled.

I wanted to relax and have fun, but also remain in control of what went on as well. Otherwise, it looked like it could turn into a freaky scene. I had already taken a hint that Vince found me attractive, and tonight I got the point even more clearly. It was obvious Vince was more than happy to be nude next to me in front of the camera. However, the feeling was not mutual. Vince was a nice guy, but I had no interest in even fooling around with him. I didn't find him at all attractive.

Burger continued painting what looked like a tribal pattern all over me. The paintbrush trailed along my legs, across my back, up and down my arms, everywhere. The cool paint tickled lightly against my warm skin. The famed composer used black acrylic so it would be easy to wash off. He finished with my face. When he was done, the effect was theatrical, to say the least. I looked like a cross between an African warrior and a Hindu God.

We started with a series of shots on the stairwell, me crawling on my hands and knees trying to convey a wild feeling to the camera. I felt like Grace Jones performing at Studio 54 as Burger clicked away with his camera.

Some time later we moved into the studio where he took some more shots. Diego wanted some shots with my dick erect in them.

Something possessed me to ask Diego if he would join in. I didn't need Ecstasy to get freaky. Being next to a strapping man would arouse me.

"Is that okay?" Diego asked Burger.

Burger nodded his approval.

A few shots later Burger was nude and in front of the camera as well. Only pictures were being taken, nothing more, no sexual acts or hanky-panky. But if anybody were to walk in at that moment God knows what thought would have sprung to mind. With me painted that way, probably that we were in the midst of some sort of satanic ritual.

We took a break so that Mr. Composer could paint Vince's body, using white. He did it quicker and was not as detailed as with me. I noticed the paint did not sit well on Vince's legs, they were too hairy. But the next thing I saw caused me to turn my head and make me sick to my stomach. Vince had the most disgustingly overgrown and neglected toenails I had seen my entire life, and I literally wanted to gag at the sight of them. I wanted to tell Vince he needed a pedicure, and fast. But I didn't want to hurt or embarrass him, so instead I turned away.

When they finished with him we took some photos together. The hideous toenails had soured my mood for it all, but I tried to act as if I was still into it. In retrospect, I should have taken Diego up on his offer of some Ecstasy; it would have made things a lot more enjoyable.

Our shoot lasted for a little while longer and then it was time for me to take off. I took a shower, and most of the black paint came off rather easily. In fact, it had already begun to dry and flake off while we were working.

While in the shower Diego popped his head in.

"So what do you think of Vince?" he asked slyly.

"He's a very nice guy," I answered tactfully.

"You're not into him, are you?" He smiled, knowing he was putting me in an awkward position.

"Um, not particularly," I answered, careful to be tactful.

Not that being tactful helped much as far as Vince was concerned. When paying me my modeling fee he was considerably less friendly.

"Here you go. Later," he said while slapping the money in my hands and avoiding eye contact. I got out of that madhouse faster than a gang member fleeing a drive-by shooting.

When I got home and told Candy about my dealings with Owen Burger, she was amused and entertained, but not at all surprised. Candy knew her fair share of characters as well.

We had settled into our regular routine of sitting on her balcony and talking crap. I loved sitting out on the patio. It was the one place in this new city where I felt completely cozy, safe, and comfortable, and had not a care in the world.

"Sounds about as weird as my date from last week," Candy commented.

"Pray tell," I laughed. This sounded like it was going to be a good story.

"Well as usual the guy turned out to be a total creep and user," Candy began.

"It all started when I was called by an agent from the Akins Agency. I was really excited because for once someone from a reputable agency was getting back to me. So I look up the guy's name, which is Greek, and I was a little surprised that he was listed as a literary agent, not talent."

Candy paused to take a drag from her cigarette. The only time she smoked was the end of the day, and only on the balcony.

"I'm asking myself why a literary agent would want to see me. It's not like I sent in a screenplay or anything. I figured he was taking on a bigger workload, so I call and make an appointment.

"My appointment was at five p.m., when a lot of people were emptying out of the place. But I see the guy, and am pleasantly surprised to find he was tall, dark, and handsome, about thirty-eight years old. So he sits me down and tells me he read on my resumé how I'm from the east coast, and this is something he is so impressed with, a New York trained actor, blah-dee-dah and all that."

"Uh-oh," I said. It sounded like this was leading in only one direction: the good old-fashioned casting couch.

"People from New York have a certain sensibility you don't find in folks that come straight to LA," Candy said, comically mimicking the agent's voice.

"Then he tells me he will pass my resumé on to the right people," she continued. "Good thing he wasn't so bad looking, or I already would have been out the door. After more chitchat, he eventually got to the real reason why he asked me to come in, suggesting we go out sometime. Normally I would have been annoyed and irritated. But I figured it couldn't hurt, maybe he is a nice guy, and my divorce from Frank is definite. So he asks me what I'm doing that same night!"

"Doesn't waste any time, does he?" I asked wryly.

"Exactly, so I tell him I have plans, and he asks me about the following night. I say okay. We meet at the Los Angeles County Museum of Art, and we actually had a pretty good time. Afterwards we headed over to his place for dinner. But the place had an unmistakable female touch. Actually there were two things that gave it away. The first was the curtains and the candles placed around the apartment. As a woman, I knew that only another woman would put in curtains like that, or a gay man. The second clue was more obvious. All over the walls were empty nails, with spaces that were perfect for hanging photos. It looked like this guy had gone through the place and tried to get rid of any evidence of a girlfriend, or wife."

"No way!" I exclaimed.

"But wait, it gets worse!" Candy laughed and put out her hands to signal she wasn't finished.

"By the time dinner was over I was over him and ready to go. But as soon as the plates were off the table, the candles got lit and he puts on a Patsy Cline CD. Now he wants to slow dance. I try to protest but he grabs me. Now this is the very first time I am so close to him. When I looked up at him, I noticed something that had escaped me the whole night. Looking closely at his hairline I could see all these little plugs, but they didn't seem to come out of his scalp. Instead, he wore what must have been an expensive weave, or whatever they call that 'non-surgical hair replacement.' Now my mood swung from boredom and disappointment to repulsion. I came up with a quick excuse for a fast exit and left in disgust."

"Good God," I grumbled, "we've encountered so much dirt all the water in the world isn't enough to clean us off."

"No kidding," Candy replied. "So the next day I bring it up to some girl I know from the audition rounds. She gets a knowing look on her face and asks me the jerk's name. Then she rolls her eyes, tells me the guy is in fact married, and that his wife lives in New York and they have a bicoastal relationship. Turns out he does it to girls all the time. He gets one of the assistants in the talent department to pull the pictures of all the attractive woman and keep them aside, and then he goes through them and decides who he wants to try and sleep with."

"Unbelievable," I said.

"Even more unbelievable was the scathing e-mail I left him. I'll show it to you later," she said with a smirk.

I stopped for a moment to light one of the candles that went out.

"You know, speaking of dirt, Adam, I'm getting really concerned with these people you are hanging with. I mean Dale seems like he means well, but mold grows mold, and look at what he does and who he is constantly hanging around," Candy said with concern.

Candy rarely got serious. But when she did, she pursed her lips together and moved them to one side of her face, and narrowed her eyes. It almost looked like she was trying to figure out a riddle.

"Oh, they're not all so bad," I sighed. "And Dale's probably one of the coolest guys I've ever dated, minus his profession. But who am I to judge anyways, now that I'm Mr. Fuck-on-camera. Besides, it's his job that concerns me as much as his drug use. He swears he's just doing crystal every occasional weekend, but he seems so high-strung this week."

"You know, I've seen so many people who are fucked up on drugs and sex in this town," Candy said quietly. "Everybody wants to be somebody, everybody wants to be famous. You are still young, Adam, there are so many options you can pursue. You have the advantage of youth, and once that's lost you can't get it back. I just want you to use it wisely, you know."

I just nodded back, looking down.

"Have you heard about any real jobs?" Candy asked.

"The accounts receivable department at Universal called me. I have an interview next week," I answered solemnly.

"That's not so bad," Candy said consolingly. "You've got to get your foot in the door somehow."

"I guess."

"Any other luck with the employment agencies?" She pursued the subject further, even though I didn't feel like talking about it.

"I don't even want to go there," I said.

"I hear you," Candy said knowingly. "It's called lack of marketable job skills. I feel the same way. I never go to those places because I know they are going to ask me to take a Word test, then an Excel test, then a PowerPoint test, and by the time I leave I'll feel so tested and demoralized I'll wish I hadn't gone in the first place."

"That's not even counting Quark, HTML, and the second language I need to learn," I stated. "Good Lord, I could go to school for years."

"You're right. And even with all those skills they'd probably want you to have two or three years experience," Candy joked. "My favorite job interviews were with Wells Fargo and Dean Whitter, at a point when I was fed up with the acting thing and thought I'd get back into sales. Wells Fargo sits me down for an exam and has me do long division, multiplication, and percentages with a paper and pencil, the kind of shit I haven't done since high school. Then of course there is a time limit, so I fail. Same thing at Dean Whitter, only they had the nerve to ask me questions like how much I made at my last job and what percentage of my income I saved. I mean, if I were making so much money at a previous job, why the hell would I need to be interviewing for a new one? I swear you can't win."

Then Candy stood up, leaned over the balcony, flung her arms out comically, and screamed, "I'm tired of putting myself out there! I'm tired of feeling rejected! I'm tired of having low self-esteem! And I'm tired of having negative thoughts!"

It was too bad no casting director was around to see this groundbreaking performance. I had to keep myself from shouting "Bravo!"

Then she turned around giggling and asked, "Does that give you an idea about how I've been feeling lately?"

"Yeah. I get it. Now let's go inside, before one of the neighbors throws something at us and Orly comes banging and screaming at the door."

"Shit!" I yelled in exasperation.

The tape gun got messed up again for the hundredth time that afternoon, sticking tape everywhere but the package. Ron was raking in the bucks from his perverted flicks, couldn't he spring for a tape gun where the blade wasn't dulled down to nothing?

"How's our newest star doing?" a familiar flat voice asked from behind.

Speak of the devil.

"Ron, you gotta give me some cash to run to Staples with. Every tape gun in this warehouse is useless," I grumbled.

"Here," he said, and pulling out his wallet slapped some twenties in my hand. "Check to see if we need any other supplies while you're at it."

"No problem," I said, looking down at the tape gun and trying to peel apart the jumbled mess.

"There's something else I need to talk to you about," Ron suddenly lowered his voice and took on an expression of gravity. He looked so stupid when he took on an air of importance. Where other people just say what's needed to be said, it was as if Ron was coaching himself.

"Let me shut the door first," he said, turning around and stepping in between the stacks of boxes.

This odd bit of intriguing behavior during what was an otherwise excruciatingly monotonous afternoon stole my attention away from the tape gun and made me take notice.

"Listen," Ron said to me in a lowered voice, "I have another client for you, a very important, high-paying client."

"Okay. Cool. I could use the money," I said.

What I wanted to say was "Is that all?" and "Haven't we been down this road before, so what's the big deal?"

Sometimes Ron's theatrics made me think he really wanted to be an actor. Shit, he probably came to this town for that very reason himself, until realizing he didn't have a prayer.

"Now, I mean this one is very important. He's not just well-known in the business like Wayne Hanley, he is a huge star," Ron said almost in a scolding tone, as if to chastise me for my casual response.

"Who? Another butt-munching munchkin?" I asked in mock eagerness.

"You're not going to believe me when I tell you," Ron said, ignoring my smart-ass humor. "And it is of grave importance that word doesn't get out. He is paying for discretion, in addition to your looks."

"That's fine," I said, annoyed at the suggestion that this whole business was the biggest thrill of my life, something I'd go flaunting around town like a homecoming queen showing off her crown and sash.

"I'm not going to go blabbing to anybody. So who is it?"

"Let me give you a hint. He is a big daddy, but not the kind of daddy we typically think of. He plays one of America's most beloved fathers on TV."

"Oh for Christ's sake, I have no clue!" I said in exasperation. "Will you just tell me already, Ron?"

"All right, all right, lower your voice," Ron said in an unnecessary panic. There was nobody around the place but the two of us in a closed room.

"Do you know the show *Life's Lessons?*" asked Ron. The name rang a bell, but I wasn't exactly sure.

"It sounds familiar," I said.

"The sitcom about the high school principal and his family?" Ron pressed.

Now it dawned on me. I'd never seen an entire episode but caught moments of it when flipping between channels, and promos when watching other programs. Amid a sea of dating and plastic surgery reality shows, it seemed to be a popular sitcom. It starred a gregarious overweight all-American Joe as a popular and well-loved high school principal complete with the typical bland but pretty wife who played straight guy to his gags, and a few children if I remembered correctly. The show also featured a number of hot-looking students and an even hotter-looking coach.

"It's not that guy who plays the football coach?" I asked, getting excited. I usually paused the remote a bit longer if he was in the scene.

"Nope. It's the star of the show himself, John Vastelli," Ron said proudly.

"You're kidding? That goofy square?" I exclaimed in amazement, staring straight into Ron's eyes.

In addition to *Life's Lessons,* John Vastelli was always doing stand-up on the comedy network and was a favorite talk show guest and awards show host. His middle-class, big slob, lazy husband act seemed to appeal to all of Middle America.

"That's right," Ron said. "America's favorite dad plays both sides of the fence. As a matter of fact, he probably prefers the grass on our lawn, but the gay lifestyle doesn't really agree with his career in terms of the image he's built up."

"I figured as much," I nodded.

"Well Mr. Dad has an itch he needs scratched and would like you to do the honors at his place tonight," Ron said in his familiar tacky manner. "And he is paying a lot. One grand. Seems he saw your work with Missy and has been thinking about you ever since. But, Adam, he is paying for anonymity. If he trusts you, he'll use you again. I told him you were a good guy, new to town, and fresh off the bus. So you gotta keep this quiet. Don't tell anyone. That means your best friend, your shrink, your priest, or whoever."

"Ron," I began stating patiently, trying not to get exasperated, "I read you loud and clear. You have made your point. Like I said, my exploits in prostitution aren't something I go bragging about across town."

"Good," Ron said with satisfaction. "Now let me give you the details. And you can get out of here a few hours early to hit the gym. I'm sure John Vastelli will love seeing you all fresh and pumped up from a workout."

About an hour later I was putting orders away and almost ready to kiss the warehouse good-bye for the day. Ron had given me a time and directions, and I was taking his advice about the gym. I was a bit nervous about this trick, so the exercise would provide a release. At least I wouldn't have to fuck with the tape gun anymore. I never got to make my run to Staples. I'd worry about it tomorrow.

I was five feet from the door when it suddenly swung open violently.

"Jesus!" I yelled, jumping back, nearly avoiding a broken nose. Looking up I saw Dale standing before me.

"You scared the shit out of me!"

"Sorry about that," he answered in bemusement.

"Where are you off to so soon anyway?" he asked.

"Oh, I just have a lot of shit to do. Ron said it was cool if I took off early," I said.

"Shit? What kind of shit?" Dale asked, grabbing my lower back and pressing my pelvis against his. Then, before letting me answer, he stuck his tongue in my mouth forcefully.

I pulled back in irritation. Looking into his face I could see he was strung out on tina. His eyes were red and dilated, and he was wound up like a mechanical toy.

"Easy, Dale," I said, trying to catch my breath.

"I'm sorry, sexy," Dale said softly with a troublemaker smile. "I'm just so happy to see you. You looking forward to tonight?"

"Tonight?" I asked blankly.

"Yeah. Tonight. The show at the El Rey," Dale crossed his brow, irritated I'd forgotten. We had planned on seeing a band we both liked out of New York for the past two weeks.

"Oh, no," I murmured.

"'Oh, no' *what*?" Dale said, his mood turning dark. He dropped his arms from around me and took a step back.

"Don't tell me you are planning on selling out on our date," he said with a brooding look. It was the first time that something in his demeanor disturbed me. For a moment I felt threatened by him.

"Baby, I completely forgot. I'm so sorry. Something really important has come up that I can't back out of," I pleaded apologetically.

"What can be more important than something we have been planning for two weeks?" Dale asked angrily.

"It's about a job," I lied. "Candy set it up. A friend of hers works with promotions at Disney and hires the junior copywriters. But his schedule is really busy, and she is going out to dinner with him and mentioned me, so I need to tag along."

I pulled that one out of my ass. Any improv acting coach would have been proud. I felt badly about lying to Dale. I wanted to tell him I had to turn a trick, but then he would have asked what trick was so important that I was backing out of our date. And then what would I say?

"Why the fuck would you want a job as a junior copywriter for Disney anyways?" Dale spat. "And you're going to talk about it over dinner, instead of going into the office? Candy doesn't seem like she hangs out with the head of promotions at Disney."

"Look," I said quietly, trying to avoid any more confrontation. "We've been over this a hundred times. I don't want porn to become my whole life. And I've been told this guy is busy."

"Whatever dude," Dale turned around. "I just hope I didn't waste a fucking ticket. Maybe Brian will want to go. Thanks for the notice."

With that he slammed the door and walked out.

I went after him. He was already down the hall and out the front door to the street.

"Dale!" I yelled. "Dale, wait up. I'm really sorry, I . . ." It was no use. He was already in his truck and burning rubber.

I felt like shit. *I'll make it up to him,* I told myself. *He'll get over it. It's the drugs that made him lose his temper.* As soon as he forgave me, I was going to have to broach the subject of his drug use. But at the moment I had other things to deal with.

As with most Hollywood stars, John Vastelli lived in the Hollywood Hills. His house was just a few minutes drive above the action on Sunset Boulevard, at the end of a cul-de-sac. It was a nice home, with a brick front, landscaped handsomely but not overly ostentatious. It could have easily been in a gentrified neighborhood in Pasadena.

I rang the bell and waited for a few minutes. Eventually I heard footsteps approach and the knob turn. John Vastelli appeared, wearing jeans and a plain white T-shirt.

"Adam?" He stretched his hand out in a shake.

"Hi," I said, taking his hand.

"John Vastelli. Come on in." Stepping aside, he pulled the door open for me.

The entrance to the house was tiled, simply decorated with a chest and few expensive oriental vases. The interior of the house was much like the outside, expensive but comfortable.

"Why don't you have a seat in the living room," Vastelli suggested. His voice was soft and polite, if a bit timid. This was not the same loud-mouth Vastelli who was always hamming it on television.

"Can I get you something to drink? A soda, wine, beer, cocktail?" he asked as I sat on a leather sofa.

"A Coke would be great."

"One Coke it is," Vastelli said, making his way to an old-fashioned wet bar in the corner. "Actually, one Coke for you and a Diet Coke for me," he winked.

I smiled back. We were quiet for a brief moment as he was bending and reaching.

"Your home is beautiful," I said. "The view is fantastic."

"Thanks," he said. "I fell in love with it right away. The guy who owned it before me was named Bosley, you know the doctor who started all the hair transplant centers? He has infomercials running twenty-four seven."

"Oh yeah," I said, thinking to myself that in ten years I'd probably need to go to one of Dr. Bosley's centers myself.

"Luckily I don't need his services yet," Vastelli smiled. "He lived in the place for over twenty years. He had a hard time parting with it."

"I can see why," I said, looking out the windows onto the LA skyline. Vastelli handed me my soda and sat across from me. I felt comfortable right away. He seemed like a good guy. He was no Wayne Hanley. The pool outside was illuminated with light against the darkness.

"Do you use your pool often?" I asked.

"All the time," Vastelli said. "I keep it heated up pretty high too. I like it steaming. Would you like to see the back?"

"Sure."

The pool area was quiet and calm. The city streets shone below in an electric grid which illuminated the sky above.

"So you're not nearly as manic in person as you are on the screen," I said after more small talk about the pool and backyard.

"Well, I'm on my downtime now," Vastelli smiled. "All that hyped-up shtick takes a lot out of a guy. Gotta recharge the batteries, you know?"

He stared bashfully at the ground. He had a very sweet and endearing quality that I found very attractive. It was certain that he was more intimidated with me than the other way around. I actually found him kind of sexy. His hair was thick and curly, and he wore it very short. His eyes were big and blue, and drooped just a bit, like those of a puppy dog. His build was stout and thick, like that of a maintenance man. He had a belly that bulged a bit over his pants, but nothing that hung over. And a barrel chest and burly arms offset his wide middle, so in reality he looked in proportion. It was a nice change from the cookie cutter, overly worked out bodies I saw all over town and on the covers of the video boxes I shrink-wrapped every other day.

"You mind if I get my feet wet?" I asked.

"No, no! Not at all!" he answered reassuringly, sounding eager to please. I took my socks and shoes off and sat by the steps. The water felt great. Vastelli sat by the pool next to me, took off his own shoes, and rolled up his jeans.

"It feels great." I leaned back on my elbows and breathed in deeply. "You weren't kidding about the temperature."

"My heating bill is my big splurge. But it's worth it. I make sure I enjoy it."

I sat back up and looked into his puppy dog eyes. It must have been so hard for this guy who had made his fortune playing the everyday straight guy to have a desire for other men.

Our expressions held long enough the way faces do when both people agree it's time to get things on. Then with his head tilting one way and mine the other, we moved forward, our lips locked. His face was flush and ruddy, the freshly shaved skin just faintly rough. His mouth tasted clean and fresh, his tongue warm. I enjoyed kissing him. I wasn't at all turned off. If anything he felt safe, comfortable, like a cozy teddy bear.

We went on for a few minutes. When we finally pulled apart I smiled; he looked dazed. He placed one of his masculine hands under my chin and ran his index finger up and down my cheek.

"You are so beautiful," he breathed softly.

"Come on. Let's get in," I said.

Standing up we took off our clothes, tossing them on the chaise lounges a few feet away.

I plunged in first, swimming underwater to the other end. When my head emerged I could hear splashing behind me. Soon he met me at the other end and pressed up alongside. I could feel his fully erect dick against me. Like him, it was thick and plump, extraordinary in girth. Glancing down I could see it was a vibrant flush color when the pool light flashed against it. A large vein ran down the middle of his shaft. Just the touch of it against me was enough to make my own cock rise, crisscrossing against his in the water. I straddled him, hanging on to his body with pleasure as we bobbed and floated all over the pool. When my dick slid up his belly my butt rose, and in turn the tip of his hard cock poked against my perineum, working its way farther back and teasing the perimeter of my hole.

The whole time we made out, nibbled each other's ears, rubbed each other's shoulders, and enjoyed each other's touch.

After twenty minutes he said, "Adam, I want to take you to my bed."

"Let's go," I answered.

He got out first, grabbing a few rolled-up towels from a nearby basket. When he made his way back to me, I was still emerging from the steps, so his erect dick was level to my face. Before he could hand me the towel I raised my mouth to the huge red head of his cock, so plump I thought it would burst. Taking it in my mouth, I heard him groan loudly above. His groans turned to yelps as I flicked my tongue along the tip and against his piss slit. John Vastelli's cock had a number of pronounced veins running up and down the shaft, which protruded so much it was almost freakish. I traced my tongue against the veins as though catching melting ice cream dripping down a cone on a hot day.

It was more than he could take. Pulling back out he panted, "We have to go inside now. Or I'm going to shoot my load before we even get there." With that he flung the towel at me, grabbed my hand, and dragged me inside.

He didn't bother turning on the lights. The room was lit only from the pool outside the windows. We sat upright for a while, legs crossed and making out, grabbing each other's cocks and stroking furiously.

I enjoyed straddling his body, and he invited me to do so. We explored each other's bodies up and down with our tongues, making pit stops at important places. I tried to fit his monster-size dick in my mouth, pushing my mouth down far enough so that my lips brushed against his curly pubes.

John was versatile and invited me to enter him first. This was after he dripped a generous amount of lubricant over his belly, so I could slide my dick up and down, using him like an amusement park ride. When the condoms came out he tossed his legs back, proving himself very agile for a big guy. As I entered him he stared up at me in lust through squinted eyes, mouth hanging open in speechlessness.

When it was his turn to fuck me I sat on him, easing my tight hole down his wide, hard tool. He was gentle at first, but then let himself go once I eased into it.

"Yes! Yes! Yes!" he hissed repeatedly, breathing hard while pumping himself into me. All I could do was throw my head back, the wind knocked out of me but enjoying every second at the same time, my dick still erect and slapping up and down against my abdomen.

I asked him to come first, to let his nuts burst their hot liquid all over my face, always a fetish of mine. When he did so I thought it would go on forever. I had never in my life witnessed a wad of jizz that big. Through squinted eyes I saw gush after gush of white ooze shoot on my hair, face, ears, neck, and chest, all of it hot and gooey. Every time I thought he was done a new stream squeezed through his piss slit, his pelvis jerking back and forth, his grip on my hair tight as he held my face close. When it was finally over I was covered and felt as though I had on a mud pack. John must have needed to be with a guy for some time to come that much, unless it was some strange genetic blessing.

When it was my turn I straddled his belly, still sticky and glazed over like a doughnut. When I came I went well beyond his head and right on the headboard, not doing so bad myself but not excreting nearly as freakishly a large an amount of come as he had.

"Come on. Lets get you cleaned up," John said, but not before grabbling my face, kissing me deep, then licking off some of his jizz for good measure. America's favorite dad was one damn good fuck.

After soaping up together and rinsing off, we stepped out of the shower. Placing a towel around my back, John squeezed me gently and whispered in my ear, "Why don't you spend the whole night, huh? I'll pay you double."

That night I slept well. It was a good thing, since repeating the whole routine in the morning required all the rest I could get.

A Party Gone Awry

The following Saturday Candy asked me to go audit an acting class with her. I figured why not. Maybe it would clear my mind a bit and, if I liked it, be a small step in getting back on track to doing something worthwhile.

Right away both of us knew something weird was going on when the class stood up and gave the instructor a standing ovation when she entered the room. One would have thought she was so great she invented a cure for cancer or something. The teacher was a fat black woman named Janet who thought she was the second coming. Apparently she had her students believing it.

At the end of the class a scenario took place that scared the shit out of the both of us. A couple was in front of the class and acting out a fight scene. Janet wasn't convinced and rebuked the couple on their lackluster performance.

"There was no feeling there, no passion!" Janet raged. "We felt nothing!"

She than proceeded to tell the guy to slap the girl across the face, a suggestion he rebuffed.

"I want to see a real knock-down, drag-out fight!" Janet roared. "Slap her across the face!" she ordered.

At first the frightened actor demurred.

"I said slap her!" Janet screamed.

The next thing we saw was the guy slapping her across the face. Then the girl slapped him back.

"Good!" Janet's voice boomed. "Now pull her hair! Don't worry, you won't hurt her!"

Both of us sat in stunned disbelief, our eyes wide and mouths open in horror, as the guy dragged the girl across the stage and she screamed in the shrillest, most disturbing tone possible.

When it was all over big Janet triumphantly pronounced, "Now that was a real knock-down, drag-out fight!"

Neither Candy nor I were impressed. We snuck out quietly, not that anyone noticed us or bothered to make conversation the whole time we were there.

"I'll be passing on that one," Candy said in a grim voice.

"That's a wise decision," I replied. "Not that I'd know too much about wise decisions lately."

We climbed back in her car to go back home, stopping to get chicken for lunch at a trendy restaurant called Birds on Highland that specialized in poultry. Across from the street from it was the Church of Scientology headquarters. It was an impressive building, old by Los Angeles standards, with turrets and an almost gothic look to it. Staring out the front window of the restaurant at it I thought maybe Harry Potter might come flying out one of the top windows.

Staring at the ostentatious building herself, Candy wondered aloud, "Do you think if I became a Scientologist I'd get a decent audition?"

Smiling and rolling my eyes I replied, "If it works, let me know."

Candy was really trying to get moving on the acting, but I could see her patience wearing thinner every day. She had landed roles in cable network shows in the same vein as *Baywatch,* and had gotten close with callbacks for guest spots on major network hit shows, but so far, the big break hadn't come yet.

After the waiter took our order, Candy suddenly got excited, jumped forward in the booth, and exclaimed, "Oh! I almost forgot to tell you! I signed you up for an audition for the *Hollywood Windows.* I put you in for Tuesday of next week, so tell your smarmy boss that you need the afternoon free. They were able to fit me in this week because all next week I have rehearsals for my scene study class showcase. I hope you don't mind us not going together. But I wanted to get in before I get too busy and consumed with something else."

Game shows were Candy's latest craze. Tight on money now that Frank was out of the picture, she was focused on extra income and free stuff until another rich boyfriend came along. Every morning she circled the contestant auditions listed in *Backstage.*

"Oh, I don't know, Candy," I said dismissively. "I really don't see myself on one of those things."

"Adam," Candy pooh poohed, "don't be so quick to judge. You never know, it could lead to some money. And then you wouldn't have to keep hanging with this seedy element, and get away from the sleaze while finding a job you like. Speaking of which, how did your interview go at Universal, the one for accounts receivable?"

"Uneventful at best," I said. "I dressed up in J. Crew from head to toe, put my best foot forward, only to be grilled by a bored-looking woman who seemed overly concerned about my phone skills. Let's put it this way, not the most thrilling job on the planet. She said she had to interview a few more prospects and left it at that."

I paused to play with my napkin for a moment.

"What scares me more, if you want to know the truth, is that I am really getting to become comfortable with the sleaze around me. It's becoming some sort of dysfunctional, triple-X family in a way. There's a whole thrill factor there. Even though I know it's getting danger-ous, you know what I mean."

"You're getting to the point where it's going to be real hard to get out of it, Adam," Candy said straightforwardly. "I mean, this is just not like you. What was supposed to be a crutch to get you through things has become your whole life. What ever happened with Dale anyway, did he cool off at all?"

I had told her that I blew off the concert with Dale, but I hadn't said why. I had been dying to spill the beans to Candy. John Vastelli wanted to see me again, sometime next week. I was more than a bit enamored of him and had been thinking about him ever since. The next day Ron grilled me on the details. I tried to be casual about it, saying it went okay, but not reveal how much we hit it off. Ron had already gotten a nice cut for arranging the tryst; I wasn't sure how much, but I assumed it was a lot.

He wasn't getting any more. His part was over, and he made easy money just for an introduction. But he wasn't getting any more money that I was making on my back, at least not from Vastelli.

I couldn't resist the urge to tell Candy. I felt I could trust her; she played the same game to get by in the past.

"You know, I bailed on him to go turn a trick," I said quietly.

"No," Candy said in a chastising voice. "Adam, that's not like you. I mean as much as I think he's not the right guy, he's still a nice guy."

"I know. I told him I needed to go out with you, because you were introducing me to a job contact," I confided.

"Great!" Candy exclaimed in mock exasperation and a giggle. "Get me involved why don't you."

"I know it sounds slimy, Candy, but this was no ordinary call. I mean big money, an important client," I leaned over my voice getting softer.

Candy's expression changed to a quizzical stare, one blonde eyebrow raised in intrigue.

"Go on," she said slowly.

But before we could speak any further our waiter arrived with the food, and we pulled our heads back as he set our chicken platters down. I felt so covert, as though I were in some sort of spy movie. All I needed right now was a piano player in the corner and Ingrid Bergman to walk through the door.

After our waiter left, I told Candy the whole story about John Vastelli. She listened in disbelief as our chicken got cold. By the time I was done, she was still amazed.

"No way!" she whispered in excitement over and over. "That big goofball! I don't believe it!"

"Shh!" I hissed, looking around nervously. "You have to swear on your life this stays between the two of us."

"Please!" Candy said in irritation. "As if you have to tell me to keep quiet. You know about every skeleton in my closet, and I trust you! Look, this could lead to something for you. Maybe Vastelli can even find you a good job!"

The thought had crossed my mind already. Realizing we hadn't eaten any of our meals, we packed the chicken to go and headed home.

"John Vastelli," Candy murmured in the car. "I still can't believe it."

"Believe it," I said.

Just then my cell phone rang. I turned it on without checking it. A voice said, "Hey." It was Dale.

"Hi," I said.

"What are you up to?" he asked casually.

"I just finished eating lunch with Candy. We went to audit an acting class this morning," I said.

"Who is it?" Candy asked beside me.

I mouthed the name Dale to her. She raised her eyebrows in a mock expression of shock.

"So how was the concert?" I asked.

"It was cool. Brian came along. Too bad you missed it."

Dale and Brian hung out often. Sometimes I wondered if Brian ever told Dale about how we fooled around during our photo shoot, the same day I met Dale. Not that it would have mattered, we hadn't started dating before that. And Dale probably assumed I had. He wasn't possessive sexually; I mean, he met me through the porn biz for crying out loud. He knew I was having sex with other people when it called for it, and we never discussed being monogamous with each other even outside the business. He wasn't naive; he probably knew that I occasionally turned tricks for money. Just not the night we were supposed to see the show, and with John Vastelli.

But I decided Brian never talked about it. Brian was too image conscious. He fancied himself a serious fashion photographer who hung out with the influential West Hollywood crowd, the people Sarah and Stephen wanted to be. He even used a separate name for his pornographic work. When other people were around on a set or a shoot, Brian was all business. He made it clear he was in it for the money only, and as soon as he became successful enough with his mainstream work would distance himself from the sex industry altogether.

"I'm glad you guys had a good time, Dale. I felt really bad about that," I said earnestly. It wasn't hard to sound authentic. I really did feel awful about bailing out.

"It's cool," Dale said. "You gotta do what you gotta do. I know you have a plan, Adam. And that's good. A lot of these guys don't, and then a few years later they find themselves used up and useless, with no resumé, skills, nothing. You are smart for wanting to get out."

"Is this the same Dale speaking that less than a week ago wanted to shape me into the biggest name to hit gay porn since Ken Ryker?" I asked.

"Babe, I can't make you do anything. You could go all the way to the top, but you have to want it," Dale said. "Anyways, that's not why I called. I'm going to a party tonight, and wanted to invite you. It's at the home of Robert Gleisman, a really hot movie director a few years back. His house overlooks a canyon in the hills. It should be a lot of fun, and a really eclectic crowd with a lot of Hollywood people, not just porn people. You up for it?"

Dale hadn't sounded this well adjusted for a few weeks. I was looking forward to seeing him. When he was together, I still had more fun with him than with any other guy I'd been with.

"I'd love to come," I said.

"How about I pick you up at nine?"

"Perfect."

"Later."

I clicked off my phone and tucked it away. I was relieved we were speaking again.

"Sounds like somebody has a hot date tonight," Candy commented.

"Yeah, we're going to a party at some director's house," I said casually. "It should be interesting."

"I tell you, Adam, a few months in town and you're already living the fast life," Candy teased.

"I'm hearing this from Miss Playboy Mansion herself?" I teased back.

At least once or twice a week Candy had a wild event to attend, including many bashes at the Playboy mansion. Candy had been going to the mansion since she first landed in LA, after a girlfriend she met got her on the permanent guest list. I had already advised her numerous times on what to wear to the endless parties held there. She had a whole page on her Web site dedicated to photos taken with celebrities at the Playboy mansion, which showed her standing with various luminaries such as Jon Lovitz from *Saturday Night Live,* Mini-Me from *Austin Powers,* and Hef himself. She was more than a little bit bummed when they instituted a rule barring personal cameras at future parties.

So assisting in putting together an outfit was my duty as her close friend. If there was a theme, like Valentines or A Midsummer Night's Dream, we could get pretty damn creative.

That evening I didn't have to get as creative as Candy. Just a tight black T-shirt, boot-cut jeans straight out of *Urban Cowboy,* and some city boots. Dale showed up a few minutes before nine.

We had to stop for gas on the way there. While Dale went to pay, his cell phone began ringing, which he had left between the front seats. At first I ignored it, but it rang and rang and rang. Finally I answered it just to shut it up. I thought his voice mail would never pick it up.

"Hello," I said.

"I have your stuff. The good shit. One hundred and twenty a gram. When do you want to pick it up?" a bitchy female voice snapped on the other end, taking me aback.

"Uh, hold on," I replied, seeing Dale approach the car.

"Here," I said to him, handing him the phone from the window. "It wouldn't stop ringing, so I picked it up."

I was worried he might be annoyed, but instead he thanked me.

"Dale here," I heard him say. Then his voice changed, became uncomfortable as he walked away from the pump. "Great. . . . I can't. . . . Not tonight. . . . It's gotta be tomorrow."

Eventually he walked out of range so I could hear no more. When he finally finished his call, we took off. He didn't mention the call, and I didn't ask.

He was calm the rest of the way, mostly filling me in on our host. Robert Gleisman was a rich and once very successful movie director, who had directed one of the highest grossing musicals of all time. It had been rereleased in theaters right before I moved from New York.

His house was in the Hollywood Hills, a fabulous 1950s-style spread straight out of a Rock Hudson and Doris Day romance. He frequently rented the place to film and television productions, a profitable side venture.

"He had the crew of *Beverly Hills, 90210* shooting a scene up there," Dale began. "Robert told me in one scene the house was supposed to be on fire, and the director stood by in amusement as the crew had to show Tori Spelling how to spray water out of a hose by simply placing her thumb on the end. The girl had never picked up a hose in her life."

There was already a string of cars parked down the road from Gleisman's house. Eventually it appeared after passing by the drive's gates. Gleisman was very warm and gracious upon meeting me. In his late fifties, he was very attractive, with a strong and handsome face, thick sun-bleached hair, and a nice build.

The party was already going full swing. A bar was set up outside by the pool, and beautiful people, mostly gay guys, stood around with cocktails. The hot tub was lit up and bubbling, as though it were inviting illicit activity. I had always wanted to fool around in a hot tub in the hills. That was so California to me, part of the illusion I had of LA before moving here. That and beautiful blond surfers, drives along the Pacific in convertibles, and bonfires at the beach. Of course, when I was romanticizing coming to live in LA I failed to think about smog, insane traffic, urban sprawl, and riots.

I spotted Brian a few feet away and nodded a greeting. He came over to join Gleisman, Dale, and me.

"Adam, every year I have an Oscar party, and this year's is just down the road," Gleisman smiled. "Brian and I came up with the idea to have men wear skimpy gold lamè thongs, and then paint them in gold metallic paint. My friends' film is considered a favorite, so I am throwing an after party for them. For every Oscar they win we are thinking of having a life-size Oscar."

I had to say I would have made an awesome Oscar, just because my shoulders are broad to point of abnormality and my waist is so narrow in comparison, the top half of my body looks like an upside-down pyramid. However, how many people at the party are really going to take time to socialize with one of the living trophies in the corner? I could see myself walking around with gold paint on for days, and I'd had my share of body painting with Owen Burger. But if it was a paying gig, as always, I could use the money.

"So what do you think?"

"Is there any pay involved?" I asked the director pointedly after he excitedly rambled on about my golden opportunity to be an Oscar.

"Ugh, no," he answered, sounding a little taken aback and surprised that I would ask such a thing. "But everybody will be there.

You'll meet a lot of people!" he went on to say, his voice gaining back its former enthusiasm.

Sure. I can just see it now, future Hollywood star discovered while parading around in a gold thong and paint. Call me pessimistic, but something told me I wasn't going to be like Lana Turner getting discovered in a soda shop. If this would have been asked of me when I was in or right out of college, or even new in town, I probably I would have jumped at the chance to hang out in the same place as a bunch of stars and Hollywood heavyweights, but by now I had been to enough parties to know guests won't take much time out to speak to the living trophy in the corner.

I wasn't kidding about pay either. Gleisman had more than enough money to shell out at least a hundred bucks to a few suckers who were willing to freeze their gilded asses off on a frigid March evening. Here the nights got damn cold. Contrary to popular belief, LA isn't a year-round summer climate like Miami, where you can prance around in a thong all year long, 24-7.

"You know, I think I'd rather be a guest and appreciate other glistening gold bodies. But thanks for keeping me in mind." I smiled at Gleisman.

"Really? Are you sure?" He sounded dumbfounded.

I'm sure he had me figured for the ultimate starfucker who would say, "I'm there!"

"I've taught Adam well," Dale joked. "He doesn't come cheap for appearances."

"Well," Gleisman said, "if you ever change your mind, let me know."

"You got it," I replied, really thinking to myself, *not a chance in this world.*

With that Gleisman excused himself to attend to his other guests. Brian, Dale, and I stood around making chitchat.

Two men were having a loud conversation nearby. One was telling the other about what he needed to do to further his dance career, going on about the importance of a good head shot. A third, more inebriated guest piped in and said, "Who cares about pictures? Everybody has one and nobody can agree on what a 'good head shot' looks like!"

I had to laugh at that one. Candy had taken tons of head shots, spending a fortune on photos when indeed no agent or casting director could agree on what a "good head shot" was. It was about who you knew in this town, not what your picture looks like.

The three of us decided to move around. A beautiful table of food was set up, and cater waiters were making the rounds with platters of champagne. Gaggles of pretty gay men stood about in Prada, and very few people were eating, as if it were a big faux pas to be seen near the food. That rule didn't affect me, as I stood there enjoying everything offered while Dale and Brian talked crap.

Keep the cheese and crackers and give me the good stuff, I thought while standing by the kitchen door and waiting for more filet medallions to come out. Keeping myself busy chewing on tiny Swedish meatballs and little strawberry shortcakes, I stuffed my face as Hollywood big shots such as Sandy Gallin sauntered by, checking the crowd out. When he smiled and said hello to me, I felt a bit embarrassed as I struggled to keep pieces of meatball in my mouth when I greeted him back. If I overdid it with the food, I practically drowned myself in champagne flutes that were constantly being circled around the room by the cater waiters.

Later on I dipped my feet in the hot and bubbly Jacuzzi near the pool. I wanted to strip off my clothes and jump in but thought I could get cramps and drown from stuffing my face like a pig with all those meatballs. Not to mention the three champagne flutes I had downed.

Dale had excused himself to go to the bathroom and Brian had disappeared a while ago to mingle. I could barely hear it when my cell phone rang above the now louder and more intoxicated crowd.

"Hello?" I yelled.

"Adam?" a soft voice asked.

"Yeah?" I yelled.

"It's John Vastelli."

I was completely caught off guard. I hadn't expected to hear from him until the following week.

"Hey. How are you?" I asked blankly.

"Fine. It sounds like you're at a party. I can barely hear you."

"It's getting pretty loud," I admitted. "I hadn't expected to hear from you until next week."

"I had a charity event to go to. It just ended. Pretty boring, but my publicist set it up. Helps us promote the show," he said.

"Never mind the good cause," I joked.

"What? I can't hear you," he said.

"Forget it," I yelled.

"I don't suppose you want to come over for a drink afterwards?" John suggested.

"I'm sorry, I can't."

"Having too much fun, huh? Sounds like a wild time," he teased.

"No, it's not that. I mean the party is fun. It's just that I came with a friend," I said.

"Oh, okay. I get you, it's cool. I know I'm calling at ten-thirty on a Saturday night, not much notice. Listen, I'll give you a call on Monday. I was thinking we could do something on Wednesday."

"I'll mark it down," I said.

"Don't get too wild tonight," John said seductively. "Save some of your energy for me."

"I'll talk to you later," I laughed.

"Later."

After I hung up I sat for a minute thinking about how much I looked forward to seeing John again. I felt infinitely more comfortable around him than any of the West Hollywood clones around me, with the exception of Dale. Then again, Dale wasn't a typical West Hollywood clone himself.

Just then I was interrupted by an accented voice behind me. For a moment I thought it was Owen Burger. But when I turned around I was greeted by the pale, angelic face of Perry Bristol.

"Is this Mr. Adam Zeller, formerly of New York City and now rising star of HUNG Video?" he asked with crisp British wit.

"Hi!" I exclaimed in delight. "I've been wondering when I'd run into you. I haven't seen you since the film festival at the Public Theater in Manhattan."

"I've been in England for the past few months. I just got back into town a few days ago. I've heard you've become quite a presence at HUNG Video," Perry smirked.

"Much to my surprise," I sheepishly admitted. "Actually, I'm here with Dale Warren. He ran off to go to the bathroom twenty minutes ago and hasn't returned. So will I be seeing you around the office now that you're back in the States?"

"Actually, my boyfriend Mitch and I are working on a feature. I wanted to talk to you about it because I remember you telling me you were in the Screen Actors Guild. There's a small part we'd like for you to read for. The name of the project is *The Voyeur,* and it's a behind-the-scenes drama about the gay porn industry, kind of a gay *Boogie Nights.* I think you'd really like the script."

Perry had already made a number of film shorts that were well received at numerous film festivals. His aspiration was to become a mainstream movie director, and he had the talent. Even his porn films, which he did for the income, had an artistic aesthetic and sometimes genius subplot. I knew if he made a film, it would be outstanding.

I gave him my information; we made small talk for a bit and then parted ways. By now my feet were prunes from sitting in the Jacuzzi. Dale still hadn't come back yet, so I decided to go look for him.

"Where are you going off to?" a muscle-bound guy with streaked hair and blindingly white teeth asked as I took my feet out of the water. He was followed by a beautiful Latino guy. Both began taking off their clothes and all the heads nearby turned our way.

"The party is just starting, papi," the Latino purred.

"Nature calls," I smiled, as the two began revealing hard bronzed bodies, tossing clothes aside and stripping out of their underwear.

"Well, come back when you've finished your business," the Latino winked, causing his friend to laugh.

"Don't worry," I teased back. "I'm sure you'll have lots of company in a matter of minutes."

"The more the merrier," the first guy said, stepping into the water, his dick bobbing around. Eventually it disappeared as he submerged his body beneath the bubbles.

I made my way into the house, passing by clusters of men all now fixated on the Jacuzzi.

While in the house I heard a splash behind me. Now people were jumping in the pool. This party was getting wild. But tonight I wasn't into any of that. I had come here with Dale. I could get sex any other time, on a porn set, turning a trick. If anything, I was having more than my fair share. I was somewhat relieved that I wasn't getting sucked into any debauchery tonight. Lately I had been feeling I was losing all control with temptation. Besides, I was on cloud nine about being approached to be featured in legitimate film, in a speaking role no less. Perry had also told me that he had secured a rock legend I had long admired into being in their film. Perhaps I would share a scene with her.

By now much of the crowd had trickled out and what was left were hard-core partiers, most of them two sheets to the wind. Couples were making out on the couches. In the corner of the room a number of people were dancing to music, their eyes closed and in another world. Screams and laughter exploded from all around me. But Dale was nowhere to be found.

For a moment I thought maybe he had left me, as payback for backing out of the concert. I began to get a little frantic and freaked out. If Candy wasn't around to pick me up, I didn't even have cash for a cab.

I spotted Robert Gleisman near the front door saying good-bye to some people. I interrupted and asked if he had seen Dale.

"Nope. Sorry," Gleisman said dismissively, going back to his conversation. Apparently I had really insulted him by refusing his offer to be a living Oscar.

Fuck him, I thought, moving on.

I made my way down the hall, where I saw people moving up and down a staircase. Many of them were holding hands and smiling lustily at one another. I passed a few more guys like that on the way up the steps. The hallway turned to the left. In the first open room there were a number of guys standing around, and few lying on the bed making out. Some of them were taking bumps of some drug or the other, most likely crystal. I peered in, looking for Dale, trying not to be too obvious. They stopped their conversation to look at me. I said hello and then walked farther down the hall. I could hear them burst into laughter from behind me.

Two doors were at the end of the hallway. The one on the left was open a crack. I peeked inside to see a couple on the bed. One was sitting on the edge with his head back moaning, and the other giving him a blow job, slurping loudly and jerking his head back and forth spastically. Neither of them were Dale. I stepped away immediately. Neither of them had noticed me. I supposed they wouldn't have given any indication even if they had; they were so into it, moaning up a storm.

I turned to walk away, then suddenly stopped, listening carefully. What I was hearing was more than just the laughter of the group in the first room and the moaning of the couple I just peeked in on. I heard grunting, a distinct grunting that was known to me.

I turned around, grabbed the knob of the door on the right, and opened it a crack.

Inside I was disgusted with what I saw. Hunched over naked on his hands and elbows was Brian. In one hand he had a vial with white powder and was reaching in to take a snort. Ramming him from behind was Dale, his face flushed and his body dripping with sweat. Both of them were gasping and groaning, and looked totally out of it. Dale's head was thrown back and Brian's mouth was hanging open like a fish.

"Here you go, dude," Brian said, passing up the vial to Dale as he pumped away.

"Thanks, man," Dale mumbled incoherently as he grabbed the vial, paused for a minute, then dumped a pile of white powder on his hand and sniffed away with vigor.

The two of them looked so gross together. I couldn't believe my eyes. The pit of my stomach began to churn. Just seeing them there spinning out of control with their drug-crazed sexual antics was enough to make me vomit. At that moment I realized what kind of element I had fallen in with, and just how far I had gone into left field in terms of life choices. God only knows if they were even using a condom.

I had seen enough. Quietly closing the door, I thought I saw Dale's eyes meet mine. If so, he was probably too buzzed on his drugs to care.

Either way, I wasn't waiting to find out. I was getting the hell out of this madhouse.

I turned and walked swiftly down the hall. When I reached the top of the staircase, one of the guys in the first room called out, "Hey, where you going?" nearly giving me a heart attack as all his friends laughed. There had to be a quick way out of this place.

Downstairs inebriated guests were hanging all over the furniture. The music was blaring. Naked people were jumping in and out of the pool. There seemed to be a massive orgy in the Jacuzzi, heads bobbing up and down, lips locked as guys made out with one another, frequently switching partners.

Salvation came in the form of Perry Bristol, in his East Village bohemian thrift rags and curly blond hair. He was walking out the door with a dark-haired guy also dressed in downtown New York fashion, complete with black horn-rimmed glasses. I guess this must have been his boyfriend Mitch.

"Perry," I yelled frantically.

"Hey, Adam," Perry said. "You're still here? Unless you want to get ravaged by the pool I suggest you take off now."

"Listen, can you guys give me a ride?" I asked, sounding clearly upset.

Perry must have sensed something was wrong, because his expression became serious and his tone of voice changed from that of a British dandy to aristocratic concern.

"Sure. Are you okay?"

"Yeah," I said, trying to regain composure. "I'll be okay. I just lost my ride and I really want to get out of here."

"No kidding," Mitch said. "We were just saying the same thing. This party is starting to get really ugly. They were drinking God knows what kind of liquid drug out by the pool. I can see this shindig turning into something out of *Beyond the Valley of the Dolls* or *Helter Skelter*. Let's get the fuck out of here."

The three of us walked briskly toward their car, a bottle-green antique Benz straight out of the 1970s. *Leave it to Perry to drive an eclectic car with an inordinate amount of style,* I thought upon seeing it, taking my mind off the ugly scene I had just witnessed for a brief moment.

In the car I told Perry and Mitch the whole story. I felt so badly they were driving me to the edge of Beverly Hills, given that they lived all the way in Silver Lake. I thanked them over again and again.

"I would really watch out, Adam," Perry said in his soft voice with genuine concern. "I feel badly, because Dale is a really good guy. Unfortunately, he's hooked on that crystal shit. It's becoming a real mess. The guy overextended himself with jobs and started doing speed to work faster and keep longer hours. But now it's taken over his life. This is just between you and me and goes no further, but Ron told me he is infuriated with him. Lately he has been making a lot of mistakes, and Ron is sick of having to pay for them. It's going to be an ugly scene there. He has begged me to step in, but we are just so busy with our film, and I'm over HUNG Video to tell you the truth. The problem is that Dale parties as much as he works, which makes matters worse."

"Perry keeps his work and social life separate," Mitch cut in. "Not that we don't have a few friends in porn, but most of our friends are outside the industry. He does his work and then leaves it behind."

"Exactly," Perry said. "Whereas with Dale, it has become his whole existence. It's so sad, because I've really seen him deteriorate."

"It's really messed up," I said. "I mean I knew he did drugs. I saw them at his place. But I just thought it was on occasion. I didn't know he was in so deep."

"Unfortunately, that's the case," Perry said. "Tonight was really a blessing in disguise, Adam; it's going to save you grief in the long run. You are smart enough to know you don't need that element in your life. If you had wanted to stay at that party, it wouldn't have been a good sign."

Minutes later we were at Candy's.

"So we'll have the casting director give you a call in a few weeks," Mitch said. "Perry thinks you're really perfect for this part, and after meeting you so am I."

"Thanks, guys. You don't know how glad I am we ran into each other," I said.

"Don't worry about it," Perry said, reaching through the front window and squeezing my hand. "Go get some sleep." He smiled, and then drove off into the night.

I entered the apartment quietly. I could hear Candy's television going in her bedroom. She probably dozed off in her bed watching it, as she often did. I was glad she wasn't up. I didn't have the energy or wherewithal to go over the lurid events of the evening with her. Instead I brushed my teeth faster than a speeding bullet, pulled off my clothes, and threw myself into bed.

A minute later I was startled by a noise. I had left my cell phone on and it was in my jeans pocket. Pulling it out, I looked at the screen. It said DALE in blocky letters. I clicked it off and tossed it on the floor.

I was done with these people. What bothered me the most about seeing Dale and Brian in their drug-frenzied fuck session is that it could easily be me months away. So far I was only doing porn and escorting, which was bad enough. But if I kept going in the direction I was heading, the temptation to become tweaked out of my mind 24-7 for $120 a gram might become impossible to avoid or resist.

My extended vacation into the realm of gay porn was over. Exhausted, I fell asleep.

Game for a New Gig

That following Monday I called in sick to my warehouse job at
HUNG Video. I had no desire to see or run into anybody. Dale had
left a handful of rambling messages on my cell phone. Some of the
messages were frantic and manic, whereas others sounded completely
spaced out.

"Adam, I'm so, so sorry I lost you at the party. There were so many
people there and I got caught up with some people I haven't seen in a
while, you know, catching up on business. Give me a call, okay?"

After I didn't call he must have figured I knew what kind of business he was doing.

"Adam, anything that went on at the party meant nothing. I was
just fooling around. Look, I let you off the hook when you sold me out
the night of the concert. Can't you just cut me some slack? Come on,
babe, call me," he pleaded on one of the more recent messages.

After a while I just erased them altogether. I was disgusted with
Dale, but most of all disgusted with myself for not getting smart
about him sooner.

When I told Candy she was really put off but not surprised.

"You know, Adam," she told me in the kitchen, "I feel like I've seen
and heard it all in this town. I'm glad you've finally come to your
senses. In the beginning I didn't want to give you too much grief
because I know how stressful hunting for a decent job is and how miserable you were answering phones at Acclaimed Talent. But your in-
volvement in that scene really went too far. I just hope you're not
planning on ever running for public office."

"Or any high-profile public job for that matter," I said.

"Well, I don't know," Candy pondered. "Look at Pamela Lee or
Paris Hilton. Shit, it seems nowadays having sex on camera is a pre-
requisite to becoming famous, so maybe things aren't so hopeless.

The point is you're getting out before things get out of control, like with Anna Lynn."

Anna Lynn was Candy's favorite illustration of the classic Hollywood tragedy. A cute blue-eyed blonde from Missouri, she came to LA through a modeling agent back home. Candy had met her in a Groundlings improv class, a class that Anna Lynn eventually stopped coming to altogether. Before long she was turning tricks with wealthy men, and out partying and drinking every night. The last she heard of Anna Lynn was that she had gotten pregnant by one of her johns, suffered a miscarriage, and incorporated the fetus into one of her oil paintings. When I heard that one I was grossed out beyond words.

"Anyway, I've seen some ugly times myself involving drugs," Candy went on. "Like the time in New York when I did too much blow and shit in my pink leather pants."

"You what?" I blurted, almost choking on my coffee.

"Oh, I never told you that one," Candy said with a guilty smirk. "One time back in New York I was on a call at this guy's apartment in Trump Tower and did way too much blow. There was another girl there as well. The guy was a total coke fiend and kept pushing more at us. I mean it was blow, blow, blow—all night long. So the whole evening I smelled this awful stench. I figured maybe one of them had gas or something."

Candy paused to take a sip of coffee.

"Actually, it really smelled like baby diapers," she reflected. "I thought maybe it was the other girl's cheap perfume. Who knows? So I ignored it for a while, but then after being sent off with my own cocaine kit, I was in the limo with the driver and still smelled it. Gross, this driver reeks too, I'm thinking. But when I got home and took off my pink leather pants, I couldn't believe it. I had thought I was just farting once in a while, but GEEEZZZZZ . . . diarrhea of the worst kind! It was so sick! Cocaine really loosens the stool, you know. I called the madam at the escort service and told her never to send me to that guy again because he got me so coked up I shit my pants. I had her in hysterics. She always got a kick out of me."

Candy laughed the whole time telling me this, hardly able to finish. I couldn't believe what she just told me and was laughing hysterically as well, tears running down my cheeks.

"My point is, Adam, live and learn, right?"

Leave it to Candy to put a humorous twist on even the most grisly subjects.

The next day I skipped work and went to audition for *The Hollywood Windows.* I was glad Candy had signed me up because at least for a few hours I wouldn't have to mull over Dale, HUNG Video, John Vastelli, or getting my life back in order from the mess I'd made of it.

The Hollywood Windows, along with *The Price Is Right,* is the mother lode of game shows, and countless people dream of being a contestant. And on *Hollywood Windows* you don't have to be a genius to win, unlike *Jeopardy.* Soon I was to find out that maybe I should have tried *Wheel of Fortune,* where you could be dumber than a stick and still win great shit.

These people meant business. Arrive dressed nicely, no jeans or sneakers. I wore my best black dress pants, nice Gucci knock-off loafers, and a blue button-down dress shirt. The audition took place in an office building not far from the Hollywood Bowl.

Upon getting there I was directed into a cramped room filled with rows of folding chairs. A variety of people were sitting in them, from nondescript housewives to pretty young girls, everyday-looking guys, office workers, and old ladies. After everyone had crammed in next to one another, a middle-aged woman dressed in black with an expensive dye job came in and announced herself.

"Hello everybody! I'm Susan!" she said in an overbearing voice filled with gusto. Everyone gave her back what I thought was a very friendly hello.

"Oh, come on!" she said in an obnoxious teasing voice. "I know you guys can do better than that! Let's try again! Hello everyone!"

"Helllooooooooooo!!!!" the room shouted back like a bunch of trained parrots. I felt like an adolescent child sitting in the peanut gallery of *The Howdy Doody Show.*

"Okay folks. I'm going to give you some forms to fill out." Susan went on to explain the forms and then spoke further about other logistics. She had a voice that would be perfect for an infomercial or a hosting job on the Home Shopping Network.

"If you are an actor, put down something else, whatever your day job is. We do not want any actors as contestants; we already have our nine celebrities on the show!" she said in a sarcastic singsong Snow White tone that assumed many of the applicants were starving actors.

It was no surprise half the people who came to audition *were* starving actors desperate for money to fund their pursuit of stardom. I wondered if anybody put down professional extra, as I'm sure they got a lot of those in here too.

We were then informed that someone named "Fran" would be coming into the room when we were done filling out our forms.

"Fran is our head contestant coordinator, so you want to be nice to her! And just a hint, she loves friendly, energetic faces!" When saying this Susan made the most grotesque phony expression of excitement I think I'd ever seen in my life. I wanted to vomit. People in the room were laughing at her shtick in a forced way, and I could tell the competition to grab attention and become a favorite in this joint was really going to heat up.

Susan left the room and gave us five minutes to fill out our forms. People began making small talk and some asked to borrow pens or pencils, as I'm sure they were terrified to ask Susan for them for fear of looking like an unprepared contestant. Susan came back into the room with Fran.

"Hello there, everyone! I'm Fran!" Fran announced.

This time the response was enough to shatter glass. "HELLOOO FRAN!!!"

"Wow! What a great group you are!" Fran said in a mock surprise voice with eyes wide open, as if we amazed her. It was so condescending and rehearsed that now I really, really wanted to puke.

We proceeded to hand in our forms and then Fran had us say our names aloud so she could check us off on her list. As soon as she started out, it was obvious she was feeling out the contestant potential in the room, hamming it up with each person so she could see how they would interact on the show.

A person who sat a few chairs ahead of me had a last name that began with a W, and Fran joked about it, telling him he was all the way at the end of the list. The guy replied he was used to it and, again, everyone in the room burst out in their now familiar forced laughter.

I was really beginning to feel that I was in some form of a lunatic asylum, or better yet, a living laugh track.

By the time she got to me I knew I'd have to think of something clever to make an impression and get on this fucking show to have a shot at winning some cash. She pointed the end of her pencil at me, signaling to say my name. This was my moment to make Fran think I was perfect *Hollywood Windows* material.

"I'm most likely last, but not least! I'm Adam Zeller, with a Z!" I said in my peppiest voice possible and a plastic grin across my face. Sure enough the room erupted in the now very familiar chuckles and giggles.

"You're absolutely right; you are last on the list!" Fran shot back in an equally peppy shout as the room laughed gleefully like a cast of idiots.

After she was finished with the rest of the list I knew far more detail about these people than I cared to know, like the guy who flew in from Sacramento for one day just to audition.

Now it was time to take a test. It was a list of statements that you either agreed or disagreed with, similar to what's said on the actual show. The statements ranged from "Horse racing is considered the sport of kings" to "Abraham Lincoln is the tallest U.S. president in history." I considered myself a relatively informed individual but was stumped by a few of the more inane questions. After everyone was finished Susan and Fran left the room to go over our little pop quizzes, telling us they would be back in about ten minutes.

Immediately everyone in the room started buzzing about what they agreed and disagreed with. There was a loudmouthed male schoolteacher behind me who had been hamming it up more than the rest of us put together. The whole time I'd been there I just wished he would shut up.

Next to me sat a plain-Jane mom with young kids at home who really seemed to know her facts when we talked about the questions. I bet she watched the show religiously every night. She was very nice, and I hoped they'd pick her as a contestant. I could see them passing her over because she wasn't slick or ethnic enough, or some stupid reason like that.

Eventually fake Fran and her sickening sidekick Susan came back into the room.

"Okay, everyone. Now we are going to read out names of people who we would like to stay for the second half of the audition. We appreciate all of you coming in today."

Just get to it, I thought as she informed us in what length of time the rejects could audition again. She read the names off and came to a stop. My name wasn't called out. Shit. I didn't even make the first cut. Not only was I a career failure with no marketable job skills, but now I was a failure as a game show contestant.

Well, I thought, *I couldn't have dressed better, behaved peppier, and wore any bigger of a grin across my now sore face.* I said good luck to the sweet young mother next to me and left the room. In the elevator the rest of the rejected contestants grumbled about their crushed hopes.

I guess I'd never be able to say out loud "I'll start with the center window!" It would have been nice to get some cash or a new car, but this didn't even make it near the top of my list of disappointments.

I got in my car and checked my messages. I had two of them. I looked at the phone in irritation; I was in no mood to listen to Dale carrying on in one of his drug-induced episodes.

Sure enough the first message was him.

"Why won't you call . . . *beep!*" I erased it before I had to listen to any more.

I was just about to do the same with second message until a soft, calm voice stopped me from hitting the delete button.

"Hey, Adam, it's John. I hope you're having a good week. I was wondering if you wanted to have dinner tonight. Give me a call, let me know. I know a quiet Italian place in Studio City. I think you'd like it. Hope to hear from you."

The message had come in only twelve minutes earlier. Hopefully John was still around to answer his phone. I dialed his number.

"Hello," a voice pronounced. He answered his phone in the same boisterous manner that he performed in.

"John, it's Adam," I said.

"Hey there," his voice lowered a bit, but betrayed a genuine excitement that I had called him back.

"I just got your message. I'd love to go to dinner tonight."

"Great. Listen, do you want to swing by my place at eight, and I'll take us to the restaurant?"

"Sounds good."

"How are things going?" he asked.

"All right," I lied. Then I thought better of it. "Well, not really. I'll tell you more tonight."

"Are you okay?" he asked.

"Oh, I'm fine," I protested, trying to downplay any sense of drama. "I'm just really looking for a change of pace. Trying to clean up my life a little, you know what I mean?"

At first I hoped I wasn't putting him off. *Fuck it,* I thought. *I need to be honest about who I am and where I'm at, if he can't deal with my shit that's his problem.* He knows what I've been around. It's not like we met at a dinner party.

"I think that sounds good," John encouraged in a chipper voice. "If you're not happy with things, you have to work to change them. We'll talk about it more tonight over dinner, okay?"

"I'm looking forward to it," I said with genuine anticipation.

"Likewise," John said in a low voice. "I have to get back on the set. See you tonight."

After saying good-bye I clicked off the phone and made my way back home. Earlier I had thought about going to the warehouse to do a little work but blew it off. I didn't want to run into anybody that would sour my mood.

That night I kept on the nice outfit I had worn to my unsuccessful game show audition. I showed up at John's house a few minutes before eight. He answered the door in slacks and a button-down shirt, and smelled great in Hermes cologne.

"Hey, handsome." He greeted me with a kiss. I felt comfortable and at home, just as I had when I left. I felt a sensation of arousal down below as he kissed me and his body brushed against mine.

We drove to the restaurant in his BMW coupe. We talked mostly about his day at the set.

"So how was your day?" he asked, changing the subject.

"Oh, all right," I lied. There was no way I was telling him that I flopped a chance at a game show. I didn't want the man to think I was buried up to my neck in loser dust.

"Just all right? What did you do?" he prodded.

"Actually, I sent out some resumés and really spent a lot of time searching the Internet for some job leads," I lied further.

"Really? I didn't know you were looking for a job. What kind of position are you looking for?" he asked.

"Oh, uh, advertising or PR, also production jobs. Maybe something with a studio or production company," I stammered quickly.

"Any prospects?"

I breathed in calmly. It was annoying to talk about.

"Not at the moment," I said quietly.

"So you're not looking to stay in the adult industry?" John asked shyly.

"No," I answered sharply, looking out the passenger window.

The conversation stood still for a while, until John started telling me about how much he loved the restaurant he was taking me to, and what I should order. When we got there the hostess led us to a quiet table in the corner. A few people glanced and lingered on John for a while, then went back to their conversations. I thought it brave of him to take me out in public. But it was a small place, and though I made a splash in the porn industry, there were countless porn stars in town. Chances were nil that anyone would recognize me. If anything, dressed the way I was, they probably thought I was a colleague or something. Who the hell cared what they thought anyway?

After some of the best penne a la vodka I had in long time, we went back to his place and retreated straight to the bedroom, spending much time with foreplay. The sex was great, even better than the first time. When we had finished we went out for a dip in the pool.

"Adam, what would you think about becoming my assistant?" John asked out of the blue.

"Are you serious?"

"Absolutely. The girl I have now is great, but she is going back to school. And I need somebody badly. Someone to run back and forth between my agent and manager, take care of personal errands, travel, appearances, that sort of thing," John said.

"You're not apprehensive about it?" I asked, not believing he was offering me a job that required me to be near him on such a close basis.

"That's the one condition. It requires complete discretion. I have to know I can trust you, Adam. I mean, I am really doing this for a few reasons. The first is obvious: I like you a lot. I think you're a great guy and I enjoy being around you." He paused.

"The second is I believe you have a lot to offer, and with this job you'll be meeting a lot of people. People at the network, at the production company, my agency, PR people, and more. I wouldn't expect you to work for me forever. As a matter of fact, if something came your way that was a great opportunity even after a short time I'd encourage you to go for it."

I couldn't believe what I was hearing. What a difference a night makes. And it couldn't come at a better time. I could kiss HUNG Video, Dale, Ron, Brian, and the rest of them off and get on with my life.

"How soon can I start?" I asked.

"I was thinking next week," John said. "I'll have you work with Stacy for a few days. She can introduce you to everyone and acquaint you with things that need to be done. Then she is heading home for the holidays and will start school full-time when she gets back, so the timing works out perfectly."

I hugged John from behind in the water, spooning up against him, and whispered in his ear, "Thanks, John."

As I sucked on his earlobe he whispered back, "You're welcome, gorgeous."

Within a week my life changed drastically. I informed Ron I had a new job offer the morning after my date with John.

"You're kidding me!" Ron said. "You have the makings of a porn superstar. You've already done it; you should be taking it all the way, boy! Get yourself a hot Web site, put out some escort ads, make cross-country appearances. You know how many guys would want to be in your shoes?"

The way Ron made it sound you would have thought I was turning down a full scholarship to Harvard.

"I know you're disappointed, Ron, but this was just a means to an end for me, an opportunity to get over hard times. I really appreciate everything you've done."

That I meant. As slimy as I thought Ron was, he was basically harmless. And after all, HUNG Video took me in when I left my job at Acclaimed Talent with nowhere else to go. If it weren't for him, I could have landed up at Taco Bell for all I'd known.

Though I didn't feel like going back there, I agreed to work that end of the week in the warehouse so Ron wouldn't fall behind on orders, and give him time to find somebody to take over. There was no shortage of him finding a broke porn star or hooker for the job. It was just a matter of finding one who wasn't a complete mess, which sad to say was harder than it sounded. Even to do work that a ten-year-old could handle.

My last day at the warehouse made me kind of wish I hadn't gone back at all. But at least I knew I had closure with Dale.

The packing tape was screeching up a storm as I raced to finish the last of the day's shipments, going through the UPS book and slapping on bar codes like there was no tomorrow. Suddenly I heard the front door burst open outside the hallway.

Shit, I hope that's not Marvin, I thought in a panic. Marvin was the UPS guy, a big and tough black dude with one of the most down-to-earth dispositions out there. His pickups were always something to look forward to during rather uneventful days in the warehouse.

"Marvin, is that you?" I said out loud without looking up.

"Who's Marvin? Your new boyfriend?" a familiar voice asked sarcastically.

I looked up to see Dale leaning against the doorway. He was a mess. He looked like he had been up for ten days straight without sleep and was completely disheveled. The growth on his face had gone beyond a five o'clock shadow and had become the beginnings of a beard. His eyes were bloodshot with heavy dark circles, and he looked like he lost weight from the way his grubby T-shirt hung off of him.

I felt my body tense up and swallowed, breathing in a bit and bracing for what was sure to be an uncomfortable conversation. He had still been calling me every day since the night of the party and I still hadn't returned his messages, hoping he'd gotten the point.

"Hi," I said.

"Hey. I came by at the beginning of the week and you weren't around. I thought maybe you'd skipped town or something. You have a problem returning phone calls?" he said in an accusatory, even threatening tone of voice.

"I really don't think it's a good idea for us to talk anymore," I said quietly.

"You mind telling me the fuck why?" he asked, moving forward a bit and folding his arms across his chest.

This was going to be uglier than I thought. I could tell already.

"Because I really don't want to be around you when you are constantly strung out on speed. That's why," I said firmly, standing up straighter and trying to put on a brave front, even though I was petrified. He was worse then I'd ever seen him, completely possessed by drugs. Who knew what he was capable of at that moment.

"That sounds pretty high and mighty coming from a fucking porn actor," he sneered, coming closer. "You need to get off your high horse. You think you're hot shit because you're from New York, well, you couldn't handle New York and you're really no better than the rest of us."

He knew how to hit me where it hurt.

"Former porn actor," I said angrily. "And you're right, I'm far from perfect, but I know I'm a better person than to invite someone to a party and then leave them to go snort crystal meth and fuck someone else in a bedroom."

"Did you enjoy watching?" Dale asked accusatorily.

"What?" I said in exasperation and anger, tossing the tape gun across the work table. "You were my fucking ride, and I was worried! Don't try to turn this around on me!"

"I said I was *sorry!*" Dale yelled, his face contorting into an ugly sob at the word "sorry." This was getting way out of hand. "You could have returned my calls and given me a chance to apologize. I gave you a second chance."

"Canceling a date and what you did are two entirely different things," I said, and then tried a different approach. "Look, Dale, I'm not angry anymore. I just don't think we should see each other."

That did it. Dale kicked a stack of boxes over and yelled, "Why!"

"Dale!" I yelled in protest. "What are you doing?"

"Look. I fucked up, babe. I'm sorry." Dale was now blubbering like a basket case. His emotions were so up and down he was like Patty Duke and Margot Kidder rolled into one.

"Look, let me take you out to dinner tonight. I'll make it up to you," he begged.

"I don't think it's a good idea," I said.

"Come on, babe," he pleaded softly. By now he had moved up to the table a few feet away from me.

"No," I said. "I'd really feel better if you'd just leave, Dale."

I reached across the table for the tape gun, looking down and taping over a box, trying not to shake, waiting, just waiting for him to leave.

A few seconds passed with him standing there. I was preparing to look up and say something when all of a sudden Dale lunged forward and shoved me with such force I fell to the ground. I hit the concrete on my right side. Luckily my shoulder and arm took the brunt of the blow, and I was able to keep my head from making contact.

"Jesus!" I hollered.

"You know what you are?" Dale snarled in contorted face and low voice. Then he yelled, "You're a user! You're a fucking brat and a user!"

He proceeded to kick me with a hard blow, his hiking boot making contact. I yelled out in pain and scurried back on the floor.

"A fucking brat and a fucking user!" Dale hollered over and over again in a demented voice.

I had managed to move back enough that I could raise myself up, despite the pain on my right side where I hit the concrete and the blow where his boot hit my left thigh. The next thing that happened put the fear of God in me. I felt my stomach knot up in fear as Dale grabbed a box cutter from the table and raised his hand. The end of the table I was near was shoved up against a wall close to the shelves. I couldn't move back farther.

"Put that fucking thing down!" I heard a voice across the room yell. "What's wrong wit' you, man?!"

I looked over to see Marvin, the UPS guy, making his way toward us from the door.

"I said put the fucking knife down, motherfucker!" Marvin ordered, sounding like the scariest thug to ever come out of the hood.

Dale was completely taken by surprise, staring at Marvin. I used the opportunity to jump over and across the table.

"I didn't mean anything by it, man," Dale mumbled, then dropped his knife and backed away from the table.

"Get the fuck outta here!" Marvin yelled even louder.

Dale darted out the door.

Marvin turned to me, grabbed my shoulders, and asked, "Are you all right, Adam?"

By now I was heaving, panting heavy breaths of fear.

"Oh God," I stammered. "I'm so glad you showed up. He was so strung out. I've never seen him like that."

"Yeah, you don't have to tell me, man," Marvin said with a shake of his head and look of disgust. "I know a base head when I see one. You wanna call the cops?"

"No," I shook my head, still in shock. "I just want to get the fuck out of here. I'm never coming back anyways."

"It's cool. I hear you," Marvin said quietly. "Just give me what boxes you got real quick. I'm gonna walk you to your car just in case that crackhead is still out there waiting to jump your ass."

Still shaking, I helped Marvin stack the boxes I had packed on the dolly. Fuck the rest of the shipments. Ron could take care of them himself. Marvin made sure I got in my car okay. After thanking him more than once I started the ignition and drove into the traffic.

After driving a block, I began sobbing, sobbing harder then I could ever remember. I shuddered when I kept thinking over and over what could have happened, whether I would have just been maimed or had my throat slit. I shook and sobbed the whole way home.

A Fresh Start

Candy was infuriated when I told her what happened. "Adam, why didn't you call the police?" she yelled in anger. "You should have gotten a restraining order. He knows where we live. I swear to God if he comes near here I'll smash his balls into bits and pieces!"

She would have too. I told her I just wanted to let it go, and forget the whole episode. I wanted nothing more to do with Dale Warren from that point on.

That night I took a few Xanax from Candy to help me sleep and felt much better the following morning. I even went to the Beverly Center the next day for some shopping therapy. I needed new threads for my new job. My intention was to be as professional as possible and use the opportunity I was being given to present myself in the best way to every business contact I came across. This was one chance I wasn't going to blow.

In the meantime I saw John during evenings when he was free. A toothbrush of my own had taken up residence next to his in the master bathroom. In magazines I would see pictures of him and read blurbs about various women he took to public events. He had a number of different "beards" he went out with. Whether he was sleeping with them I didn't know, and I hadn't asked. As a famous everyday all-American Joe carrying a successful sitcom on his shoulders, he had to do what he had to do. The bottom line was he was good to me.

Never did he demand things of me, that I be around for him at his disposal as far as our sexual relationship was concerned. It was always "Do you want to come over?" or "If you feel like it."

With the holidays a few weeks away, his assistant Stacy showed me the ropes. Stacy was a fresh-scrubbed and friendly young girl with an average build and average weight. But she carried herself with a sense of confidence and authority. I really liked her. She had been accepted into the graduate program at USC Film School, the most prestigious in the country.

"John is such a sweetheart," she told me when we were driving around our first day together. "He really is the best boss I've ever had. This is not an easy job to give up."

"So how did you two meet?" she asked me later that same day.

"Oh, a friend put us in touch," I said, and then quickly changed the subject.

Stacy wasn't stupid. I'm sure she had come to a conclusion regarding John's sexuality and personal life. But it was clear she liked and respected him, so it wasn't an issue. If anything, the way she spoke about John made it sound as though she were protective of him. If she had any suspicions about how John and I met, she kept it to herself. Though she came in his house for work purposes every weekday, we had never crossed paths until I got started on the job myself.

Stacy introduced me to his agent and everyone on the set, the publicity people with the network, even everyday people such as the dry cleaner, landscaping service, and maids. Luckily John was signed with William Morris, not Acclaimed Talent. I would have dreaded having to go back to that place every week, although it would have been fun to rub my new job in Matthew's face.

"John's a casual guy," Stacy told me. "But don't be fooled. He is worth millions and pulls in as much as a Kelsey Grammer or Jennifer Aniston. He's just not the kind of guy to surround himself with a huge entourage like Puff Daddy or someone like that. A lot of other stars earning the money he makes employ full-time chefs, housekeepers, bodyguards, and more. It's really amazing when you think about it."

Overall, the job was a cushy one. Some of it was banal, like picking up and dropping off dry cleaning and waiting for a piece of furniture to be delivered. But at fifty grand a year, I wasn't complaining. For me, the job was a godsend. The highlights, such as accompanying John on appearances, far outshadowed any drudgery.

When he did *The Tonight Show,* Jay Leno came back into the dressing room, shaking hands with everyone including myself. It was out of this world. At a holiday comedy review Stacy and I hung out backstage with all the other performers and their people, everyone mingling around and chatting it up, having a good time. It was unlike anything I'd done before. Overall, I didn't feel like I was just a minion, as was the case at Acclaimed. I was actually meeting people, and enjoying every minute of it.

I drove to Vegas to be with my parents for a few days over the holidays. It helped that I was in good spirits, and that I was able to buy my family some nice gifts. As a college student I always felt like such a drain on my folks. So it was fun to spoil them for a change. I bought my father some great kitchen appliances, some Buddhist reading which he was into, and mountain biking gear. I bought my mother an outrageously expensive Louis Vuitton handbag, a Hermes scarf, and Barnes & Noble gift certificates.

As usual, I got along well with my father. But my mother and I hit it off famously. They had no idea about my escapades in the adult film industry. I had told them I was working as a receptionist the whole time, and had met John Vastelli through my job at the agency.

I had a close call, however, when I ran into Sarah and Stephen while helping my mother with some last-minute shopping at the mall. Sarah was in town visiting her own family and had invited Stephen along. His family was probably relieved to be rid of him for the holidays.

My mother had gone to the shoe department in Macy's and I was milling around the men's department.

"Hey, sistah!" I heard from behind me.

Looking up, I froze in a bundle of nerves.

"Oh, hi!" I replied in mock delight, trying to play it cool. I was planning on seeing Sarah when I looked up her sister, but on my own time and without Stephen being around.

"What are you two doing here?" I asked innocently.

"What does it look like?" Stephen asked, lifting up handfuls of shopping bags and doing some curls with them, flexing his perfect biceps.

"Stephen's staying with us for the holidays, experiencing a Vegas Christmas," Sarah laughed.

"So you've been very busy since we've seen you last," Stephen said slyly, cutting to the chase. "We all saw those magazines with you in the buff. I have to say that I haven't seen any of your performances, but Fred gave you a thumbs up. And Fred is a tough critic. You know he only tells it like it is. As a matter of fact, I believe his exact words were that if he knew you were that hot in bed, he would have spent less time making small talk with you and tried to get some action instead."

It was an underhanded compliment. Both Stephen and Sarah were giddy with gossip, their white teeth gleaming with devious Crest-White-Strip smiles. But I didn't have time for a spitting match. My mother could be coming from the shoe department any minute, and I was sure Stephen wouldn't drop the subject in her presence. On the contrary, he would have loved spilling the beans in front of her, and giving the A-list something to laugh about when he got back to LA.

I just shrugged it off.

"You know what they say, when the going gets tough, you, uh, do what you have to do!" I stammered with an awkward smile, tripping over my words.

"Well, you landed up doing a lot more than I ever would have guessed," Stephen laughed. "Can we look forward to any future exposure from you?"

"I don't think in that capacity. But then again you never know. Life is funny that way. The fans really seemed to like me," I added.

Stephen was about to say more when I broke him off and quickly said, "Listen, I really need to be getting back home. Sarah, I'll give you a call soon." I pecked her on the check quickly and started walking away.

"Great seeing you both!" I exclaimed before turning around.

"Don't be a stranger, Adam!" Stephen said as I made my getaway. "The whole town knows you're not shy, you don't have to be with us."

"Later!" I said, not looking back, disappearing down the escalator.

I found my mother in the shoe department.

"Ready to eat?" I asked.

"Well, I thought I might try these on," she deliberated, picking up a shoe and holding it up for me.

"What do you think?"

"I think they'll make you look like you're a hundred," I said, trying what I could to get her out of the store as soon as possible. "Come on, let's grab something to eat. I'm starving."

With that I dragged my mother out of the mall, careful to avoid a close call. I guess it would be awhile before I could put my recent X-rated endeavors out to pasture.

I was back in LA right after Christmas and floored at what awaited my arrival. I was at John's house, helping him sort through some paperwork when he said out of the blue, "Hey, Adam, I left some documents on my nightstand. Can you grab them for me?"

"You got it," I said, and zipped to the master bedroom.

From across the way I could see the nightstand was completely cleared off with the exception of a slim white box, wrapped in a red bow. Looking down, I read "Merry Christmas Adam." Opening it up, I was stunned to see a stack of hundred dollar bills, one after the other.

"Holy shit," I whispered out loud.

There was easily more than three grand in there. This was too weird. I felt like a kept lover in some movie. At the end of the bills was a note that read "There is more in the nightstand drawer."

I opened the drawer with a shaking hand to find a perfectly wrapped box inside. The seal on the top read Cartier. I painstakingly took apart the perfect gift wrap, pulling gently on the satin bow. A glimpse of velvet greeted me as I took off the lid. It was definitely a watch box. The velvet top snapped back revealing a classic Cartier watch with a crocodile band and diamonds surrounding the face. No one in my family owned a piece of jewelry that expensive.

"You like it?" I looked up to see John grinning broadly at the doorway.

"John," I gasped in shock. "This is too much. I can't accept this."

"You can and you will. I'm your boss, and it's a job requirement. A sure way to piss off your new boss is to refuse a gift."

Generosity was one of John's greatest attributes. He had been generous buying gifts for the whole crew and cast of his show. The year before he had taken them all on a trip to Hawaii during hiatus. That's why Stacy had said the decision to go to back to school was so painful, he really was the best boss she ever had.

John and I put the task of sorting mail aside for the moment and spent the rest of the afternoon in the sack. When we were finished, he put my new watch on my wrist, and we took a nap, my Cartier-clad arm resting across his chest.

Zinnia

John was cohosting a network New Year's Eve special and needed my help. I spent the next few days going to rehearsals with him and racing around to get everything in order. I was beginning to become familiar with a number of women that John would take out with him in public. There was Susan, a nice woman who worked for John's production company. Another woman, named Olivia, was a writer on his show.

I especially liked Olivia; she was pretty in a very organic and earthy way. She often came over to the house with a female friend named Grace. I suspected she was actually a lesbian, and Grace was her lover. But they never spoke about it or brought it up. When Olivia came by most of the conversation revolved around *Life's Lessons*.

There was a third woman that John would date on occasion, and whom I disliked at first sight. Her name was Zinnia, and she went by that one name alone. But Zinnia was far from being a Cher or a Madonna. She was a starlet in the 1980s whose biggest claim to fame was costarring with a famous football quarterback in his motion picture debut. Hired on the basis of her sultry looks, they alone were her one asset; otherwise she lacked in the talent department. She managed to stretch her fifteen minutes to a few spreads in *Playboy* and a stint on a nighttime soap opera. But that was all back in the day. Now she seemed nothing more than a Hollywood hanger on, a freeloader whose outfits made Paris Hilton and Pamela Anderson look like Sisters of the Holy Order.

What bothered me even more was somehow I felt I had spoken with her before, somehow crossed paths with her. And it wasn't because she had once been on TV during my childhood. It was something more. I just couldn't place my finger on how, why, and where I knew her from.

"John," she would gush when she came over, "I love that new dining room set you have. It's absolutely exquisite!"

When they went out John paid for everything, and she was guaranteed free entrance to every big-time affair and party in town. For Christmas John was more than generous, buying her diamond earrings from Tiffany.

"Oh, my God!" she shrieked when opening them. "John, you shouldn't have!"

Yeah right, I thought. *If he didn't do the "shouldn't haves" you'd be out the door so fast there would be skid marks.*

It killed me that John had to live his life as a secret and maintain a facade with the help of such a phony freeloader. But any revelations or questions of his sexuality would have destroyed the image and career he had worked so hard to build. Certainly, no one would buy his down-and-out everyday guy routine.

Still, he seemed to get a kick out of Zinnia, complete with her face-lift, joker lips injected with more collagen then Melanie Griffith's ten times over, and grossly out of proportion implants. She flattered him and doted on him, so I thought their association was harmless enough, until I told Candy about her.

Candy was still my one and only confidante, the one person I knew I could go to with anything.

We were both enjoying a quiet night at home after the exhausting bump and grind of the holidays, equally pooped out. Sitting out on the balcony with Chardonnay in hand, I had been telling Candy how cool Regis Philbin and Kelly Ripa were on the New Year's broadcast when the subject of Zinnia came up. I hadn't yet mentioned Zinnia to Candy, which was surprising given that Zinnia was exactly the kind of tragic figure we could share more than a few laughs over.

"I would have liked to have spoken more to Kelly Ripa if it weren't for John's beard for the night, this monument to plastic surgery named Zinnia. She just wouldn't shut up," I muttered.

"No!" Candy yelled, startling me.

"No what?" I asked, completely perplexed.

"He does not date her!" she stated in disbelief.

"Yes, they've known each other for about a year now, met through acquaintances. You know something I don't know?"

"Do I ever," Candy said with suspense, setting up one of her stories.

"What have you heard?" I asked eagerly.

"It's not what I've heard. It's what I experienced with her."

Candy proceeded to tell me a story that left me disliking Zinnia much more then I had before, if I thought it at all possible.

"It all started one day at the gym, when I kept making eyes with this gorgeous six-foot-two muscular baby-faced stud and supposed Diesel model," Candy began. "Afterwards I went to get a manicure and pedicure. At the salon this woman asks me if I go to the Workout Warehouse, where I belonged at the time. The woman was a sultry brunette in her late forties who had seen better days. Her tits were huge and it appeared as though she had some other work done, which I guess in LA is pretty much expected. But what stood out about her the most was that she had a dark complexion yet wore this weird yellow-green foundation on her face that was way too light for her skin."

"Yes! That's her!" I interrupted, getting all excited. "She does wear greenish foundation!" Then, making a confounded expression and straying from the subject at hand I asked, "I wonder why she wears it anyway? It really bugs me."

"Because she's a fucking idiot," Candy quipped. "So back to my story. At that point I had no clue who the hell she was. But it turned out that she was friends with the hot guy at the gym, and proceeded to let me know that he had told her how gorgeous he thought I was. Then she introduced herself, and I never would have guessed it was her. In addition to looking a lot older, she was so squat and short."

"No kidding!" I agreed. "She has the build of a gnome. So go on."

"But that makes sense. I mean, what's his name is notoriously short," observed Candy, referring to the quarterback who gave Zinnia her movie role.

"So she asks me if I am going to the Midsummer Night's Dream party at the Playboy mansion. I told her I was. 'Well, you have to come with me and my friends in my limo!' she insists. So not having many girlfriends, I was happy to be invited and looking forward to meeting some new faces. She gives me directions to her condo and a time to come over."

I was sure this was going somewhere crazy. If it involved Candy, chances were one hundred to one that there was a wacky scenario to unfold.

"So the night of the party I put on a peach-pink Grecian girl costume, apply my makeup, and go to Zinnia's," Candy continued. "Back at the salon she had asked me if I'd ever been in the pages of *Playboy*. I told her I sent in photos in the past but all I ever got back was a form letter. So she told me to bring over some photos, and she would personally pass one on to Hef. I arrive at seven-thirty and find a blonde television actress and a guy who is supposedly Zinnia's fiancé. Also there was a local designer and a few sluttish-looking chicks, but what threw me off were these two fat guys who didn't seem to belong there at all.

"Everyone wanted to take a look at my photos, and after they had all been passed around they narrowed the choice to one. Zinnia put it in an envelope with a note and off we go to the Playboy mansion."

Candy paused for a moment to take a sip of wine. I was wondering where the hell this story would end up.

"We all cram into the limo, with the two fat guys sitting in the middle. During the drive it's revealed to me that these men had apparently paid Zinnia ten thousand dollars just to sneak them into a party at the Playboy mansion. As we drive up to the gate it dawns on me why I'm really there: to serve as a cover and bait to the front guard. I was right by the window along with the other blonde chick, which makes sense because it's widely known the security at the mansion likes blondes. Zinnia was counting on us being there so the limo could get in without being checked. Sure enough we got passed in."

"You are kidding me!" I said in astonishment. "What a desperate scam, charging people to sneak them into a party. Now I've heard it all."

"Yup," Candy said, nodding her head with conviction. "You know what's even sicker? When we get inside she turns around and tells me we should do lunch someday, and leaves me for the rest of the night. I never saw her or spoke to her again. I ended up having to hitch a ride home with someone else. So there you have it. You know what pisses me off the most? The bitch never gave me back my pictures. It's not as if Hugh Hefner ever saw them."

"What a skank," I said while shaking my head in disbelief at her Playboy party scheme. "She is so repulsive. What the hell is John doing with her?"

"Oh, she's so phony, Adam, he probably has no clue," Candy said. "When she wants something she is ever so charming and gracious, but as soon as she gets it from you, you're dropped on the ground faster than a hot potato."

I sat brooding for a moment about how I was going to bring the matter up with John about the one-named snake and her green-yellow foundation. In a way, John was using Zinnia too. As long as she got her gifts and perks, she seemed just fine with it.

I decided I wasn't going to worry about it. I had stressed enough the past few months. For now, I just wanted to enjoy my life and the amazing opportunities that had just appeared. And even though things got ugly at HUNG Video toward the end, I had no regrets. Without HUNG Video I never would have met John Vastelli. My sexy stint in porn had opened up a whole new world for me.

"Hey, let's put in a Mae West movie!" I suggested to Candy.

"Hey, big boy." Candy swaggered with her hand on one hip and the other puffing up her hair in her best Mae West impersonation. "I love the idea. Why don't you come up and see me some time?"

The Glamorous Life

The weeks following were bliss. I truly realized in LA its all about who you know and what you do. My job put me in touch with a whole new class of people that I just wouldn't have gotten to know beforehand. I had practically moved in with John, spending half my time there and the other half at Candy's. It was really perfect that way. Even though John was on the set during the days when I worked with him and he rarely had twenty seconds, having Candy's place ensured we had time apart so we wouldn't crowd each other.

At times it was difficult carrying on such a covert relationship. I had to be careful of what I said around him in public, keeping our communication completely emotionally detached and strictly business. But at the same time, it added to our passion. At night John could let it all go, his whole facade, his whole image, his whole act. And he released his tension through sex, which seemed to get more enjoyable as time went on. John had lost a lot of shyness, taking more control, getting into role-play.

He even sent me to the Pleasure Chest on Santa Monica to pick up some toys. Though I had experienced a lot, I still hadn't experienced sex toys. For some reason I always associated sex toys with divorcées, swingers, or bored suburban couples who needed to put zing in their lives.

But with John I found that sex toys were fun. Here we were two grown men performing sex acts on each other yet it had the same feeling as two innocent children at recess. Through it all we explored more and more of each other's bodies. Every tuft of hair, every goose bump around John's nipples had become familiar territory for me. When his legs were swung back in the air and my tongue traced the pink line of skin that traveled from his testicles to his anus, I knew exactly where to nibble and what flesh to pinch and snag between my teeth, listening to him moan in pleasure throughout.

Our favorite toys were the Electro Anal Beads, Impulse Orgasm Balls, and Impulse Flashing Penis. It drove John wild when I sat on his dick and he fucked the shit out of me while I stuffed his ass with the Impulse Flashing Penis. He couldn't seem to get enough of the vibrating, pulsing, and escalating variations of motion, and changing levels of speed going up and down and up and down. We burned through two packs of batteries in no time at all.

Life was good. Traveling among the most powerful people in town while picking up papers at William Morris or bringing items to the studio lot, coasting around LA in John's brand new Range Rover. I followed him at functions where stars the likes of Jennifer Aniston, Halle Berry, and Tom Cruise stood next to me sipping cocktails. Of course, John always had a date with him. I always looked forward to it when it was Olivia. The three of us would laugh and cut it up in the limo. But on the public occasions when he took Zinnia along, I dreaded her company. She always treated me as if I weren't present and name-dropped the whole time, laughing in her shrill and pretentious manner.

"I was at the Ivy today, and Jennifer Lopez was sitting right next to us," she would gloat. "We got into this thirty-minute conversation because we share the same Pilates instructor."

I wanted to smash her overly made-up olive green face through the car window.

I hadn't told John about Candy's experience with Zinnia yet. I didn't want to appear meddlesome or jealous. Although when he walked down the red carpet arm in arm with her I had to suppress the urge to keep my fist from knocking her straight into Joan and Melissa Rivers. When Zinnia saw an *E! Television, Entertainment Tonight, Access Hollywood,* or other major network camera she took charge, practically dragging John in front of Jann Carl or the Rivers duo. It was like watching a greedy child go berserk at an Easter egg hunt.

"Somebody shoot her with a tranquilizer," I muttered under my breath at one such event.

A successful and famous actress who, unlike Zinnia, had survived the 1980s overheard me and laughed, "She's still trying to stretch those fifteen minutes, even twenty years after the fact, huh?" then winked and disappeared down the red carpet, leaving me surprised and amused.

One night after going to dinner with John and a group of colleagues, including Zinnia, I could hold my tongue no more. She dominated the conversation the whole evening, talking about nothing and turning what would have been an otherwise dynamic and charming evening into one massive migraine. She even got up and left the table a few times to show she knew people at other tables. As soon she came back she took over where she left off, blabbing incessantly about this person or that person, the best restaurants, stores, or whatever other crap came flying out of her mouth. I should have introduced her to Stephen and Sarah. They would have gotten along famously.

"I don't know how you can stand her. She is so obnoxious," I told John when we got home. "She never shuts up or gives anyone else a chance to speak, except when the topic turns to work because lord knows that's foreign to her. And when you talk about the show she still has to open her mouth with drippy, ass-kissing compliments. Her nose is so brown no amount of yellow-green foundation can cover that up."

"She's just very Hollywood, Adam. Besides, she's entertaining," John said dismissively.

"Entertaining?" I repeated in dismay. "Exasperating is more like it. How did you ever get to know her anyways?"

"I've known her for years, when I first came to town. Before I became famous," John said quietly, almost cryptically, as he looked straight ahead.

"Well, there's nothing wrong with seeing an old friend once in a while, but when they're as overbearing as that—"

"Adam, can we not talk about it!" John snapped, cutting me off and burying his head in his hands.

"Sure," I said, somewhat stunned. "I'm sorry I said anything."

"Look," John said, bringing his head up and gazing into my eyes, "I don't want to think about her right now. I want to think about you." With that he kissed me. "Come on, lets go to bed." He stood up, grabbed my hand, and led me to the bedroom.

A few nights later I was at Candy's and we were sitting out on the balcony. I had run lines with John all night and he needed to read some scripts his agent had passed along, so I decided to leave him alone for the evening.

"He just freaked out," I told Candy as she lit up a cigarette. "It was the weirdest thing. I had never seen him flip out like that."

"Well, it sounds like you definitely hit a raw nerve," Candy said knowingly.

"Do you think there's blackmail going on?" I asked.

"I don't know," Candy said as she put on her analytical face, brow furled, lips pursed together, and eyes squinted. "Knowing her, it's a strong possibility. But if it were just that, why not just pay her off and keep her away?"

"The limelight, the right parties," I stated, "that's the payoff."

"I don't know," Candy said dubiously. "There's got to be more there. What surprises me is that he doesn't have any shit on her. I'm sure the skeletons are just clawing to get out of her closet."

"Are you kidding? She probably wrote the line that any publicity is good publicity. A washed-up sex symbol with a dead career? Anything he could throw back at her would be an appearance on *Howard Stern,* money for a tabloid exclusive, and the talk show circuit."

"Not if it meant going to jail," Candy sang sweetly.

"What do you mean?" I asked.

"Let's just say I've heard drug rumors from other girls at the gym and around town. And I don't mean using. I mean supplying. And the latter is rare in that it is one bit of publicity that is still not good, thank God. Nothing more pathetic, loser ridden, or shameful than going from television to dealing narcotics," Candy said firmly.

"If it's true, maybe we can get her out of the picture for good," I whispered hopefully.

"I'll do some digging around," Candy winked. "I'm still pissed about not getting my pictures back. She probably sold them on the Internet."

Taking Out the Hollywood Trash

The next day my mind was taken away from Zinnia when I received a surprise call from Perry Bristol. He was to begin filming *The Voyeur* in a month, and true to his word wanted me to read for a part. The project was a behind-the-scenes comedy drama set in the world of gay porn, about a young and misguided aspiring filmmaker who becomes obsessed with a destructive male "gay-for-pay" porn star.

Though at this point I wanted to distance myself from the world of porn, I knew this film would be brilliant. And in a way, it could symbolize leaving that brief part of my life behind for other things. Besides, I hadn't completely lost the acting bug that had driven me to come to LA to begin with, a desire that had been pushed to the wayside among all the craziness.

When I broached the topic with John, he was supportive. The role only called for me to be away from a few days of work.

"Take as much time as you need, Adam," John told me.

I was to read for the role of Kurt Bottoms, a washed-up, bitchy porn star with an attitude. Seeing as how my last days with HUNG Video had turned out, finding motivation for the role wasn't something I was worried about. The part was small and brief, but well written with some great lines. The bottom line was that it presented the opportunity to act in what I knew would be a good film, and perhaps the priceless chance to build an acting career.

Going to extra lengths to appear trashy for my audition, I went so far as to bleach my dark hair. Despite the fact it took my hair forever to take to the bleach, leaving my scalp fried with nasty scabs, the end result looked good. John thought it was sexy, which made me happy. Candy hated it.

"Ugh. Why did you do that, Adam? It looks so cheap!" she said with brutal honesty.

"Good. It's supposed to look that way."

The day of the audition I changed into a tight tank top and baggy gym pants, finishing off my smutty, West Hollywood hustler look. I arrived and was greeted by the casting girl, a spunky and friendly gal named Lisa. With glasses and a super casual look, she fit the profile of the typical production girl. I signed the audition list and took a look at the two other actors in the room: both spaced-out-looking young blond guys. I guess my instinct to bleach my hair was right on target.

Neither guy looked particularly interested or eager. Actually they looked uncomfortable. If anything they were most likely completely freaked out and put off by the explicit lines, that and the fact that the role called for a simulated sex scene, with the character of Kurt Bottoms getting fucked by one of the lead actors. Big surprise, considering I was up for the part. That might make most actors apprehensive about taking on this particular job. Let's face it, this wasn't the kind of part that Tom Cruise would have taken early in his career.

After waiting a few minutes to read, Lisa came to get me. Sitting in the room was Perry and Mitch.

"Hey, Adam!" They greeted me simultaneously.

"My rescuers, taking me away from the party turned ugly orgy!" I laughed.

"No kidding," Perry said grimly. "A good thing we left when we did, and that you're not hanging with Dale anymore."

"What do you mean?" I asked. I suddenly got a sick feeling in my stomach, and my face got hot. I hadn't heard Dale's name since the day he attacked me.

"He's hit rock bottom, Adam," Perry said in a quiet tone. "Things got so bad that sure enough, Ron fired him. I guess it was an ugly scene. He was throwing things around the office, the graphics guys had to restrain him and call the police. Last I heard he was seen around town getting thrown out of a bar. Hopefully somebody will get him in rehab soon."

I didn't say anything. It was too depressing.

"Well, enough of that," Mitch exclaimed, turning the conversation around. "We have been dying to hear you read, Adam."

I just hoped I could after getting so upset at the mention of Dale. I immediately began to block him out of my mind and get back to the matter at hand.

The first lines began with my character in a pool telling his costar that he'd better hurry with their scene, because he has a stripping engagement that night. From there it went into some really bad porn dialogue, which was fun to read. God knows I had seen some really dumb people in front of a camera firsthand. The day at HUNG Video where I handed out lubricant came to mind.

I also had lines in one other scene, and ironically the setting for this scene was Missy Manhandler's birthday party. Within the gay porn industry, Missy's birthday party was one of the most important social events. Therefore Perry was re-creating it in the film. He informed me that Missy was even making a cameo, singing on stage in drag and in all his outrageous glory.

It would be fun to see Missy again, this time in women's clothes and fully made-up.

We read through the scenes twice. The first time I made the mistake of looking straight into the camera lens, instead of at Lisa, who I was reading my lines with. But I nailed the character perfectly, getting an enthusiastic reaction from all three of them. The second go was nothing less than perfect. I left feeling confident I had bagged the part.

The following day I had a message from Perry telling me all three of them thought I was perfect for the role, and it was mine.

The producers would be getting to me with all the necessary paperwork within the next week, being that I didn't have an agent. For the next few days I waited, thinking about being in front of the camera again, in a legitimate and well-written film. I was being sent official papers from real, legitimate, producers!

Although there weren't many big names involved, there was one famous person I was looking forward to meeting. She was one of my favorite female rock singers, and in one of the best new wave acts of the late 1970s and early 1980s before going solo. These days she did a lot of acting in independent projects like *The Voyeur*. Perry mentioned there was to be a cast reading within the next week, and would let me know the details in the next few days.

But before that time, I was to have my first and hopefully only run in with Zinnia. Luckily, before it occurred, Candy had done some snooping around.

"Guess what!" I yelled at Candy over the phone. "I got a part in a movie! A true speaking part in a legit major movie!"

After I got done telling Candy the good news she said, "This must be your lucky week. It seems everything is going your way!"

"What do you mean?" I asked.

"I caught her! And not only did I catch her, but I caught her on camera!" Candy squealed.

At first I had no idea what she was talking about.

"Caught who?" I asked, completely puzzled.

"The despicable skank! The bane of your existence at the moment! Hollywood's most notorious leech! Need I go on?" Candy huffed in exasperation.

"Zinnia?" I gasped.

"Bingo!"

"What happened?" I asked in breathless anticipation.

"Well, you know how I quit Crunch to go back to the Workout Warehouse?" Candy never did get over the see-through showers. "She still works out there. The Diesel model is still there too by the way. Man is he ever hot!"

"Just get on with it!" I snapped.

"Anyhow, my trainer tipped me off to the fact she does 'business' out in the parking lot, behind the building. So I'm sitting in my car using my cell phone, sure enough I see her there, yellow-green foundation and all. She is talking on her phone, and then a man in a suit approaches. If she was smart she would have conducted her little transaction in her car. By this time I hung up with my call. Sure enough, I see her pull out a white bag of powder and pass it to the guy. But not before snapping the image on my camera. And as clear as it can get on camera too!"

"No way!" I said in astonishment.

"Oh yes, and baby, I have the images in print for you to pick up at home!"

"You know, you are truly amazing. You really are," I said in all honesty.

"Thank you doll! My pleasure. See ya shortly!" Candy cooed.

A few nights later Zinnia stopped by John's unannounced.

"Where's John?" she snapped, without so much as a hello.

"He's putting in a long day at the set. Won't be home for a few hours," I said coolly, standing by the door. "And hello to you, too," I added.

"I need to use the phone," she ordered, pushing me aside and letting herself in. "And if you can get me a Diet Coke I would appreciate it."

"Did I miss something, or am I suddenly on your payroll?" I asked angrily. She would have never dared speak to me in that way if John were around. Typically she just ignored me.

"Listen, faggot!" Zinnia spat with venom, turning around, whipping off her sunglasses, and shooting me an enraged look. "John and I have known each other a long time and we got a little deal going. So I'm not going anywhere. Now I know he's ramming you, but I don't really give a fuck. You see, he knows I can smash his career to smithereens, and honey, he won't be able to pull an Ellen DeGeneres and survive it. So I suggest you get your fudgepacker ass to the bar and pour me a Diet Coke."

She pointed to the bar in satisfaction.

"And throw in three cubes of ice, you fucking fairy!" she added for further humiliation.

I was seething. I could feel my face getting hotter and hotter. Boiling blood was crawling up the back of my neck like a bubbling brew.

The wench had pushed me to the brink. And I let it rip. Getting up in her face and baring my lower teeth I seethed, "Listen you miserable, used-up, has-been cunt. I know all about your little games—you pile of shit. Blackmail, payoffs, scams, the whole the fucking deal. But I'll tell you one thing that looks worse in the press than a closet-case actor. And that's a has-been starlet that has turned to blackmail and dealing drugs to maintain her Hollywood lifestyle, you pathetic excuse for a human being. So now I'm going to make a suggestion. And that is you never show your botched-up, plastic surgery–ridden, yellow-green face in this house ever again. You got that?"

I pointed at the door just as she had pointed me to the bar. The stumpy little bitch looked at me with wide-eyed horror. Evidently she wasn't used to people lowering themselves to her playing field where they could get that dirty. But she hadn't known what Candy and I were capable of, especially when we put our heads together. She would rue the day she messed with us.

"Who do you think you are, you pretty-boy faggot? You have no fucking idea who you are messing with!"

"Oh, I think I have a better idea than you know, bitch!" With that I marched over to the coffee table where my briefcase bag was, newly bought at Prada care of John's generous Christmas gift.

"You see, I've been on to you for a long time," I said, and with that pulled out a laser photocopy of the wench passing her narcotics outside the gym. I practically slapped her across the head with it.

Zinnia's face turned from yellow-green to blazing red.

"Is that what you do on the clock?" she seethed. "Spy on people?"

"I didn't have to," I said in satisfaction. "There are other people you've screwed over who will do the work for me. Now, I don't know what you're lording over John. He didn't even want to talk about you. But it's over. I want you to get the fuck out of here and never come back, you understand me? Because if so I'll make sure your picture is pasted over every front page in the country as a washed-out coke whore, and I'm sure the police department would just have a field day tormenting your spoiled ass. So let's call things even, okay? You get lost and we'll forget this little episode ever happened."

Zinnia stood there enraged, tears of anger in her eyes. It was actually more disturbing than enjoyable to witness her reaction. The bitch obviously had some deep pathological disorders. It was a frightening reflection to think that there were people like her in society. I swear if she had a knife in hand she would have stabbed me right then and there.

Thankfully, she grabbed her bag from where she had flung it on the couch and made her way to the door instead.

"You better watch yourself, you fucking queer," she turned around and snarled before leaving. "You see, this little exchange here, this was nothing," she twirled a long red lacquered nail in the air to illustrate her point. "I've been playing at this kind of game for a long time. You have no idea who you just messed with."

With that she slammed the door, her heels clicking loudly down the front walk. I went to the front window, watching her climb into the driver's seat of her black Porsche, practically squeezing out of her tight low-slung jeans, rhinestone appliqué crop top sparkling in the late afternoon sun.

I tried not to reflect as much on her ominous threat and instead enjoyed the battle I had just won.

Playing Stupid

For the next week I worked as usual, enjoying life. John was in good spirits, having just signed on for the lead in a major studio film that was to shoot in the summer, while *Life's Lessons* was on hiatus.

I hadn't seen Zinnia since our confrontation, and as far as I knew, John hadn't heard from her either. I decided to keep the details of what I found out secret. If John brought her up, then I'd tell him about it, otherwise why give him something he might worry about—though in reality having something on her should have made him happy.

By the time the week flew by the day of the cast reading for *The Voyeur* arrived. Most of the cast showed up. The leads were all attractive and in their twenties, the kind of types you'd expect to see on *The OC.* There were two male leads, one playing the hot and straight porn star and the other the young camera guy obsessed with him. Also there was the female lead, a pretty girl with a dark sultry look who had the role of the suffering stripper girlfriend of the gay-for-pay porn star. The rock legend wasn't present for the reading, but I expected that. Somebody read the part in her place, and I read a few of the other bit parts as well. The male lead playing the porn star had done mostly television work, and once had a recurring role on *Baywatch.*

Between Candy and myself, I think we had come across half the cast of *Baywatch* in one way or another, maybe because cast members on that show rotated more often than inventory at a supermarket.

The same night of the reading I attended a party with John and his "beard" I liked best, Olivia. It was a charity affair at Morton's, and the paparazzi were outside snapping away with their cameras. Once at our table John and Olivia immediately joined the rest of the table in showbiz talk while I sat on John's other side. At one point I grew bored and decided to take a walk to the bar and check out the exquisite ice sculpture.

"Adam, is that you?" a voice asked me from behind.

I turned around to find HUNG Video's very own resident photographer Brian standing behind me. Looking handsome and polished in a black suit, he was certainly a different vision from when I'd seen him last, spun out on crystal with his beet-red face flopped on the bed while his ass got stuffed by Dale.

"Hello, Brian," I said stiffly.

"What brings you here?" Brian asked in a bubbly manner. He must have had no idea I had witnessed his drug and sex fest with Dale.

"A friend," I said curtly. "And you?"

"I'm here with Robert Gleisman."

Just then Gleisman himself came up from behind and gushed, "Why if it isn't Adam the perfect Oscar! You haven't changed your mind, have you?"

"No, I'm still going to have to pass on your offer," I said. I could just see myself the next day, running between William Morris and the set of *Life's Lessons* with remnants of gold paint all over my body, the symptoms of pneumonia setting in from subjecting myself to the frigid air clad in nothing but a gold lamé thong.

"That's too bad. You don't know what you're missing!" Gleisman said with a toothy smile.

Sure I do, I thought—*a skin rash and a lung infection.* I was just about to excuse myself when Gleisman noticed my Cartier watch and exclaimed, "What a beautiful Cartier! Santa must have had his eye on you!"

I brought my hand back in self-consciousness. It was only the second time I wore my watch.

"Oh, it's just a good fake," I scoffed.

"I know watches, my boy, and that is no fake," Gleisman responded.

I was at a loss for words.

"So what are you doing with yourself these days?" Brian asked, now looking thoroughly intrigued. "Ron said you're no longer hanging around HUNG. We've missed you."

"Oh, I have a job as an assistant," I said.

"Really? An assistant for whom?" Brian coaxed.

I paused for a moment, wondering if I should divulge who I was working for to Brian, especially seeing as he knew Dale. Candy swore she had seen him driving past our building some time ago, though I had yet to run into him in person.

But at the same time why should I have to keep my life a secret? Why should I have to keep running from the past, especially people from the past? Still, I decided against it.

"Um, for a few producers," I fibbed. Before either of them could ask me for names, I quickly added, "I really should be getting back to my table. It was good seeing you guys. Bye."

I took off faster than a road runner with a bad case of diarrhea.

"Where have you been?" John whispered affectionately under his breath while the rest of the table was in conversation.

"Oh, just admiring the ice sculpture," I kidded.

Later that evening, Brian came meandering near our table. From the side of my eyes, I could notice him peering inquisitively at my table, checking out who I was with. Since moving to LA, it seemed as if paranoia followed me everywhere.

The Voyeur

In addition to my job, *The Voyeur* helped me keep my mind off my worries. One of my scenes was scheduled during the first week of shooting. The location turned out to be the same house where the cast met for the reading. And it was the perfect setting, tucked in a canyon with a gorgeous pool in the back that held a breathtaking view of the city below.

A few large trucks were parked out front. Inside the house many people were milling about, and cords and wires ran across the floors. Gruff-looking crew guys walked past with lights and gels, and I was careful to stay out of their way. A friendly production assistant with a walkie-talkie directed me to the holding area upstairs, where most of the other actors in the scene were waiting.

An older actor whom I recognized from playing a lot of character roles on television was sitting nearby. I knew from the cast reading he was playing one of the porno company producers. A pad of paper and some watercolor paints were in front of him, and he was doodling to pass time. He asked if he could paint me, and I told him to be my guest.

"So do you have a background in porn yourself?" he asked coyly.

"What do you mean?" I asked, immediately self-conscious.

"Well, the other day we had some actual porn actors on the set, so I thought maybe you did that kind of thing as well," he murmured while dipping his brush into a cup of water.

"No. I know Perry from New York, and since I'm in the Screen Actors Guild he thought I would be good for this part," I answered assuredly.

Feeling heat rising up the back of my neck, I was determined to be treated as a professional actor. And why shouldn't I? I had an expensive theater background and was in the union, just like these other people. The only difference was I didn't have an agent. If this jerk thought he was any better than me, he'd better think again.

His masterpiece was interrupted when one of the production assistants grabbed me for makeup.

I had smeared self-tanner all over my body the night before, so I wouldn't look like a plucked chicken or Dracula on camera. Somehow it didn't take that well, even though I put on a lot. It wasn't streaky or blotchy; I just didn't look that tan.

Since most porn stars do have a tan, I suggested to the makeup artist that he might want to put a darker or more orange foundation on my face.

"We don't want it to clash too much with your body," he dismissed, brushing aside my idea.

So much for looking like I had a little color on camera. Forget *The Voyeur.* I might as well be in *Casper the Friendly Ghost,* or better yet, *Night of the Living Dead.*

I went back to the holding area, determined not to let my pasty complexion get on my nerves. I was going to make this a positive experience, come hell or high water. The whole time I kept reminding myself this was my first speaking role in a major film, and I was going to enjoy it.

When I got back to the holding area the snotty old queen of a character actor was gone and the hunk of the movie was there instead.

"Hey, what's up?" he nodded casually, in typical macho form.

I said hello and went over to the other side of the room to grab some hair gel out of my bag, which I brought with me knowing only I could fix my hair right. My hair grows in more directions than one would find on a compass. *Oh well, as long as it doesn't all fall out I'll be happy,* I thought.

The studly *Baywatch* actor was doing his best impression of being chill. I had to give this guy credit. He didn't strike me as being remotely gay, or having any gay tendencies, but then again, my gaydar wasn't the best. In the script it is clear his character only has sex with men for money.

But still, it was pretty brave taking on the role of a man having sexual contact with another male, period. I suppose he took it because the script was well written, and lead roles for relatively unknown actors are far and few between. And in Hollywood, there is no shortage of buff, pretty-boy actors like the one sitting in front of me.

Now it was on to wardrobe. In the beginning of the scene I was to wear a bathing suit, in the middle a business suit, and in the end a towel wrapped around my waist. But the costume designer, a funky Dutch girl who lived in Silver Lake, hadn't decided on a bathing suit.

To my horror, out of a box she pulled out a few of the most hideous thong bathing suits I had ever seen in my whole entire life. One was especially ugly, and consisted of a black string around the waist, a black string up the butt, and a black and yellow zebra print on the barely there material that was supposed to hold in the crotch. My eyes grew wide with fear as I imagined it on my pale body.

"You're not going to make me wear that one, are you?" I asked. At least I prayed not.

"I don't know. I kind of like that one. I think it's perfect for the scene!" the designer said with her thick Dutch accent and a wide grin on her face.

"Why don't you try both on, and I'll take you outside to show Perry and see what he thinks," she decided.

Needless to say the crew was given their first big show of the day when I walked out to the pool twice in two different G-strings. I could tell more than a few were less than thrilled, glancing at me uncomfortably. When I had to parade around the second time there was less reaction. They knew what the film was about, so they must have been prepared to see anything. After all, they weren't working on a Disney production. Unfortunately Perry went for the hideous black and yellow bathing suit. Then again, it didn't really matter too much. I wouldn't be wearing it in the scene for too long.

Meanwhile, back in wardrobe, *Baywatch* boy was throwing a little fit about his bathing attire.

"I'm telling you. I'm not wearing shit like that. My character isn't like these other guys!" he said to the designer, with a disgusted look on his face.

The bathing suit in question was actually a more conservative silver Speedo, cut very wide. The U.S. Olympic swim team wore less than that.

Here he was giving the designer grief when I had to wear something even Richard Simmons might consider too gay.

Furthermore, this guy had been on *Baywatch,* where half the wardrobe consisted of Speedos. This little tantrum over the bathing suit was the first display of discomfort from the hunky lead. The designer was not amused, telling him that is exactly what his character would wear during a porn shoot, and the wardrobe was already approved.

Apparently she won the battle, because when we were told to take our places he was wearing that bathing suit over those rock-hard buns of his. Before being led to the pool, I had been given a fluffy terrycloth robe and was escorted by one of the PAs. The take in the pool went well. I was now Kurt Bottoms asking the lead if he was a fast fuck, because I had to go dance in Las Vegas.

"I hope you're quick, because I have a gig to get to in Vegas," I sneered the line in my most nasal voice.

After Perry yelled "cut!" the crew erupted in laughter, so I must have been amusing.

"The bored and petulant expression on your face was priceless, Adam," Perry said.

When it was time to get out of the pool, the assistant designer held my robe open for me to step into. It was kind of cool, and I felt like I was being treated like Rudolph Valentino.

I'd better enjoy this moment while it lasted, because it sure as hell didn't happen every day.

Sometime later the cast and crew broke for lunch. After lunch the rest of the afternoon didn't go quite as smoothly, and consisted of me being bent over while the hunk is supposedly fucking me up the ass.

In this take the viewer wouldn't see anything except my head and his upper body, and then they were planning a long shot where you could see us going at it from the side, but with our lower bodies covered strategically by a reflector.

I was literally hunched over grabbing onto a railing with the hotshot lead actor pressed up against me from behind.

We each had our bathing suits on the whole time. The hard part was getting the rhythm of our movement right. Perry was trying to get us to gyrate in such a way that it looked like I was really getting it up the ass, but it just wasn't happening. Instead his groin and my ass were smacking into each other like two bumper cars on the Santa Monica Pier. Perry was getting a little impatient, and in his excitement over instructing how it was done in actual porn he ended his lesson with, "You know what I'm talking about, right, Adam?"

Perry knew I had "dabbled" in gay porn since my arrival in LA, but I wasn't expecting him to bring it up on the set.

"You mean you've done this before?" Mr. Beefcake leading man asked, standing behind me in surprise. At least someone had thought of me as a legitimate actor, until now.

I gripped the railing tighter in frustration.

"Uh . . . sort of," I answered, dismissing his question. I was still hunched over and now getting agitated. Imagine standing in front of tens of people trying to simulate a sex act with you as the recipient, and an uncomfortable costar. Not an easy feat.

It still didn't go right. Again Perry gave us some pointers, and once more, ended this time with, "You know what I'm saying, right, Adam?" in an encouraging tone, as if I was the porn expert and could take matters into my own hands and show Mr. Baywatch how it was done.

Perry had no clue that I had no desire to be considered the porn expert or thought of as an experienced porn actor, much less be reminded of the fact I appeared in an actual porno. I simply wanted to be treated as just a legitimate film actor. Was that so fucking hard? Too much to ask for after years of appearing in plays, taking classes, and even joining a goddamn union along the way?

"I don't know!" I snapped, obviously irritated and catching Perry off guard, but at this moment I really didn't give a shit.

Why did he feel the need to point out my porno past not only once, but twice? Taking a hint I didn't feel like getting into the specifics of how a simulated ass fuck should flow and what it should look like, he finally told my costar to thrust himself against me and that I remain passive and let myself be pushed forward, which worked.

Shortly thereafter it came time for me to say my last line, my character asking impatiently for his pay so he could go to his gig in Vegas. When that was done I was wrapped and free to go.

That evening John and I stayed at home and ordered in his favorite Chinese takeout from Chin Chin on Sunset. I told him in detail the events of my first day on the set.

"Hey, I'm proud of you, babe. It's a start, and I'm sure the film will do real well. These guys sound like they know what they are doing." He beamed.

"You are so sweet, you, know that," I said, grabbing the back of his head and pulling his forehead toward mine. "Even though it's a theatrical release that I still wouldn't feel comfortable bringing my mother to, you just made me feel like a million bucks!"

"Hey! You don't know your mother wouldn't like it. Didn't she like *Boogie Nights?*" John asked.

"I don't think that movie is her thing either," I said.

"You might just be right about that," he agreed, biting into an eggroll.

"Have I told you just how happy I am you've come into my life?" I asked, nibbling on his ear.

"Don't tell me, show me . . ." his voice trailed off, eyes closed and head falling backward.

We proceeded to enjoy the rare comfort of a quiet night at home. No entourage, no riffraff, no crowds and cameras to deal with—just the two of us.

Dale Pays a Visit

I wasn't so lucky a few nights later. John had an event to attend and would be out late. I decided to spend the night at Candy's, do some laundry with her, and just hang out.

Unfortunately, street parking wasn't abundant that particular evening. After driving around the block a few times I settled on a spot a block and half away. Walking briskly toward the building, I heard a car door slam behind me and the unmistakable sound of footsteps coming my way.

Be cool, I told myself. Before I turned around I heard a familiar voice say, "Hey, Adam, wait up, man!"

It was Dale.

I broke into a sprint toward the building.

"Get away from me before I call the cops," I threatened.

"Just listen to me!" Dale implored in a panicked voice.

"Help!" I yelled.

"Listen!" He had caught up with me and grabbed me by my shoulder, forcing me around to face him. I pulled away and put my arms up, ready for whatever was to come.

"I don't want to hurt you, dude! I'm sorry. I'm sorry for everything. I just need a little money. Can you do that for me? Huh? Anything— fifty bucks, twenty bucks?" Dale begged.

He was worse than a mess. He looked downright indigent. He reeked of body odor and his face had not been touched by a razor in weeks. His hair was greasy and shaggy underneath a soiled baseball cap, while his face looked gaunt and broken out. There were numerous bumps on his face and neck. It was as if all the chemicals he was putting into his system were trying to escape from his body through his skin. Apparently he had been habitually picking at them as well, as many were open ulcers that were either scabbed over or oozing.

"Oh my God, Dale. You need help. Are you trying to get any help?" I pleaded.

"I know dude, I know!" he whimpered, tears streaking down his face. "I'm trying. But in the meantime I have nothing to eat. Please, help me out," he sobbed.

I just stood there in disbelief.

"Please!" he begged again, this time with even more desperation.

All of a sudden I heard, "Get the fuck out of here!" Candy was leaning over the balcony, phone in hand.

"Adam, are you okay? I'm calling the cops! You better leave, motherfucker!" she screamed.

Dale looked at me with sudden desperation.

"Please!" he begged once more.

Shaking, I grabbed my wallet, managed to pull out some twenties, and handed them to him.

"Dale, please go find some help. Maybe the community center. If you want me to make some calls for you . . ."

"I know. I'm going to. I promise," he said.

"The cops are coming!" Candy announced. "I'm coming down there too with a bat!"

Bless Candy's soul. There was a lot she owned, but one thing I knew for sure she didn't own was a baseball bat, but she had my well-being at heart.

"Look, you better go," I said.

"Thanks, Adam, I love you for this man. I'm sorry I fucked up. I'm sorry I hurt you," he sobbed.

With that he ran back to his car, turned on the ignition in a flash, and screeched off into the night.

This time Candy made me file a restraining order. Not that it was going to do much good. Chances were Dale had probably lost his place by now and couldn't be found.

Orly came out of her apartment to see what all the fuss was about, wearing nothing but a Victoria's Secret negligee much too inappropriate for her age along with all her jewelry, of course.

"Ad-deem! You must be very careful with all zee crazee peeples in dees town!" she scolded, then proceeded to flirt with the cops and ask them unrelated questions about the neighborhood for minutes afterward. I thought she was going to invite them over for a nightcap.

When the cops finally left, Candy and I sat at the table with some tea and tried to calm down a bit.

"Oh, fuck it," I said. "This ain't doing shit to calm our nerves. Let's crack open a bottle of wine."

"Good idea," Candy agreed.

Tonight there was no joking, nothing to make light about. It was just sad and pathetic. Watching another human being destroy themselves had to be one of the most painful experiences in life.

"Oh, my gay nerves. Oh, my gay nerves," I repeated over and over again. "My gay nerves are fried."

"You'll be okay," Candy muttered as she struggled with the cork. "The human body is pretty resilient. It has a way of mending itself."

"It better. I think it's aged twenty years just in this past year alone. Talk about sensory overload, and ups and downs," I said.

"You wanted an exciting life. That's what brought you to the big city," Candy remarked.

"I had visualized exciting in a dynamic, invigorating, thriving way. Not exciting in a crazed, directionless, demoralizing way," I whined.

"Look at it this way, Adam, we're experiencing the wild side early on," she reasoned, then changing the subject asked, "So why did you give him money?"

"I just felt so sorry for him. Even though he attempted to cut my face up that day in the warehouse, I think it was just the sheer desperation. It's like he is completely disgusted with himself and what he is doing, he just doesn't know how to stop."

"Or not disgusted enough to want to stop. You know what they say. Once you hand out a few crumbs you've got them pecking at your door for good," Candy cautioned.

"Actually no," I remarked, "I never heard that."

"Okay, I just made it up," Candy said in a testy yet humorous tone. The first bit of humor all night. "I just hope he doesn't come lurking down the street again, all right!"

"I don't think so. I think that's the last we'll see of him."

"What makes you so sure?" Candy dismissed.

"I don't know," I answered simply. "I just get the feeling."

My second day on the set of *The Voyeur* wasn't scheduled until a few weeks later. The days until then had been quiet. I hoped all my troubles were behind me. This scene was at Missy Manhandler's birthday extravaganza and was being filmed in some hole-in-a-wall bar on Fairfax that had been re-created inside to resemble a decent club. I thought it might be stranger than my first time on the set, only because with Missy being there I was reminded even more of my days at HUNG Video.

The bar had regular drag performances, so there was a stage and a dressing room in the back. When I arrived for my call time, the cast and crew were sitting down to lunch. I drove my car along the side street where the trucks, catering, and dressing room trailers were set up and waved to Perry and Mitch, who shouted greetings and waved back. When I had parked my car I sat down and joined everyone to eat.

What did make me excited about today was my wild getup wardrobe had given me. It consisted of my own white cowboy hat bought on Melrose, a silver leather jacket, silver boots, silver lamé G-string, and a silver holster with two toy guns that shot off confetti. I only had two lines, in which I drunkenly approach and interrupt the lead character then shoot my guns off in the air and saunter away.

Before my scene was set up, the rock diva that was the star of the production had some dialogue to shoot. The directors and a few crew people personally escorted her from her dressing room trailer to the bar. After I was in my getup and sitting in the makeup chair she walked by, looked me in the eyes, and practically purred hello.

This woman was the fucking essence of cool. A downtown New York legend I'd loved since childhood had looked me up and down in my sexy cowboy gear and greeted me. That moment alone made being involved with the film worth it, no matter how successful it turned out.

Being the biggest name attached to the project, they wrapped up the rock goddess first and then it was on to the rest of us. After lunch many people began to arrive on the set. Because the setting was a party, plenty of extras were needed. I hid out in the dressing room of the club with the Dutch costume designer and her assistant, both of whom I had bonded with.

The dressing room was plastered with pages ripped out of fashion magazines such as *Vogue* and *Elle*. On the ceiling was a fabulous poster of Diana Ross from the 1980s, on which she wore her hair in a new wave, Mohawk sort of style. The drag queens that normally performed at this dump had a field day decorating their dressing room, which appeared to be an ongoing collage in progress.

Soon Missy arrived on location, already dressed to the nines in all his magnificence. He had scared the shit out of some poor PA who was trying to direct him into a tight parking spot, and blamed the poor sucker for causing him to bump his car into the one parked behind. Wearing a white platinum wig, colorful airbrushed eye makeup, and a black latex outfit with black ostrich feathers, Missy Manhandler was a sight to behold. His backup band was just as outrageous, and ready for the rock number they were going to perform in the film onstage.

Missy wasn't the only porn superstar on set. Evidently Perry was friendly with straight porn legends as well. Ron Jeremy, the male porn actor otherwise known as "the hedgehog" was in the scene as well. He sat near the door to the street in a chair, resembling a pudgy, droopy-eyed dog.

I had heard that Ron Jeremy never misses a chance to ham it up in front of the camera in a mainstream project, and craves a successful legitimate acting career more than anything else in the world. Evidently *The Voyeur* was no exception.

When it came time for my scene we had to rehearse it a few times and get the blocking straight. I was to enter and interrupt the two leads at just the right beat. The first time I did it was ridiculous and I had no idea what I was doing, popping out of nowhere like a gay wizard. After a few more rehearsals we finally got the timing down. In between these run-throughs and the actual take, Mitch took me aside and quietly told me, "Just make sure you are careful when you approach the lead. He doesn't want to be touched."

I looked at Mitch like he must be kidding.

"I haven't touched him at all," I responded point-blank.

I'm not an oblivious person, or some yokel who never left the farm. I could tell this big "star" had issues. I wanted nothing more than to perform well and get on with my business. Please. It sounded as if it was all part of my diabolical plan to make a pass at the guy. Give me a fucking break. This was exactly the sort of ego bullshit I despised.

"Why, was he bitching about me doing that?" I asked incredulously, and frankly, pissed off.

"No, don't worry about it. He's just sensitive about it, that's all," Mitch said, quick to change the subject, not wanting it to become an issue. He rolled his eyes as if to tell me he had dealt with the same crap from him on previous occasions.

Apparently Mitch and Perry had to work hard to keep their star happy. I guess his insecurity about taking on this scandalous role escalated in the past few weeks, from worrying about bathing suits to becoming paranoid about other actors getting too close. Never mind the fact he simulated anal sex with me the last time we saw each other. Evidently he lost respect for me when he found out I had appeared in actual porn flicks. Or maybe seeing me again just reminded him he wasn't at the level of Brad Pitt.

Needless to say, I didn't give two shits about him. My reasons for being here had nothing to do with fawning over the lead actor. I was here to be professional and do well for personal reasons.

With all that in mind I gathered up my pride and after a few takes wrapped the scene, ending each time with my toy guns provided by the prop guy exploding confetti into the air. When that was over we broke for another meal, and I spent time blabbing with Missy and some of the other actors from my other day of filming.

I stuck around for Missy's big performance, which was really quite entertaining. Missy Manhandler covered the old Blondie classic "One Way, or Another" with gusto. I was placed at the front of the stage, but I would have stayed and watched it if I were off camera as well. Standing in the crowd I waved my hat around like I just arrived at some twisted gay rodeo.

"I'm gonna getch-ya, getch-ya, getch-ya, getch-ya!" the whole room screamed like a bunch of maniacs at the end of the number.

The day dragged on and on, with the countless party scenes being filmed.

After a while I grew tired of sitting in the drag dressing room, which at this point was beginning to look very grimy, especially with countless people parading in and out. That coupled with all the junky crap I kept eating from craft services made me more than eager to get home. It didn't seem that I had anything else to do, and Perry and Mitch didn't have time to notice I was there anymore. So I took off the wild outfit, put on some normal clothes, said my good-byes, and drove home.

I had finished my first real speaking role ever, and I was feeling really cathartic, almost like a heavy weight had been taken off my back. At least I had done some legit acting in Hollywood.

I thought back to how I used to dream about being in movies as a kid. I owned all these huge photo books of the old movie stars, biographies, even Oscar trivia books that I would read over and over. It was a realm I could escape into, a means of dealing with the pain of not belonging, not feeling accepted. I was obsessed with this image of old Hollywood, a world that really didn't exist anymore. I was always a dreamer, but becoming less so as time wore on.

Still, though all my dreams hadn't been answered, I was living a damn good life with the best job I ever had and a man I adored. Our relationship might have been covert and undercover, but it was the best relationship I ever had. Until an event happened that turned my life upside down and once again tore my world apart.

It was a Monday, and I was taking a break from running some errands to work out at the gym. As I was leaving my cell phone rang.

"Hello," I said.

"Adam," it was Candy. "Are you okay?"

"Yeah, I'm fine. Why are you asking me that?" I began to freeze up.

"So you haven't seen it yet?"

"Seen what?" I was now agitated.

"Adam, you are on the cover of the tabloids. I was at Sav-on Drugs picking up some stuff. There I was at the checkout line digging through my purse when I looked up and saw a headline that read 'His Porno-iffic Assistant.'"

"You're fucking kidding me," I said in a daze.

"I only wish I was," she replied. "There are two pictures juxtaposed on the front. One is a still of you nude from behind, turning and smiling at the camera. They used lettering to cover your ass. The other is of you and John at a function, and you are whispering in his ear."

"Oh no," I said

"I picked up a copy so you can take a look without having to buy it yourself. Do you need to come by and see it?" Candy asked sympathetically.

I slouched against a nearby wall in a state of shock. I couldn't even respond.

"Adam? Are you still there?"

"Yeah." I breathed weakly. "I better come over. Shit," I whimpered.

"Are you okay to drive?" she asked.

"I guess I'd better be. I'll see you soon," I said and hung up.

A flushed, hot sensation overcame my body. It felt as though all eyes were on me, from the gym to where my car was parked. I tried to keep myself from shaking. The overwhelming urge to vomit came over me. If I thought my gay nerves had suffered before, they were taking a beating right now. I leaned up against the elevator wall that took me from the gym level to the garage below. A handful of trendy types were inside with me. My eyes were closed and I was breathing in and out heavily.

"Doing all right?" a guy I knew from the gym asked me.

"Oh, yeah. I'll be fine," I lied, smiling faintly.

"Rough workout, huh?" he smiled.

"Yeah, very rough," I breathed.

After what seemed forever I reached my car. During the whole drive over to Candy's I kept begging God that John wouldn't be upset and that he wouldn't hate me. After all, he knew what I was about before he met me. The question was would he want anything to do with me now that word had gone out his personal assistant was a gay porn star.

On the way to Candy's my phone rang a few times. I didn't answer it. At that moment I just didn't have the strength.

Candy was in the kitchen leaning against the counter when I came in. Looking down at the table I saw the image of myself in my naked glory smiling back at me on the cover of *America Weekly.*

"It's worse on the inside," Candy muttered. "Just totally mercenary."

"There's no pictures of John and I in the act, are there?" I asked frantically.

"No, thank God," Candy said.

For the next few minutes I didn't say anything, I just looked down, reading every word of the piece, which came complete with more racy images of me.

"America's favorite dad, John Vastelli, who plays beloved high school teacher Phil Langella on the show *Life's Lessons,* has hired a gay porn star better known as Adam Zee to be his assistant." The piece began, "Zee, whose real name is Adam Zeller, has been accompanying Vastelli around town for the past few months, sparking rumors of a love affair between the two men. Though Vastelli dates a number of women, which in the past has included '80s' sex vixen Zinnia, the all-American comedian has long been the source of gay rumors . . ."

The article went on in detail about the few adult flicks I starred in, how I walked away from the industry to work for John, and how it was rumored I stayed at his home often. In essence, though sensationally written, the article was for the most part the truth. Whoever rigged this story either knew me, John, or the both of us very well. The gay press was going to have a field day with this. There were probably forums already set up on the Internet to discuss the topic.

"What do you think John's going to say?" Candy asked.

Just then my phone rang.

"We're about to find out," I said, picking up the call. It was him.

"Adam, we need to talk," John said.

"I know," I responded.

"You've seen it?" he asked.

"Oh yeah," I breathed out heavily.

"My agents and the network is already talking about damage control," John said.

"What do you mean?" I asked.

"Grab a pen. I'm going to have you meet me at this address. Do not come to the house. There are probably photographers snooping around waiting to take some photographs," he ordered.

I took down the address and agreed to meet John in an hour.

"This doesn't sound good," I told Candy.

"Look, don't rush to assumptions, Adam," Candy tried to comfort me. "He might just think you the two of you need to stay apart for a few weeks, until the whole thing blows over."

"Oh, that's great for my job! He probably hates me now, wishes he never met me or became involved in my mess of a life," I sobbed, throwing my hands in my face and sliding down the kitchen wall until I was slumped over into a pathetic ball.

"Adam, you're going to have to be strong," Candy cautioned.

"I'm sick of trying to be strong. I can't even remember how I got to this place anymore. A year ago I was in New York temping. How did I get to this?" I wailed.

"That doesn't matter. You're here and you have to deal with it." She paused a moment and then said, "I wonder who the hell is behind it."

"Who knows," I huffed, looking up with streaked eyes and a blotchy face. "Could be Brian, could be Ron, could be Zinnia. I'll never know. All I know is in an hour I have to face John, and I'm so scared he'll want nothing to do with me."

My fears were legitimate. An hour later I met John at the home of one of his business associates in Beverly Hills. He was sitting on a white sofa inside, his shades still on. Seeing someone wearing shades indoors is never a good sign. They are the ultimate Hollywood defense mechanism.

"Hey," I said. As I approached him for a kiss he put his hand up, making his position clear early on.

"Sit down," he said gently.

"John, you don't think I had anything to do with this, do you?" I asked incredulously as I sunk into the overupholstered chair across from him.

"No, Adam, I don't. As a matter of fact, if anything, the whole thing is my fault. I should have known better than to become so closely involved," he stated.

"Oh, John, don't say that," I replied, completely crushed.

"Please, Adam, don't make this any harder than it has to be. This isn't easy for me at all. I felt so free with you, and was so into you I wanted to forget that I have to be careful. I've worked my ass off for so many years to build up my career; you have no idea. And the ironic part is that I can't share it with who I choose to. But if that's the sacrifice I have to make, then I have to live with that," John said grimly.

"John, is it really the end of the world? I mean look at Ellen, she got her career back . . ." I began before John cut me off in a rage.

"Yeah, only years after her own fucking show got canceled. And Rosie came out and now she's the world's most pushy dyke as far as the media and public are concerned. Jesus, Adam! Look at my show, and my audience! This is Middle America! Do you think they're really going to buy it after they find out in real life I'm shacking up with a guy? A guy who is a fucking porn star and a whore for Christ's sake!" he exploded.

I sat in the chair stunned as tears rolled down my cheeks. I had never seen John so angry, and never once believed he could be so enraged. He had always been a gentle bear with me.

"Oh shit," John muttered. He got up from the sofa and began pacing back and forth, putting his hand up to his forehead in emotional exhaustion. "I'm sorry I said that to you, Adam. You know I care for you. It's just that so many people depend on me, a whole cast and crew. If the show gets canceled they lose their jobs. There is just so much at stake here than just us, you understand?" he asked, finally pausing to look at me.

I just nodded my head, staring straight ahead through blurred eyes.

"Oh man, I can't do this anymore," John sighed. "Look, let's just play it cool for a while. I'm going to have a car service take your things from my house to your apartment. You won't have to worry about money for a while; I'll take care of that. If you get into trouble call me. But otherwise, we have to keep our distance, all right?"

Again, I just nodded my head, rose up, and made my way to the door. If he couldn't take it anymore, he had no idea what I was going through.

"Babe, I'm sorry. Please understand, please understand," I heard John's voice choke up from behind.

"No problem," I answered in a bitter voice as I walked like a zombie to the front door of the strange house. "It's the kind of life I'm used to, starting over."

With that I slammed the door behind me, stumbled to my car and slammed the door. After collapsing for a moment over the wheel I got myself together and drove to Candy's.

"Oh, come on, Adam! You haven't left the house for days!" Candy lamented. She then marched over to the blinds and jerked them up, letting a flood of early California sun in the room which painfully blinded me.

"Ohhh," I moaned groggily, suffering the pain of photosensitivity. "Put them back down."

"No!" Candy refused. "It's still my fucking home, and I'm ordering your ass up whether you like it or not. Besides, I'm making waffles. So drag your self-pitying ass into the kitchen now!"

I threw off the comforter and marched down the hall toward the kitchen in my Calvins. The only people I had spoken to in the past few days had been my parents. A friend of theirs brought the tabloid article to their attention. Otherwise they never would have seen it. My father handled it better than my mother.

"You know, Adam, you have to take a good look at the decisions you make and the choices you make," my mother said coldly.

I kept silent, not mentioning the fact that when I graduated college with zero dollars in my bank account I had wanted to come back home and get on my feet. It was so easy to point the finger at somebody when you're not in their situation. Yet at the same time she was right. I had made some poor choices and was paying for them.

"Did you ever stop to think about how this might hurt you, not to mention your father and I?" she asked coldly.

"No. I was too busy thinking about paying the rent and putting food on the table," I said numbly.

My mother always spoke for my father. Yet when he got on the phone all he did was ask how I was doing and told me that he loved me.

Despite having my life plastered on the front of a national publication, they didn't ask me if I needed to come home. Not even for a visit.

If this experience didn't teach me that I was never going to have the close-knit family life I wanted so desperately, nothing would.

About a dozen reporters and television producers left messages. I didn't return any calls. Lord only knew how they got my number. Ron had probably sold it to them.

"You should at least find out if they will offer you any money to sell your side of the story. Look at John. He dropped you like a hot potato. His spine must be made out of sawdust," Candy told me.

"Dropped me with a few thousand dollars," I said. True to his word, John had everything brought to Candy's, all my clothes, my Cartier watch, and a check for three grand which I had yet to deposit.

"It's too soon for me to make a decision if I want to talk to the press or not," I continued. "Besides, that might just make me look worse. Maybe when this blows over we can salvage our relationship."

"Where, in hotel rooms by sneaking up the back stairs?" Candy huffed. "Is that really the kind of relationship you want? Face it, Adam, he is never going to jeopardize his TV career. You deserve better than that. You never know. Maybe the publicity could lead to something, an acting role or a reality TV spot. You might as well try to turn lemons to lemonade. I say ride the publicity while you can, before his PR people smooth the whole thing over and it becomes yesterday's news."

"Well. If worse comes to worst I can always revive my porn career," I said. "Ron and a bunch of other top studios like Falcon have already called me offering money to sign me as an exclusive. I can just see the names of the films they are planning. *Anal Assistant, Hollywood Houseboy, Stud to the Stars,* and worse."

"Let's not go there yet. That's only the last resort," Candy quipped. "I'm just glad I dragged you out of that moldy bed. How many waffles do you want?"

We made waffles and popped in a Mae West film afterward. The choice for the night was *Klondike Annie,* where as a nightclub singer Mae stabs a man in self-defense and goes on the run disguised as a Christian missionary in Alaska. Never mind none of the other characters seem to be suspicious of a missionary with full makeup, bleached hair, and a swagger. It was *Sister Act* before *Sister Act* ever happened.

"You know, Mae West didn't make her first film until age forty, so she gives me hope," Candy joked.

For the next few hours Mae and Candy kept me entertained without a thought of anything.

Performing for a Party

After days indoors and not even a visit to the gym Candy convinced me to tag along with her to a party for her hairdresser Ricky. I was still despondent. John had not called me once, not even to find out how I was doing. I felt hurt and dispensable. Candy thought that getting me out would take my mind off him.

The night of the party Candy and I headed to the area of Ricky's apartment. We found the address, which turned out to be a typical two-story Spanish-style building. Thinking the right apartment was on the ground floor, Candy and I rang the bell.

A wooden peep hole in the door was pulled back to reveal a metal mesh screen. Behind it we could see a very sexy dark-haired guy wearing a white wife-beater tank top that showed off an exceptionally muscular physique. Candy and I glanced at each other. At this point I knew we had knocked on the wrong door but was glad for the mistake.

"Hi," I said blankly. "Is this Ricky's place?"

"Actually he lives upstairs," the guy answered. The minute he opened his mouth I knew he swung my way, which in turn excited me. We apologized for disturbing him.

"No problem. I'm actually heading up to his party in a while myself." He smiled. Now I was glad Candy dragged me along. I knew there would be something there to keep me entertained and help me forget about John, even just for the moment.

"He had a great build," Candy said encouragingly as we went up the steps. "Your type, huh?"

"Oh yeah," I said without hesitation.

Ricky answered the door upstairs and we went inside his place. We were among the first arrivals, which explained not hearing the sound of festivity and the roof being raised. Hanging out in the kitchen we poured ourselves some vodka and cranberry as the apartment steadily became more packed. Of course I waited for the sexy downstairs neighbor in eager anticipation. Candy teased me about it.

"Look at you! You're on the prowl now!"

"Hey, Ricky. Who's that guy who lives downstairs from you?" Candy asked.

"Oh, you've met Tray? Isn't he delicious?" Ricky gushed. "By the way, Adam, I saw you in that tabloid, and . . ."

"Ricky!" Candy scolded.

"Candy made me promise not to say anything," Ricky continued. "But I thought you looked fabulous, and whether it is true or not the whole thing is just fabulous."

"Thanks, Ricky," I smiled. "I appreciate it."

"Of couse, darling! Ricky always tells the truth!" he said with glee, and with that scurried to the other room to greet new arrivals.

About an hour later Tray made his entrance, bringing along an overweight female friend. When he saw us in the kitchen he said hello. "Glad to see you guys found the place."

His friend had recently relocated to LA and taken a job as an employment recruiter. I would have offered my resumé to her until she went on to explain her company specialized in placing CEOs and high-level executives. Thankfully I had spared myself the embarrassment. Besides, I was here to forget about my troubles. Nobody needed to hear about the disastrous state of my affairs regarding my professional life, or lack thereof.

Though talkative, Tray had a soft-spoken manner and puppy dog eyes that were endearing, and made him seem more alluring than before. We continued to speak in the kitchen until the lighting of the cake and blowing out of the candles interrupted us.

"Everybody quiet!" Ricky's butch lesbian roommate growled.

Ricky then stood up on a chair and made a rather serious and dramatic, not to mention self-serving speech about how difficult his year had been and proceeded to thank everyone for standing by him and supporting him. One would have thought he was auditioning for Shakespeare in the Park.

"As you all know, this has been a very hard year for me," Ricky began.

Come visit my world and we'll compare sob stories, I thought.

Thank God his guests eventually got creeped out and uncomfortable enough to run up and hug him, brushing off the melodrama with some joking around. Someone had the good sense to put the music back on.

"That was a rather somber display," I commented afterward.

"No kidding. I was like man, Ricky! You're bringing us down!" Tray laughed.

It was clear there were sparks flying between Tray and myself. Candy and his friend were standing aside now and speaking more with each other, while the two of us gazed into each other's eyes and chatted up a storm. Tray was an aspiring actor. He told me he saw himself playing cop or detective roles on television. I thought he might be convincing. While soft-spoken, he had a gritty quality as well.

We had moved into the other room and were sitting on the couch. Ricky had popped in a new collection of Madonna videos in the VCR to show to his friends as everyone drank and made merry. Ricky loved Madonna.

I yearned to be with Tray at that moment. I desperately desired another man's touch, the abandon of having unattached sex at that moment. It was the perfect cure for my doldrums and woes. The last guy I'd been with was John, and now I needed somebody to wipe him from my memory, a fuck to help me forget about him and clear the slate.

My mind drifted back to a plan I had been hatching for the past half hour. I kept commenting on how much I loved Ricky's apartment, and how cute the building was. Then I directed the conversation to Tray's apartment, asking if the layout was the same, and who his roommate was. Of course, this was all part of my ulterior motive, which was to have Tray invite me into his place so I could get some play.

"Actually, even though my apartment is directly below Ricky's the floor plan is different, especially the kitchen area. It's kind of weird," Tray explained to me.

Now it was time to make my move.

"Really? I'm trying to visualize it. I'd love to see it," I said casually, anxiously awaiting what kind of reaction I'd get.

Tray saw right through me. He gave me a mischievous smile and looked as if he was contemplating what he should do next. "Well, my roommate is spending the night at his girlfriend's," he said.

He had mentioned earlier his roommate was straight, and that they had met in an acting class.

"I guess we can go down there for a few minutes and I can show you around," he went on while smiling sexily and raising his eyebrows suggestively.

Other guests were aware of the sparks flying between us as well, and I found out later that we were already the subject matter of much of the talk at the party. Ricky had even come up to me a few minutes earlier, when Tray stepped in the bathroom, to get the scoop. Ricky mentioned another one of his friends had his eye on me. I didn't even care to ask who it was. Right now it was all about Tray.

I turned to Candy, who was chatting with some other people, and told her I was going downstairs for a bit. Candy said okay with a knowing smile. Like everyone else, she had been keeping a close eye on the developing situation between muscle-man Tray and me.

When I followed Tray out the door, the party had flowed outside, so there were people hanging out on the staircase and driveway. Most of them were smoking and carrying on. I paid no attention. My eyes were fixated on the muscular frame in front of me.

Tray opened the lock and I followed him inside. After flicking on the lights, I followed him around, glancing at the interior and trying to pretend that I gave two shits about the structural differences between the upstairs and the downstairs units. When we were finished I stood with my back to the front door.

"So how do you like the place?" he asked me slowly.

"Very much," I answered quietly, wondering who would do what next.

My question was answered when Tray reached behind me and flicked the light switch off, leaving us standing face to face in the darkness. Our lips met a second later, tongues lapping together in each other's mouths. All night I had been waiting to grab on to his strong frame, which felt like a rock-hard sculpture as I rubbed my hands up and down the muscles of his back, finally gripping his round, firm butt.

I could tell that once this guy decided to get it on, he did it with zeal. He picked me up and sat me on the kitchen table, gyrating wildly against me. Of course I'd been wondering how hung he was, and was delighted by his girth and length. My shirt and his tank top flew off. My hands went over his enormous pecs again and again.

I jumped down from the table so we could grab at each other's pants, releasing our eager dicks, which sprung up to greet each other. The tip of his dick went back and forth against mine, stopping now and then to poke and lay against my stomach. We stood there for a while, continuing to make out furiously, groping and grabbing at each other, bodies pressed together tightly and rubbing away. I could hear laughter and commotion outside, and see figures walking past the windows through the blinds. But I didn't think twice about it, as we had seen guests outside on our way down. Besides, the lights were out, and I didn't think it was possible to see anything through the windows. In the heat of the moment, it was the last thing on my mind.

Tray pushed me toward the bedroom, flopping me down on the bed. We kicked off our shoes and released our legs from the grip of our pants, which had since fallen to our ankles. Without warning, he shifted around on top of me, shoving his huge and swollen cock down my throat, and taking my own dick inside his mouth. I gripped on to his beautiful hips, grabbing hold while he bobbed up and down on my face. We changed positions a few more times, and in the middle of what was so far the best sex I was having in a long time, I noticed voices and laughter near us growing louder and more excitable. Eventually Tray jumped up suddenly and stepped halfway off the bed, sealing the blinds quickly. He looked back at me with a childish but still sexy grin.

"What happened? Someone peering in?" I asked, breathing heavily. If there were people peeping in at us, I had no idea. I was focused on one thing only, the hot stud in front of me and his beautiful anatomy. The window could have been a mile away as far as I was concerned.

Things heated up to a point where we couldn't hold it anymore. Actually, Tray came first. Usually I was the one that couldn't hold off coming, but this time I would have loved to go at it even longer. He stood up from the bed, groaning out loud and trying to squeeze the slit of his dick shut and hold in his load until he had his other hand in position to catch all his wad, so it didn't go flying all over the floor. I stood up and bit and sucked on his nipples. He started to yell as his orgasm began, and I kneeled down so I could witness him spurt his load up close, catching some on the side of my cheek. I followed suit right after him, less conscientious about messing up the floor.

We went into the bathroom and cleaned ourselves up, and wiped up the floor as well. My guess was we had been downstairs for about twenty minutes. All eyes were on us when we reentered the room, but I was so relaxed and happy I didn't think about it twice. My mood hadn't been this worry free in a long time. The music was still going loud, so I couldn't hear if anybody made any comments. Candy was sitting on Ricky's couch when I came back. She looked up at me with a big smile.

"Hey, Adam!" she said enthusiastically, just a hint of a teasing tone in her voice.

The heavyset friend of my latest fuck smirked knowingly as she greeted us. I guess the whole party suspected that he wasn't showing me his stamp collection. While I was getting my rocks off Candy was growing bored. The party was dying down and it was time for us to leave. I left with Tray's phone number. I hoped we saw each other again. If nothing else, maybe I had finally found myself an occasional fuck buddy.

On the drive back home Candy told me that half the party had witnessed the muscular stud and I getting our groove on through the blinds.

"But the lights were off," I said, honestly thinking it was impossible.

"Hello, Rebecca of Sunnybrook Farm!" Candy sang in my ear. "How brightly lit was that driveway? You don't think that might make it possible to see inside?"

"So did you come down and take a peak at us getting busy?" I asked teasingly.

"Eww. That's one thing I don't need to see," she said with a look of disgust on her face, then proceeded to grill me about the details.

So what if half the party knew I was screwing around? Thousands of other people could watch me have sex on their DVD players and VCRs. I didn't give a shit. The past few weeks had been some of the worst in my life. I needed a good screw to lift my spirits and help me forget the heartbreak. That it was with one of the most magnificently built guys I had been with was just icing on the cake. I went to bed that night feeling a lot better.

My sexual satisfaction was to be short-lived. The next week was to bring on more grief and disillusionment to my life, though I wouldn't have thought it possible.

Things started to slide further a few days later when I decided to keep in touch with Tray by what I thought was a sweet idea. During our conversation that night we discovered we were both old movie buffs, discussing our favorite old-time stars and films at length. I had a few books sitting around that I had already read. One was a biography of legendary World War II musical actress and pinup Betty Grable, while a few others were novelty books, with subjects such as *Hollywood's Biggest All Time Flops*. I thought Tray would appreciate them.

I left them outside his door with a note. A few days later he still didn't call. Finally I caved in and called Tray to see if he got them. He gushed over the phone about how surprised he was and how sweet it was of me, and that we would definitely have to hang out again. He told me he had meant to call me but was busy with his job waiting tables. Our conversation ended with him promising to call the next week.

"Okay, whenever you have time," I said, knowing better than to sit by the phone.

That night Ricky met Candy and me at the Abbey. Ricky went on at length about what a scandal I caused at the party.

"I was glad I could be of entertainment. It seems my antics are meant to amuse the whole world," I said sarcastically, referring to me being fodder for the tabloids.

I went on to tell Ricky I thought Tray was hot.

"Adam, he may be the body beautiful, but I wouldn't give him any more thought," Ricky said point-blank. "Tray likes to have his share of fun, which includes lots of circuit parties, running around, and many sexual partners. He's not one to think of seeing a second time, you know what I mean?"

"Gotcha," I said. In other words, if I were to look for someone to help me get over John, I should keep looking.

I put Tray out of my mind and sipped my martini. What did I care? It wasn't as if I was some innocent victim of love. On the contrary, I went right after the guy like a lion on the hunt. I honestly hoped Tray enjoyed his books. I wanted a good piece of ass and some sexual plea-sure to soften my misery, which I got from him. Unfortunately, it wasn't the only thing I got from him.

Hitting the Breaking Point

Exactly a week after Ricky's party I was in the kitchen putting away some groceries. I had all but forgotten my escapade with muscleman Tray. After stacking yogurts in the fridge, I suddenly felt the need to urinate. I hadn't peed that morning, which was highly unusual, but really didn't give it much thought.

I went to the bathroom, my bladder full and ready to be relieved. As I stood over the toilet with my limp dick out ready to take a whiz, I immediately sensed something was wrong. When feeling this ready to pee I usually gushed like Niagara Falls. But for some reason I was having trouble releasing, even though I had the urgent need to go. It was like I was clogged up.

The next thing I knew I was gripped with a painful burning sensation bad enough to make me gasp and bend over in agony, and I had to keep myself from screaming out in pain. It felt like I was forcing myself to pass razor blades through my penis. I moaned as I continued to urinate, wanting to stop because of the scorching discomfort but at the same time desperate to empty myself.

When I was finished I stood there, gripping my crotch with both hands and my face wincing up. I was stunned, to put it mildly. I knew I was in trouble. My recent conquest had given me more than a good time to remember him by. Along with it Tray had passed on some kind of nasty VD, perhaps urethritis or gonorrhea. I stared at the numb expression that was on my face in the bathroom mirror as I washed my hands, slowly soaping them up and rinsing them off in a daze. This was not what I needed in my life right now. I had no stable job, just been dumped, and was now reminded of the fact that I had no medical insurance and something was wrong with me. How much more shit could get thrown my way?

I drove to the nearest business I could think of that carried *Frontiers* or some other publication that would have info on where I could get myself checked out. I found a free clinic on North Schrader Boulevard in the heart of Hollywood, and dialed the number immediately. A girl answered the phone and I asked somewhat spastically if I could come in within the next few hours. I scratched the counter in frustration when she told me there were no openings left, but walk-in hours were every day from 11 a.m. to 3 p.m.

"I'll come in tomorrow," I said in frustration, and threw the phone across the room. I was even more frustrated by the fact I had to pee again, and this time knew what was in store for me.

After another torturous session over the toilet, I flopped on my bed and flipped through the pages of the papers I had brought home, hoping to clear my thoughts and forget about my infected dick and dismal job prospects for a while. I skimmed over the frothy articles and stories, making my way to the back where the personal and adult ads are placed. I was just about to close the rag up and toss it aside when an image struck me as I flipped through the end of the weekly.

I greeted it with disbelief and dismay. Taking up about a quarter of a page was an advertisement for phone sex, with yours truly staring at the camera with a stupid forced grin and in the gayest pose possible. My torso was twisted in a way so that my shoulders faced the camera and my pecs popped out more than they normally would. The lower half of my body was in profile, and I was sticking my butt out as if I was getting ready to give a lap dance. I wore a phony sort of sultry expression on my face. My eyes squinted a little as if to look piercing and my lips pouty as to look bigger. The sex-line number was printed strategically at my groin, covering up my privates.

Great. Just wonderful. I had graduated from being in a few porn movies to being splashed across national supermarket rags to now being the model for sleazy sex services.

My mind couldn't take any more. If I kept focusing on all the shit I was buried in up to my neck, I would explode. It was like a cruel joke: the more I tweaked out about all the crap I had to deal with, the more was thrown at me. In an attempt to zone out, I flipped on the TV and watched reruns of *The Golden Girls* until eventually falling asleep.

The next morning I ran out of the apartment without saying a word to Candy. I was one of the first people in the waiting room of the clinic. I sat on some sofas watching television chat shows when I was eventually called in by one of the nurses. She was a sensible, no-nonsense woman and asked me what my concern was. She could tell I was freaked out and upset, perhaps more so than most people who came in who were probably more embarrassed and uncomfortable than anything else. I imagine your average person just wanted to get whatever they had cleared up and than clear themselves out of the clinic.

Leave it to me to be much more demonstrative and emotional. I went into my whole sob story of meeting Tray for one night and my downfall. She sat and listened, probably having heard it all before.

"It's not worth it," she said in a straightforward tone. "Look at what happened. You have to suffer, then come down here and deal with all of this for five minutes of pleasure. You're worth more than that. You give yourself time to get to know someone first," she stated firmly.

It was strange to be hearing a voice of reason especially when everyone I surrounded myself with seemed borderline crazy. To be sitting across from a practical, unassuming individual for a change was almost a comfort, though obviously I would have preferred not having needed a trip to the VD clinic. Did things have to get this extreme to find a sensible person in LA?

Before she finished I sat there and listened in horror as she went on in detail about cases where people had picked things up from making contact with people's throats. Having something passed on to you was demoralizing enough; I didn't want to think about people walking around with an STD in their mouths. After leading me into a room and examining me, she said she did notice some discharge down there.

"Let me give you this," she said, and handed me a pill along with a liquid antibiotic of some sort to chase it down with. "That should clear it up. We won't know what it is for sure until your results come back in a week. I'll schedule you for a follow-up around then."

Instead of leaving, I stuck around to get an HIV test as well. I had always tried to be as safe as possible, but at this point I wasn't sure of anything. I had been with so many people since arriving in LA I couldn't keep track. I began manifesting the worst in my mind. What if I had caught AIDS? Then what would I do? Maybe I was being punished for all my evil deeds. My thoughts churned over and over with "what if." I began sweating and shaking, twitching my right foot so uncontrollably that the other people in the lobby looked at me in irritation, the guy next to me getting up and moving to another seat.

I was broken from my trance when a cute Hispanic guy came down the hall and announced my number. I followed him down the hall into a small office and sat down. Unlike the nurse I had earlier, he was soft-spoken.

"Hello, I'm Eduardo, one of the counselors. How are you doing?" he asked.

Well gee, let me think, I wanted to say. *My eyes are popping out of my head from anxiety, I'm trembling uncontrollably, and I'm chewing on my lip like it's a stick of gum, what do you think?*

Instead I settled on "Fine."

We began with routine questions about my sexual history.

"How many partners have you had in the last year?" Eduardo asked at one point.

Oh shit. I couldn't even recollect.

"Umm, let me think," I stammered.

I sat there for a few minutes. There was Dale, John, Wayne Hanley, Tray, other clients, and numerous porn stars from the handful of films I made for HUNG. Finally, Eduardo asked, "Can you give me an approximate number?"

"Twenty-five," I said.

The questions got more excruciating, such as how many times was anal sex involved, did I receive or give, and so forth. I knew the whole process. I had been tested numerous times before. But it was agonizing to try to remember the details of individual sex acts on the scene of each porno set, and every night as a male whore for hire. At one point in our conversation, the subject turned toward work.

"I'm currently unemployed," I mumbled.

At that point I did something I had never done before. I looked at the poor guy, tears welled up in my eyes, and I started sobbing. I just completely broke down. Everything came out at once. I was making a complete display of myself in front of a complete stranger, bawling my eyes out. Losing a guy I loved, being out of a job, picking up an STD, and seeing my image splashed on a tacky phone sex ad was more than I could take.

In a way it made sense I was having an emotional breakdown here and now. I was in an office, speaking with someone whose job it was to hear information that was completely confidential, almost like a therapist. And what I desperately needed right now, other than a decent job, was a therapist.

The poor guy looked at me with deer eyes and passed me a box of tissue. It was safe to assume such an unexpected outburst from a grown man was not something he was prepared for first thing in his day. Then again, I had to take into consideration the kind of work he did and where I was. From the outside I appeared like someone who should have his act together. Nothing could be further from the truth.

"You know, the state of California has public assistance programs that you are probably eligible for," Eduardo said meekly.

While he was trying to be helpful, that bit of information only had me sobbing harder. Holy shit. Now the subject had turned to welfare. I had dealt with a lot of issues and circumstances in my life, but never in my wildest dreams did I ever think I'd even be touching upon the subject of my going on welfare. What was even worse was that in the back of my mind I thought it might not be such a bad idea. If things kept on going as they were, I might soon find myself in line. Eduardo the HIV counselor was probably horrified at this point.

I finally got a grip on myself, and we solemnly proceeded with what was supposed to be a routine HIV test.

"Would you like the names of those services?" Eduardo asked as I got up to leave.

"No thanks," I said. "I'll be okay. I'm just going through a rough spell."

I just wanted to go home.

On the brighter side, I had to pee before finally getting out of there. I found the bathroom in the hall and prepared myself for pain.

The nurse must have given me something strong, because whatever it was had already kicked in. There was considerably less discomfort than last time. I hoped the rest of my life, especially my HIV test results, turned out as well as my urinary tract.

Bowing Out with a Boa

That night Candy was getting ready for a party at Koi, one of the restaurants to be seen at in town.

"Are you sure you don't want to tag along?" Candy asked while strapping on a pair of gold Manolo Blahnik stilettos. Her look this evening was particularly stunning. She had on a beige cashmere tank top sweater with a padded bra that made her breasts look even bigger than they already were. A sequined gold and nude skirt that cost $2,500 from Blumarine, which she had seen Jennifer Lopez wear in a photo shoot, lit up the room.

"No, I think I'm just going to hang out here," I replied. While Candy looked breathtaking, I was frazzled and looked like shit. I felt gross too, as though I were infested with the encounters from my past, both mentally and physically.

"You sure you don't want to change your mind? There will be an open bar and sushi," Candy teased as she touched up her lips with some Chanel gloss. She was a whirling dervish while getting ready— sandal straps one second, lip gloss the next—but always came out looking like a million bucks.

"No. Thanks but no thanks," I said.

"All right," Candy sighed in resignation with a hint of disapproval. She felt I was becoming a permanent hermit, succumbing to serious agoraphobia.

"How do I look?" she asked, spinning around in her sequined number.

"Sensational," I smiled.

"If you change your mind, call me." And with that she clicked her way out of the apartment, shutting and locking the door behind her.

I would soon regret not accompanying her, despite my depression. I tried to lay down with a book but was too fidgety and nervous, worried about my HIV test results. Thinking the television would distract me more easily, I turned it on. After flipping through the channels I came upon none other than John hamming it up on the screen before me.

I had forgotten that *Life's Lessons* aired that night. Instead of changing the channel I froze, watching John and thinking about how happy I was with him, how right it felt. I sat numb for minutes watching the whole program and wishing that things could have been different. The urge to call him was becoming impossible to fight. I had little pride left, and I didn't want to seem any more pathetic and dangerous, misguided and misdirected to him by contacting him in my current frame of mind.

Suddenly an uncharacteristic rage took over me. After beating the pillows hysterically and spooking out the cats, I realized I needed to calm down. I darted into Candy's bathroom.

Her vast collection of cosmetics took over the counter, compartment after compartment of Lancôme, Chanel, Shiseido, MAC, Bobbi Brown, and more set up in clear compartments purchased at Bed, Bath, and Beyond. Ignoring the mess, I pulled open her medicine cabinet. After knocking over a few bottles I found what I was looking for, her bottle of Xanax. Grabbing a handful, I popped them in my mouth, chasing the pills down with tap water gathered in the palm of my hand.

I need something better to chase these down with, I thought, and went into the kitchen where I found a bottle of merlot open on the counter. I couldn't be bothered to pour it into a glass, so I just started guzzling it down from the bottle.

All of a sudden I felt really hot. I started stripping my clothes off right then and there in the kitchen, piece by piece, flinging each garment around with reckless abandon.

"Score!" I yelled as my underwear caught onto the ceiling fan.

"What this place really needs is some music," I hollered out loud in a drugged-up stupor that was really beginning to hit. Prancing over to the stereo system, I punched the buttons until ABBA's *Greatest Hits* came on. Soon I was spinning around in the room like an escapee from Bellevue.

"Dancing Queen, young and sweet, only seventeen," I bellowed in the most tone-deaf, off-key, ear-splitting singing voice imaginable. No *American Idol* reject had anything on me.

I grabbed a hot pink feather boa Candy had draped over one of her lamps in the living room, which she kept around so we could crack each other up with our Mae West impersonations.

Dancing over to the stereo I turned the volume dial up all the way, the music blasting so the walls shook. It felt so good to forget about everything. I wanted this feeling to last forever. No more worries about the future, no more regrets about the past. No more feeling scared, negative, like I wasn't skilled enough, not smart enough. No more feeling like a freak.

A minute later I heard banging on the doorway. It was Candy's neighbor Orly, yelling to turn down the music.

"Cahn-dee, Ahh-dum, turn down zee mus-eeec right now!" Orly hollered in her broken English.

"Fuck off, Orly!" I yelled, and then darted for the bathroom, tripping on the boa around my neck and skidding on the floor along the way. Crawling the rest of the way I felt the cool tile of the bathroom, hoisted myself up, and grabbed the remaining bottle of Xanax, dumping them down my throat and coughing.

Stumbling toward the kitchen I grabbed the wine, spilling most of it on the boa and my naked body but getting a bit of a swig in my mouth.

"I called zee po-leeese!" Orly yelled, banging furiously on the door.

"Go away!" I moaned.

The room started spinning faster and faster around me. I felt hot, so hot. I needed fresh air. Through my blurred vision I could see the opening to the darkness outside, the gauzy curtains that framed the balcony. Stumbling toward the open door of the balcony, I crashed into a side table, knocking over a lamp and a vase.

"Shit. Candy's gonna be pissed," I slurred.

Finally I crossed the threshold from the living room to the balcony. The cool evening air smacked against my hot skin, offering just a slight wisp of invigoration. Pulling myself up against the iron railing,

I stood against the late night breeze, hot pink feathers flying around me and sticking to my mouth as I tried to spit them away.

"John, John, I love you. I love you so much," I mumbled, feeling queasy and hanging over the railing, my head feeling heavy.

Behind me the faint banging of the door and more voices could barely be heard under the blaring ABBA music as "Mamma Mia" now blasted.

Air, I need more air, I thought as I leaned forward further. The next thing I knew a sharp pain hit me in the stomach, causing me to buckle over. My body jutted further. Then everything went black.

Staying Alive

It wasn't a pang of pain in my stomach but a pain in my eyes that greeted me as I awoke to a blinding flood of light. For a moment I thought they were the lights of heaven, until my squinty eyes and blurry vision cleared and I saw Candy sitting next to me in her familiar pale blue sweat suit.

"Where I am I?" I whispered.

"Cedars Sinai," Candy answered bluntly.

"What happened?" I asked.

"Well, where do I begin," Candy started in a no-nonsense tone. "After raiding my medicine cabinet it appears you decided to take a dive off the balcony in nothing but a pink feathered boa, almost getting us evicted in the process. Miraculously, all you ended up with was a broken wrist and mild concussion after hitting the grass instead of the cement. Oh, did I mention they managed to pump your stomach and get most of the Xanax out?"

"Oh Jesus. I am so sorry, Candy," I moaned, picking up my head a bit to look at the cast on my right arm.

"Ohhh," I gasped in pain. My head felt like a rock.

"That would be the egg-size bump on your head," Candy muttered. Then, taking hold of my other hand, she squeezed it hard, placed one hand on my cheek, and emphatically told me, "Adam, don't ever do that again. No matter how bad things seem, they change. Don't ever, ever pull that shit. Promise me?" she ordered while her blue eyes stared into mine.

"I promise," I replied gently.

"Good." She winked, and then kissed me on the forehead.

"So they told me the medics did their best to keep it professional after arriving on the scene to find a large, muscular, naked man laying on the ground with a hot pink boa tossed around his neck. You're the talk of the whole building. When I came home I couldn't get Orly to shut up. She followed me from the apartment all the way to my car, and wanted to come to the hospital as well. Thankfully I was able to talk her out of it. She was very concerned though, despite the fact you disrupted her beauty sleep with raging disco music."

"So I guess I messed up big time," I sighed.

"You messed up, but by the grace of God you didn't wind up dead," Candy said. "Which brings me to another matter."

I looked at Candy with worn-out eyes.

"What? Dare I ask?" I said.

"It was in all this morning's papers. I could hardly believe it myself. I never bought the paper, but needed something to do while waiting for you to wake up, and I already have every magazine the gift shop sells at home."

"What?" I exclaimed, flabbergasted. "My falling off the balcony completely inebriated on pills and booze made the paper?" I asked in fear.

"No, not you," Candy rolled her eyes. "Calm down."

"Here," she said, laying the paper on top of me. "I'm not even going to tell you. I'll let you read it for yourself. But I have to warn you, it's upsetting."

Using my good arm I picked up the paper. The front headline read "Actress Killed in Drug Deal Gone Awry." The subheadline said "Zinnia, one-named starlet who rose to fame in the '80s stabbed to death in her home."

Placed underneath was a publicity shot from Zinnia in her heyday when she was still a smoldering beauty, before her looks became wrecked with aging and excessive plastic surgery. But what shocked me even more was a mug shot of none other than Dale right beside her. The caption read "Dale Warren, 31, of West Hollywood has been booked and held on a million dollars bail for the stabbing death of Angela Watson, 45, better known as Zinnia."

"Holy shit," I whispered in astonishment. "I don't believe it."

"It was on all the morning news shows too. They had *Good Day LA* on in the waiting room and that's all they were talking about," Candy commented.

"Oh man, Dale," I said out loud. "How could you do it? What a waste. Oh man," I repeated in shock.

"Horrible, isn't it," Candy said grimly. "At least we know he won't be creeping around our place anymore."

I was in shock. All of a sudden my mind put two and two together and staring at the paper I suddenly remarked, "That was her! That's who it was!"

"That was her who? What are you talking about?" Candy questioned.

"That night Dale and I went to Gleisman's party," I recollected. "He stopped to get gas and I answered his cell phone when he got out of the car. A nasty woman's voice snapped that she had his stuff, not even bothering to make sure it was him. No wonder she seemed so familiar, and it was always creepy to me whenever she was around John. She was supplying Dale with drugs all along."

"Wasn't very careful or discreet about it either," Candy observed. "Doing transactions in parking lots, not even making sure who she was speaking to on the phone, having crazed addicts in her home."

"You know, I think she was just so frustrated, Candy. So bitter she just didn't care about that any more," I remarked.

A lump filled up my throat. I felt so guilty, despite all the craziness around me and events happening so fast, maybe there was more I could have done for Dale. He had been so sweet in the beginning, such a great companion.

"Oh, Candy, I let him down. I totally let the guy down. He had a problem and needed someone to take control of it for him, someone who cared enough. And all I was thinking about was myself, what kind of job I needed and where the next buck was coming from. Turning tricks while a friend was in trouble," I finished in tears.

"Hey," Candy said smoothly, "stop that. You tried to tell him. Look, Adam, I'm sure he was way overboard with his addiction before you ever stepped into the picture. And maybe if he hadn't tried to kill you, you could have done more. But I'm sure a lot of people tried to get him off that stuff, but others can only do so much. You can bring a camel to water but you can't make them drink." Then she stopped and asked, "Did I get that saying right?"

"Yeah."

"Anyhow, you've gone through so much these past weeks. You need to rest and be good to yourself."

I had been through a lot. But I made a vow at that point never to become so self-consumed that I couldn't be of help to someone in my life ever again.

Candy left to get some things done. I was to be discharged within twenty-four hours. All I could think about as I lay in my hospital bed was that through a series of unfortunate circumstances I came to know two people, and now one was dead and the other headed for prison. And one of those people I had cared for at some point. In my short time in LA I witnessed Dale become ravaged and brought down by drugs, and the grisly reality of it left me glum and sober. After my own episode the night before, feeling sober was something I needed at the moment.

Almost two weeks later I wobbled into the clinic to receive the results of my HIV test, still wearing a cast on my wrist. In the lobby I waited anxiously, but in much better form than my first visit. Finally Eduardo came into the room carrying my file, and greeted me in a peppy and sunny disposition. I took it as a good sign.

"What happened here?" he asked, noticing my cast after trying to shake my right hand.

"Oh, just a minor accident," I said, brushing it aside. "I took a spill outside my building."

"Nothing serious I hope?" He began leading me down the hallway.

"Oh no, not at all," I smiled. "It's coming off in a few days."

We both sat down. I took a deep breath. He got right down to business.

"Okay, Adam, your test results came back negative," he said, showing me the paperwork and pointing to the word "nonreactive."

"Great," I breathed.

Before leaving Eduardo inquired if I was doing better, and told me to keep practicing safe sex. I left feeling refreshed and renewed, and promised to come back in three months to be sure.

With my hospital bills from the fall wiping out all the money John had given me and the cash I had from Christmas dwindling down to nothing, I would have to find a job very soon. And that was okay. I'd take any job. At a hotel, at a department store, where I could make the bills and pay the rent. It didn't matter if it was day-to-day drudgery or not the best job in the world, because it wouldn't be forever.

I was putting together a long-term plan, and it was going to involve going back to school again and starting anew, this time with greater focus. My time in LA taught me some valuable lessons about what I wanted in life. And I felt good about the decision to start again, without the sense of wariness that clouded me when coming to Hollywood.

God wasn't finished with me yet, and I wasn't finished with myself either.

Cut to Flashback

The e-mail was close to being deleted along with all the other junk mail finding its way to my in-box until I looked more closely. Though I didn't recognize the address, instead of the usual GET OUT OF DEBT or HORNY TEENS! BARELY LEGAL! it read VOYEUR NEW YORK DEBUT. The whole experience had all but been forgotten among the loads of classes, assignments, and work on my plate. I had already been back in New York more than a year by this time, and couldn't be happier.

It wasn't too much of a surprise. I figured the film would have a run in a few artsy movie houses in New York and LA. It made the rounds of quite a few film festivals like Toronto, Berlin, and Sundance before finding a distributor. Perry and Mitch had a whole *Voyeur* Web site created with updates and latest news posted. My name was even listed in the Internet Movie Database, a record of my one true credit as a movie actor. Actually two credits, if I counted *Sect of Lucifer*.

What did come as a surprise was when *The Voyeur* experienced a record-breaking run at the Quad Cinema on 13th Street, and went on to play in other major cities and even smaller ones, such as Cleveland and Fort Lauderdale.

Good for them. Those guys deserved it. God knows they put enough blood, sweat, and tears into the project.

Glancing at the movie listings and advertisements in the paper while sipping my morning coffee, I reflected momentarily on whether I would have been able to land an agent if I stuck around LA, now that *The Voyeur* was a success. My conclusion was no. It would take more than a few minutes on screen in a racy role to land even a semi-decent agent.

Not that it mattered much anymore. That was all history. Due to deadlines and a heavy workload, there was no way I was going down-

town for the premiere. Besides, I already went to the screening for
cast and crew before I left LA, and that was more than enough.

Almost two years have passed since I left Los Angeles. The last few
months I spent there were remarkably peaceful and enjoyable. Knowing I'd be leaving soon, I concentrated on the good my surroundings
had to offer. I think I went for a hike in the hills or a swim in the West
Hollywood Park almost every day.

The decision came to me soon after my release from the hospital.
All of a sudden my need to be in the limelight, to feel loved and receive attention and adulation from others had retreated. I was just
happy to be alive, and ready for a new direction. My disappointments
had beaten away a lot of lingering hang-ups. They were instead being
replaced by lessons in humility. My life wasn't going to be like the
lives of those celebrities I had read about with envy and adulation. But
there was a whole entire world full of wonder and possibilities outside
of the glitter and glamour of Hollywood.

A month after the murder of Zinnia I was asked to take part in an
E! True Hollywood Story about her and the grisly events surrounding
her death. It seemed the producers learned about my association with
Dale, probably through Ron, and remembered me being revealed as
John Vastelli's gay assistant. I declined to become involved.

Candy thought I was crazy.

"What, you are giving up the chance to be on E! Television?" she
asked in shock.

"It's just not something I care to relive on camera," I said point-
blank. "I'd just come off looking like a queer Kato Kalin anyway."

The tabloids had tried to get me to sell the story of my love affair
with John Vastelli. No matter how bad of a crunch I got in financially,
I have yet to broach the topic in public or sell out to the tabloids. Even
facing paying off student loans for years to come has not made me
succumb to spilling the beans, something I am very proud of. Of
course, it's not out of morals alone. Though I loved the man, I'm no
Mother Theresa. It's just that in order to be free and move on to a successful life I had to make a clean break from the past or forever be stig-
matized as the ex-porn star/secret boyfriend of a famous closet-case
star.

Speaking of which, John has managed to keep his sexuality at bay to this day, though rumors still persist and bubble to the surface every now and then. His star keeps rising with Middle America flocking to his family action-adventure movies and tuning into *Life's Lessons*. I almost have to laugh when I think about it, it's like "hear no evil, speak no evil, and see no evil."

He called me once, a few months after my embarrassing suicide attempt. His call came as I was picking up groceries at Pavilions Supermarket.

"Adam?" I heard a faint voice as a shopping cart crashed next to me.

"Yeah? Who's this?" I asked, preoccupied with stuffing broccoli stalks into a clingy plastic bag that was anything but accommodating.

"It's John," he said nervously.

My perfect stalks of broccoli I just spent minutes searching for hit the floor.

"Hey," I said in shock. "How are you?"

"Great. Same old thing, working hard, you know how it is. So how have you been?" he gushed. It sounded like he was overcompensating with affection, or maybe suffering from guilt.

"Better. I'm doing better," I answered, still stunned.

"Adam, I've missed you. I've thought about you so much," his voice hushed.

"Same here, John. Me too," I said, my voice now tinged with regret, laced with a bit of anger.

"Listen. I want to see you, are you doing anything tonight?" John breathed.

I just stood there.

"Adam? Are you still there?" John asked with concern.

"Yeah. I'm here."

"So what do you say? Can you come over?" he persisted.

"John, can I ask you something?" I asked, clearing my throat. "If I see you tonight, will I see you again after that?"

"I don't see why not," John answered.

"Will it ever be out in public, or just late-night rendezvous like it was when we met? Because if that's the way it's going to be, I can't go back to that, living a covert life where we see each other once in a blue moon. What I feel for you is more. I can get a late-night fuck anytime I want."

"Babe, we went over this. I just can't risk it," John said.

"And I just can't go on feeling badly about myself, John. I've been through a lot since I got to this town. And I just can't live like that."

"Oh, babe, please. Do you need any help?"

"It's not about money!" I yelled out in the produce section as everyone around me turned to look.

"I know it's not, Adam. I just feel so bad I can't be with you like that, all the time. I want to show you I care." His voice broke.

"Look I have to go," I said. I just couldn't go on.

"Please, babe. Please come by and see me," John begged.

"I can't, John. I need more than that," I insisted. I couldn't believe myself. I was so weak when it came to temptation. Usually I gave in so easily. "But I love you," I added.

"I love you too," John sobbed.

I hung up the phone. Refusing to meet that man was without a doubt one of the hardest things I did in my life. Even a few years later, I yearn for him every once in a while.

By the way, I still have my Cartier watch. Despite being a broke student, I have resisted the urge to sell it. It's in a safety deposit box.

I never did find out who sold our story to the tabloids. My money was on Brian; he might have even been in on the deal with Ron. Zinnia would have been too scared of becoming the ultimate social pariah and going to the clinker. Truthfully, it didn't matter. If it hadn't had been them it would have been someone else. What mattered was that a life with John and an open relationship would never be possible until he came to terms publicly with his sexuality. Until that day I wish him happiness, but even with a rewarding career I'm sure John spends much of his time being miserable.

As far as the porn companies were concerned, they quit calling after it finally became apparent to them that I wasn't going back to an X-rated life.

Instead I got a job working front desk at the Beverly Wilshire Hotel, a job that kept me content and paid the bills while I prepared to return to graduate school to earn my masters in journalism. If I'd gained anything by coming to LA besides short-lived notoriety, it was plenty of insight and stories to share.

Occasional bouts of anxiety struck when I worried about getting accepted to graduate school. I'd fared better than I expected on my GREs, taking them at a testing center in El Segundo, not far from the airport. It felt like I spent all day there. Surprisingly, the quantitative or math portion came easier than expected. The analytical part was a bitch. Trying to figure out whether Betty was sitting next to Tom or if Tom was sitting next to Bernard around a goddamned conference table had me dizzy.

Eventually the exams were taken, essays written, recommendations secured, and applications filled out and sent off. Now it was in God's hands or up to the universe where I'd end up. Of course I'd land somewhere. I just hoped to heaven it was one of the schools I'd applied to.

I set my standards high, figuring if I was making the commitment to go back to school, I might as well reach for the top. All the kicks in the ass I'd taken the past few years must have made me more brazen and sure of myself. This time around school was going to be the single focal point of my life, the number one priority.

No drifting off and thinking up ways to become famous, like before. No fucking around or screwing off like my first go at a higher education, literally and figuratively. Especially with all the student loans I'd be paying back for years to come. My choices were narrowed down to Syracuse, Columbia, Berkeley, and Northwestern. Reading my acceptance letter to Columbia, I ran up and down the halls of the apartment building screaming with joy. Orly came out of her apartment with phone in hand, prepared to call the police as she did the night I fell off the balcony.

For six months between leaving LA and coming back to New York I lived with my parents but didn't see them that often. My time was spent busting my ass waiting tables at Planet Hollywood in Caesar's Palace, saving up as much cash as I could in addition to the small fortune in student loans I'd have to take out. Remarkably, my mother and I got along pretty well. We had both grown in the past year, and she was happy about having one of her children attend an Ivy League school. In fact, only on a few occasions did she lose it over toothpaste residue in the sink or drips on the counter.

Saying good-bye to Candy was the hardest thing about leaving LA. How odd it was that my soul mate for the past few years had turned out to be a larger-than-life blonde bombshell, more close to me than any man I'd ever met. Our relationship was completely unconditional. Two people on similar missions of self-discovery, the hard way. Two people supporting each other through the crap life hands you, or in this case the Hollywood machine. A straight woman and a gay man, different bodies, yet such similar minds. Two people willing to put themselves through hell for what they thought was love, adoration, success, and validation of being worthy.

She had been bummed about my leaving for weeks.

"I feel when you leave I'll have nobody to talk to," she cried more than once.

"I'm only a phone call away," I kept telling her.

"Not the same thing," she'd reply.

Before leaving California a slip with an envelope was attached to my windshield wiper. This was on my third to last day in town. Just like my arrival in LA, a parking ticket marked my departure.

I took this as an affirmation from the universe that I was making the right decision.

I cringe whenever I see or hear anything about Wayne Hanley, which is quite often. Whether it's a business article, a biography in a bookstore shelf, or a tidbit in page six, the man is all over the media. He recently gave the biggest single donation of money to a university or educational institution on record, a cool few hundred million. Too bad he isn't donating money to help pay off my student loans. I'll still be a charity case myself for a few more years.

But I'm not as fresh and young as I was a few years ago, so I'm sure he'd have no desire to impale my throat with his monster schlong. Especially when he can find dozens of prettier boys right off the bus to satisfy his sexual desires.

I stopped speaking with Ron, Brian, and the rest of the porn crowd months before leaving LA. One night at the Abbey I spotted Brian in the crowd. When it looked as if he was coming my way I darted in the other direction.

I keep in touch with Candy through regular e-mails and occasional phone calls. She's moved on as well. The gold digger mentality she had when it came to men has been spent. No more ads in *LA Weekly* seeking out sugar daddies, no more getting involved with men for weekly shopping sprees at Gucci and Dolce & Gabbana. Instead she has channeled her fashion obsession in a more healthy way, by becoming a personal shopper and stylist, a gig she does with expertise and aplomb, talking away with clients over everything from ink to pink.

Occasionally I wonder if my brief porn past will ever come back to haunt me. On the rare occasion that I frequent a gay bar a guy will approach me here or there and ask if I was in videos. But for the most part, it seems like forgotten history, a bygone era. Then again, I don't think too many of my colleagues at Columbia have the time or the desire to rent triple-X-rated gay flicks. And realistically, it's not as if I was Jeff Stryker or anything. My fifteen minutes of fame in the porn scene were brief, though eventful.

Besides, there is so much X-rated crap pasted and posted all over the place. The countless faces on sleazy Internet sites are a dime a dozen. If I ever go on to anything of importance in the public eye and it does catch up with me, I already have my sob story down pat. Actually it's not really a sob story; it's just the unfortunate truth. I was a misguided and poor son of a bitch who needed to eat, pay rent, and buy gas. End of the story.

In the post–Clinton-Lewinsky/reality television era, it probably wouldn't be as big of a deal if my past did present itself. Not when porn stars like Jenna Jameson are being featured on TV alongside Julia Roberts. Everyone knows the saying about skeletons in the closet. Well, one could say I not only have skeletons in my closet, but bones and skulls falling out of my cabinets and drawers as well. Digging up the dirt on me would be an easier task than finding the checkout aisle at your local supermarket. But I've come to terms with it, and try not to look back with regret. My past is part of who I am now and there's no changing it.

Otherwise LA seems like distant smog in my mind, and a world away from where I'm at now. I don't go into too much detail about my time out there when it comes up in conversation. Usually I'll tell people I tried pursuing a career in entertainment, making it sound as if I was working for a studio or something. Then I'll quickly change the subject.

I seldom, if ever, mention the aspirations I once had to become an actor. Not out of bitterness. It's just something that I prefer to put to rest. For the first time in my life I feel that I'm at the right place at the right time, which until now had been a completely unknown feeling. And boy, do I ever enjoy the peace of mind that comes with it.

My heart goes out to all the drifters out there chasing a dream. But my old dreams have been put out to pasture for more appropriate ones. Maybe someday I'll bring the recollections of my time in the city of angels and dust them off. As an aspiring journalist I'll save what I could have contributed to episodes of *E! True Hollywood Story* and *Biography* for a project of my own.

And who knows? Maybe it will prove to be inspiration for things to come, and I'll be able to make better sense of my time in La-La Land.

ABOUT THE AUTHOR

Andy Zeffer is Features Editor of *The Express News* in Fort Lauderdale, Florida. His work has appeared in the *Provincetown Banner*, the *New York Blade*, the *Washington Blade, Southern Voice*, and *US Weekly*. In a previous life, he was an actor, appearing in Woody Allen's *Celebrity* and the hit independent film, *The Fluffer*.